David Burnell was born and bred in York. He studied mathematics at Cambridge University, taught the subject in West Africa and came across Operational Research as a useful application. He returned to study this at Lancaster and then spent his professional career applying the subject to management problems in the Health Service, coal mining and latterly the water industry. On "retiring" he completed a PhD at Lancaster on the deeper meaning of data from London's water meters.

He and his wife live in Berkshire but own a small holiday cottage in North Cornwall. They have four grown-up children.

David is now starting work on the next book in the "Cornish Conundrum" series.

A Cornish Conundrum

Happy reading!

Daid Burnell

Twisted
Limelight

David Burnell

Skein Books

A Cornish Conundrum

TWISTED LIMELIGHT

Published by Skein Books, 88, Woodcote Rd, Caversham, Reading, UK

First edition: May 2017.
Second edition: August 2017

ISBN-13: 978-1546326182
ISBN-10: 1546326189

The front cover shows Crooklets Beach at Bude in North Cornwall. The upper Bude Canal is in the background. I am grateful to Dr Chris Scruby for taking and fine-tuning the main photograph; and also the photo of me shown on the back.

BUDE

NORTH CORNWALL

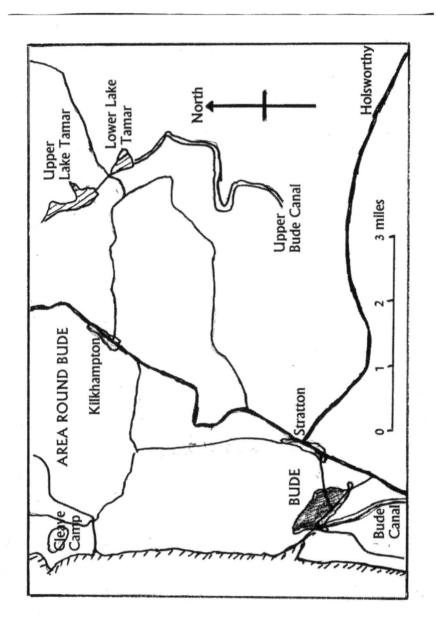

PROLOGUE

The battered van rattled down the Cornish lane, drew up outside the old thatched cottage and stopped. The driver leaped out, stepped up to the front door, knocked hard and listened for a response. But rather to his surprise no one was at home.

There was no choice but to find the key. As was so often the case he found it under the mat. He stepped inside the kitchen and looked round. It didn't have the appearance of a place waiting to be emptied, rather of somewhere that had been abruptly forsaken. There were still dirty mugs and a half-empty carton of milk on the table.

This was not what he expected. Exasperated, he strode through the rest of the house and found it all in much the same state. No tidying had been done here. His job was practically impossible: he would first need the help of a experienced housekeeper.

After a few moments, frustrated, he returned to the kitchen. And paused; was that a sound he had just heard?

He stood completely still and listened hard.

There was a background hum from somewhere outside but that wasn't his problem. Yes, there it was again. He frowned; it sounded like an irregular banging. It came from inside the house; what on earth was it?

As he waited his ears grew more attuned. He sensed it came from a door in the corner – was that, perhaps, the entrance to a cellar?

He tiptoed over and the sound grew more distinct.

There was a key in the lock. Quietly he grasped and turned it – it moved easily enough, seemed well oiled. He wouldn't be the first to go down here. Beyond he could see stairs going down, although the bottom was pitch black. There was no obvious light switch in view.

He recalled that there was a torch in his backpack. In his line of work he quite often had to go into attics or cupboards.

A moment later he was back at the top of the cellar stairs, his torch now pointing the way. He had no excuse for delay and started down, step by step.

At the bottom was another door, also locked but with a key sticking out. Was it sensible, he wondered, to come on his own into a strange house and then barge in to an empty cellar?

Then he heard the sound again. The banging sounded more desperate now; it sounded like a cry for help. Despite his lowly status here as a one-time visitor he couldn't stop now.

Slowly he pushed open the door, stepped inside and swung his torch round the space beyond.

And saw, to his horror, a young woman with waves of red hair, encased in a metal cage. Her gag prevented her crying out but she was kicking the bars in fierce anger.

She saw him and then her eyes widened.

Something was wrong, though. She wasn't looking directly at him.

4

Before he could speak there was another noise behind him. He started to turn his head to see who she'd seen – if it was the owner, was it too late to remonstrate? – but he was a split-second too late.

A heavy metal post came down hard on his head and he knew no more.

CHAPTER 1

George Gilbert, analyst and occasional amateur sleuth, heard a crash behind her.

Turning, she saw that something – or someone – was trying to force their way in through the shop doorway. First a dishevelled mop of honey blond hair appeared at about the height of George's knees. Next came a slender body, finally a pair of legs. It was a woman. It was easy to tell that as she seemed to be wearing no more than a grubby grey bathrobe.

George had just been starting to examine an old copper lamp. She turned back to the antique dealer, astonished. 'Does this sort of thing happen often?' All she could think of was that it might be some sort of rag-week stunt, maybe for Barnstaple. But she could see Martha looked equally shocked.

George turned back to the new arrival. The woman was extremely dirty – she was covered in mud – and looking more carefully, the analyst could see that her hands and knees were tied together. The poor woman was in no position to walk – no wonder she was coming in on her haunches.

She seemed to be trying to speak but for whatever reason no sound was emerging.

George looked at her more carefully. 'Wait a minute, don't I know you?' Given the newcomer's state it was hard to be sure,

6

and it was a long time since college, but had they not once been fellow maths students at Cambridge?

But to take this line of research any further the newcomer needed to be able to speak. 'I think she needs a glass of water,' said George. 'And do you have a knife or a pair of scissors? I'd better have a go at those ropes.'

'Try this,' said Martha, offering her a knife from a cabinet which was labelled as displaying "the days of the slave trade".

'Goodness knows when it was last used but it looks sharp enough.'

The new arrival looked apprehensive. Then her face lit up in relief as George managed to force the knife through the rope around her wrists, release them and then, a minute later, to free her legs. George could see that deep marks had been left on both wrists and ankles by the tight bindings: the poor girl must have been tied up for some time and in a lot of discomfort. There was also an ugly gash on her left leg.

She offered a hand to help the newly-freed woman to her feet. But not surprisingly, she was far from steady as she pushed herself slowly up and then tottered towards a nearby Regency chair.

As she did so, Martha returned from the rear kitchen with a large glass of water. 'Here you are, my dear.'

The woman reached out rather unsteadily, seized the glass with both hands and started to swig. Twenty seconds later the contents had entirely disappeared.

'I'd better get some more,' said Martha. She disappeared once more to the kitchen.

'Thank you.' The drink seemed at least to have had a positive effect on her ability to speak.

She turned to George. 'Yes, we do know each other. But first things first, I need to get out of here. My captor will be back soon. I managed to get out of his car but as soon as he's back he'll realise I'm gone. He'll know I can't get far.'

'Not without help,' commented George. 'But my car is parked outside too. I can help you get away. Come on.'

She reached towards the other woman and helped her out of the chair, noticing the layer of mud she had left behind. She shut her mind as to how much this might reduce the value of the chair. Then she helped the potential escapee struggle toward the door and out onto the pavement.

It was just after nine o'clock in the morning. Bude would be much busier later on, this was August, the height of the holiday season, but at this hour there was no one else about.

'My car's this yellow Mini-Cooper. Lie out of sight on the back seat, at least till we're out of Bude.'

George opened the door and helped her new companion inside. She threw the car rug over her as an extra layer of protection. Then dashed back to the shop and called, 'Martha, I'll be back later. I'm taking her somewhere safe. It's really important that you don't say anything about this to anyone. She needs all the protection she can get.'

Shutting the shop door, the analyst returned to her car, settled into the driving seat and started the engine. Her heart was thumping and adrenalin pounded as she drew carefully out into the road.

8

'Hey, was your captor a tall man with a beard and dark glasses, wearing a thick grey sweater?' asked George a minute later, as the car threaded its way round the Bude one-way system.

'How the hell did you know that?' came the muffled response from the back seat.

'Well not many people take photographs of my car. It's special enough to me but not historically significant. It was just I noticed this chap. He got to the end of the road with the antique shop, looked down the street, saw something he didn't like and then turned to photograph us. Maybe you'd left a trail of mud on the pavement? It's a good job you've got your head down.'

'Don't like the sound of that. How fast will this car go?'

'Well, if it is your captor, it'll take him a minute to walk down to his car before he comes after us. There's no real reason why he should suspect I've got anything to do with it – he's bound go into the antique shop first to see if you've hidden in there. With a bit of luck Martha will confuse him. She's got a good line in waffle and she's hard to stop once she gets going. And then he might get tangled in the early-morning traffic. I'll take the coastal route out of Bude rather than a main road. That also might throw him.'

George did a loop round the shopping area and down the Strand. Then she turned right at the mini roundabout by the bridge, past the long-stay car park and the Falcon Hotel, then up the hill on the coast road which led to Widemouth.

She kept glancing in her mirror but so far the road behind was empty.

'D'you think we should re-introduce ourselves? I was George Goode when you last knew me but I married a Gilbert.'

'I'm still Maxine Tavistock. I never married. Thank you for getting involved. You've probably saved my life.'

But this wasn't the time for small talk. There was silence for a few seconds and then, 'Maxine, can you remember anything about the car you escaped from?'

'It was some sort of Golf, I think. Or maybe a Skoda. Blue and fairly muddy. I never got to see its number.' A pause and then, 'Why are you asking?'

'Well, I just spotted a blue car coming round the corner at the bottom of the hill behind us. It might not be our friend but it was travelling fairly fast . . .'

'Might this be one time when we could ignore the speed limit?'

'Maxine, we're already doing forty five in a thirty limit. Aha.'

For George had seen another yellow car pulling out of a driveway ahead of them. And the chasing car was for the moment out of sight, round the bend in their rear.

Abruptly, George jammed on her brakes. Tyres squealed as the car lost speed. Then, abruptly, tyres shrieking, she swung off the road, round the corner of a building and into the yard of an MOT depot. Fortunately there was no one about. At the same time she kept glancing into the mirror. Half a minute later a blue car shot past the depot entrance and continued up the road.

'I think we'll stay here for a while, Maxine. I saw another yellow car ahead of us. With a bit of luck that'll distract our pursuer. And when he does finally catch it up he'll realise he's been chasing the wrong car and maybe give up altogether. How long d'you reckon we need to give him?'

But she was not given much choice. Five minutes later George saw a man coming out of the building, heading towards them. No doubt he would want to know what she was doing and if she needed an MOT. She recalled her muddy, half- naked passenger in the rear seat: it would be best to move on and avoid awkward questions.

Giving the man a cheerful wave, George turned the car in the yard and headed for the exit.

'How would you like to come back to my little holiday cottage and get yourself cleaned up? We're both small and slim. You could borrow some of my clothes till you got your own back, stay as long as you needed. Then maybe you could tell me what this is all about. You might need some medical help for that gashed leg as well.'

'That sounds great. I'd rather not go home at the moment. Where's your cottage?'

'It's further down the coast: a tiny village called Treknow, the far side of Tintagel. Twenty miles away. But don't worry, we don't have to go anywhere near the A39. We can get there along a quiet coast route.'

Maxine pulled off the car rug and sat up.

It was quiet enough but the fear of meeting Maxine's former captor and the need to watch for possible aggressors curbed their conversation. Just after Millook George did ask a general question but the silence from the back seat made her realise that her companion had fallen asleep. That was good: she'd probably missed out on sleep the night before.

The silence gave George time to ponder on this unexpected event and how it might affect her. The whole thing was bizarre, made even more peculiar by the fact that she knew the woman in the back seat from twenty years earlier.

The two had never been in the same friendship group but they had both been reading the same subject – maths – in the same college. That meant they had spent plenty of time together, walking to lectures along Kings Parade and on assignments. Maxine had been the one she had gone to for help when the problems were hardest. Her overall memory of Maxine was that she aware of her talents, oozing in self-confidence, but no party animal. It was hard to imagine her behaving in any way that might get her into trouble.

She was also extremely clever and had obtained one of the top firsts in mathematics in her year. The two had drifted apart when Maxine had stayed on to do a PhD at Cambridge in some obscure branch of Number Theory while George had started work in London. They'd hardly seen each other since.

On the other hand, the college connection might help the two to trust one another more in this nightmare than if it was two complete strangers that had just been thrown together.

From what she had seen, a vicious crime had been committed which needed reporting to the police. What Maxine could re-member, and what she was prepared to say about it, would determine whether or not the perpetrators could be brought to justice.

George was not in Cornwall on holiday; she was down on a business assignment. Even so that did not need to take all her time.

Helping Maxine to secure justice had better be added to her list of projects.

CHAPTER 2

Maxine stayed asleep until they had reached Treknow. The jerk, as the Cooper drew to a halt outside Ivy Cottage, woke her, saving George from the problem of how to transfer her indoors.

The car was left parked on the roadside. It was the most minor of roads but she now regretted the distinctive colour and make. It was unlikely that the captor had got her car registration number on the photograph but with a modern camera it was a worrying possibility.

Then the thought came, was there any way that she might be able to swap her car for another vehicle for the next couple of weeks?

That was for later. For now she helped the limping Maxine up the garden path. 'There's a step down as you walk through the door,' she warned. But the warning was a split second too late and her old college friend stumbled into the cottage and ended up sprawled on the slate floor, howling in frustration.

George helped Maxine to her feet. 'Sorry. I did that the first time I came here. The bath's upstairs. I'll help you up there and then bring you a cup of tea while you treat yourself to a long soak.'

Climbing the stairs took longer than expected – Maxine's leg

14

had stiffened, she seemed to be feeling aches and pains all over – but eventually the pair reached the bathroom. George left her to sort out the bath herself while she went downstairs to make a pot of tea.

Three minutes later a hideous noise seized the cottage. There was a scream from the bathroom and then a completely naked Maxine stood quivering in fear at the top of the stairs.

George raced upstairs to offer consolation. 'Maxine, I'm so sorry. I'm afraid that's what the plumbing does here if you fill the bath too quickly. I've had several plumbers look at it but it's never been fully resolved.'

Trial and error over several years had given George some remedial actions. She stepped inside the bathroom, flushed the toilet and turned on the cold tap at the sink. After a few seconds the noise hiccupped and then subsided.

Cautiously her friend followed her back in.

'Enjoy your bath, Maxine. I'll bring you some tea in a few minutes.'

An hour later the two women were seated in the lounge with mugs of coffee, both fully clothed. Remembering she might have been photographed, George had changed out of her exuberant red and green sweater into something more subdued. Maxine had made good use of George's shampoo. Her blond hair was no longer a dishevelled tangle, but hung down neatly at shoulder length. She had kitted herself out from George's wardrobe in black jeans and a multi-coloured jumper.

The plumbing had behaved itself and there had been no

further causes of alarm.

George had taken the chance, while Maxine bathed, to ring Lugg's garage in Delabole and arranged for her car to have a leisurely service, 'the slower the better.' As part of the deal negotiated, her car had been swapped for a well-used red Fiesta. The garage had even sent someone to drive to her cottage and swap the cars over.

It was a pleasure, she thought, to enjoy the benefits of local services, taking advantage of contacts built up over the years.

'The most important thing now,' declared George, 'is for you to tell me a much as you can remember about what happened. I'll make notes, if you don't mind. Then we can decide who we need to report to.'

Maxine looked uncertain. 'The trouble is, some of this story is covered by the Official Secrets Act. Even though you and I knew each other a long time ago, I can't tell you everything without a lot more checks.'

George brushed the worries aside. 'Maxine, I'm a business analyst these days. I deal with commercial secrets all the time. I don't need to know everything if you don't want to tell me. I don't even need to know your job in Bude. But how you came to be tied up in the back of a car, practically naked and a prisoner, is surely not an Official Secret. I promise you I'll be very discreet. I'm not going to rush off to the Daily Mail or anything. Just tell me what you can.'

Maxine paused for a moment, arranging her thoughts and deciding what she could disclose to her friend. Then she began.

'I've been down in this area for just over a month. I'd rather not say why, if you don't mind, it's probably not relevant. While I'm here I'm staying in a smart bed and breakfast place in Bude that overlooks the golf course.'

'So when you're ready to get your own clothes back, that's where they'll be?'

'That's right. Just round the corner from the antique shop actually. This tale starts in my guesthouse. I'd had an unusually long working day and I got back around ten pm. I was exhausted. I decided I'd have a hot shower to relax myself and ease the strain, maybe freshening up would also help me to sleep. So I undressed and stepped into the shower.'

Maxine paused, in some distress.

'There was something wrong with the shower room light. When I pulled the cord by the door it didn't come on. Didn't think anything of it, the bulb must have gone and needed replacing – it must happen sometime. I was just trying to remember whether there was another light over the sink which I could use instead when I sensed there was someone else in the room with me.'

It sounded terrifying but George knew better than to interrupt. Maxine paused, swallowed hard and then recovered enough to continue.

'I asked, "Who's there?" but there was no reply. Then someone reached forward to seize me. They held a piece of cloth over my mouth. It had a peculiar smell, slightly sweet but with a trace of chlorine. I struggled like mad but he'd got my arms held tightly, I couldn't dislodge it.'

'You poor woman,' murmured George. It sounded horrible.

17

'I held my breath for as long as I could but finally I had to breathe in. That's when I blacked out.'

'Maxine, you poor thing. How absolutely terrible. So what happened next?'

'I presume they must have found the bathrobe and thrown it over me. Then they carried me down the stairs and out to a car. When I came to I was lying outdoors in some sort of farmyard and they were busy tying up my wrists and ankles.

'I heard one of them say something like, "We'll get her talking tomorrow." Then they opened a hatch in the yard and lowered me into it. I think it was a coal cellar.'

There was silence in the peaceful lounge, a striking contrast to this tale of horror. But there was no value in the tale stopping before the end.

After a moment George asked, 'And next morning?'

'You can imagine, George, I didn't get much sleep. This coal wasn't those smooth, smoke-free nuggets – it was hard and sharp-edged. I felt groggy, it took a while before I wanted to try anything. After a struggle I managed to balance and stand up – it's not easy when your wrists are tied together – but the hatch was still well above me.'

She paused, remembering it all again. 'There must have been some other way out to access the coal from the farmhouse but it was pitch back so I couldn't see. I was cold and thirsty and my leg hurt: I'd scraped it on the pile of coal when they threw me in. And they'd tied me up tightly, it wasn't very pleasant.'

Maxine rubbed her arms as she recollected her discomfort.

'I hardly slept at all. Many hours later the hatch above me

opened and I saw daylight. "Here's something to drink," one of 'em said. They lowered a large bottle on a string but somehow I didn't trust them. They saw I'd grabbed it and shut the hatch again. I didn't try to drink it but managed to tip it over the coal.'

'What came next?'

'They left me alone for an hour or two. I realised I was desperately thirsty: had I done the right thing to dump the water?

'Then the hatch opened again. A tall man, wearing a mask, lowered himself down, got hold of me and held me up high. Then a second man, also wearing a mask, reached down and grabbed my wrists. So between the two of 'em I found myself pushed and pulled out of the hole. They weren't exactly gentle.'

Maxine gave herself a few caresses as she relived the process.

'Next they carried me indoors, sat me on a chair in the kitchen and started the questioning. I'd feared that would be coming from what I'd heard the night before. I'd done my best in the long hours of the night to work out ways that I could slow the process.'

She paused again, recollecting. 'I kept telling them that everything they were asking me about could be answered from my tablet. Of course, they quickly realised that they'd not thought to bring that, it was still in my room in the bed and breakfast. That caused a massive argument: the man in charge was furious.

'After that his partner was told to take me with him in the car back to Bude while he went to collect it. I was sent with him, locked in the boot, so I could confirm he'd got the right machine when he returned.'

'But how on earth did you get out of the boot?'

19

'They were stupid. The boot lid was locked and they'd wedged the back seats so they couldn't be pushed down from behind but they'd forgotten that you could also get out another way. There was a small hatchway in the rear seat . . .'

'So there is. I think it's so you can carry skis inside the car rather than on the roof.'

'I'd seen the thing as they pushed me in. As we went along I fought to kneel so I was facing forwards. Then, as soon as the driver slammed the door, I pushed against the hatch until it folded forward and I could crawl through into the back seat and then, head first, out the rear door. It was locked but I could still open it from the inside. The antique shop was the nearest doorway from where I got onto the pavement. But it was a hell of a relief when I got inside the shop and saw someone in there that I knew.'

George decided that now was time for a break and another mug of coffee. Maxine had obviously had a terrifying experience over the last twelve hours. Though her description had been terse and unemotional it must have taken courage even to voice it.

George was certain that this tale needed to be told to the police. But she and Maxine had known one another from way back and she'd also helped in her escape. That gave a special bond between them. George reckoned that she would almost certainly learn more from Maxine right now than would an unknown police officer.

'Here's my suggestion,' said George as she placed two mugs of fresh coffee down on the table. 'I know this will be hard but I'd like to go back over your story and check the details. I deliberately did my best not to intervene while you were talking. But if you rack your brains there might be extra details that you can remember.'

'Maybe,' said Maxine without much enthusiasm. The main fact she was aware of, right now, was that she was no longer captive. What else mattered?

But George dealt with reluctant interviewees regularly in her work. 'OK. Let's start with the villains. How many d'you think there were?'

Maxine thought for a moment. 'The shower room in my B & B is not large. The intruder wouldn't know how long they'd have to wait till I got in so I don't believe more than one could hide there. I'm sure there was no one else in my room – when I went in I put the light on and opened the wardrobe door to hang up my jacket. So . . . the abduction from my room was probably the work of a single man.'

Maxine paused to consider the next stage. 'I was unconscious during the journey to the farm so I can't tell how many were in the car. It might just have been the man from my room. But there were at least two by the time they threw me down into the coal cellar, they were talking to one another.'

'What about the questioning next morning?'

'I only saw two. But I had the impression that they were both answerable to someone else. The thing is, the interview didn't get very far before they realised they would need to go back to Bude.'

'Was your clever story about the tablet true or just a way of playing for time?'

Maxine considered. 'I'm really sorry George, I'd rather not answer that for the moment.'

George felt irritated but knew it would not be helpful to start an argument at this point. Their relationship was still fragile. There must be other things in the story that were not "off limits".

'Fair enough. What can you remember about the farm?'

'When I got there it was late and there were no lights on so I saw virtually nothing. Next morning . . .'

'Yes?'

'There were no signs on the walls so I can't tell you the name of the farm or anything. The yard was small. The kitchen looked like it could do with redecoration. There wasn't much furniture and it was very old.'

'The key question is, would you recognise it if you saw it again?'

'Probably. Assuming they hadn't changed it, of course.'

'And how far d'you reckon it was from Bude?'

'Assuming they didn't mess about and drive in circles, I should think the journey took no more than forty five minutes. I didn't have my watch, of course, but the driver had the radio on and John Humphrys was announcing the time every few minutes.

'The first ten minutes he drove very slowly – I guess along narrow lanes – and then he speeded up. But there was nothing in the noise of the engine to suggest that he was pushing the speed limit. Trouble is, there are a lot of farmhouses within twenty miles of Bude.'

George sighed. 'So it won't be easy to find the place they took you to. But can you remember anything else that might help identify the villains, their car or the farmhouse where you were taken?'

'Both men I saw were tall and fairly slim, wearing dark glasses. They didn't have particularly Cornish accents. It's not much to go on.'

'It's better than nothing. And you're around to tell the tale. You might think of more later. Now, d'you feel strong enough to take all this to the police – or do you have another suggestion?

'Could I think about that for a bit? It's all very complicated.'

George had half-expected a reaction like this, her friend was probably suffering delayed shock. She had one more card to play. 'OK then, why don't I get the local doctor over to check you out? He's been a friend of mine for ages; he's immensely discreet.'

Maxine looked like she was about to refuse then realised she had no good excuse. She was not in a position to refuse all types of help. 'That'd be great,' she conceded.

'I'll call him at once,' replied George.

CHAPTER 3

Police Sergeant Peter Travers, tall and rugged, looked around the table at his newly acquired team in Bude. Whatever might have been the case in the past, there was no over-staffing today.

On one side were two women, Jess Holland and Holly Berry. Holland was a wise, maternal figure who'd been around for years. Berry was mustard-keen but still under thirty.

Opposite them was another pair of constables, Jamie Sampson and Joe Tremlitt, who did the bulk of the patrol work around Bude. The younger (and fitter) of these, Sampson, would be redeployed to Plymouth in the winter months when Bude offered far less scope for police work.

And at the far end was a special officer of unknown rank, never seen in police uniform, Colin Caldwell. Travers had not requested his presence, he was just there. He'd been told that Caldwell's role was to cover links with Cleave Camp, the government listening station, further up the coast.

There should have been others. Two had claimed their annual leave for August before Travers had taken charge. Another was off – stricken, he said, with a mysterious lurgy.

Travers himself had lived in and operated out of Delabole for years. Responsibility for the team in Bude was a recent addition to his remit, part of the latest round of government-imposed staff savings. In more generous times it might have been accompanied by promotion. The previous woman in charge of Bude had been an inspector but was now retired.

His arrival as the new man in charge had been greeted with underwhelming enthusiasm. It would have helped if he had come with the rank of Inspector – that would at least have shown that the Force in general valued his abilities. The time since Easter had been an ongoing battle of wills between the sergeant and the staff he had inherited.

For an hour the meeting dealt with a series of issues carried forward from their previous meeting. Interest could best be described as modest.

'Right. That's the ongoing stuff. What have we got that's new since a fortnight ago?' asked Travers. His staff produced written reports, of course, he insisted on that, but some interaction might spice up the meeting.

Jess Holland began. 'A young man came in to the station late yesterday afternoon with a disturbing story. I didn't know what to make of it.'

Travers had been out on an incident in Crackington at the time and hadn't heard anything of this. 'Go on.'

'He was called Jake. He's the greengrocer's lad from the shop at the top of Fore Street. His dad employs him to set out the stalls outside the shop in the morning and to take them in again at night. I don't think he's especially bright but he's willing enough. He has some sense of responsibility.'

'Yes . . . ?'

' Jake had recently found himself a second part-time job, with a man who did commissioned house clearances. But now, he tells me, this chap seems to have disappeared.'

'What's his name? The house clearance man, I mean.'

Holland glanced at her notes. 'He's called Fairclough, Barry Fairclough. Apparently he operates as a chimney sweep in the winter months and focuses on house clearance in the summer.'

'So he's well embedded. No need to push off and try his luck in another part of the country?'

'Not as far as Jake knew. He helped Barry whenever there was a clearance that involved heavy furniture. Barry was fit, he said, but he couldn't do it all on his own. In these old cottages some of the furniture is decades old and can't be separated into pieces. It's not flat-pack.

'Jake's clearance job was mostly on Saturdays. But Barry hadn't called on him for the last three weeks.' Holland glanced at her notes again. 'He last saw him, he said, on the first Saturday in July.'

Travers had a hunch, which he would have found hard to justify, that this might be serious; but he knew that it was best if others felt that for themselves. He glanced round the room. 'OK. What do the rest of you think? Is this a Missing Person we should do something about? Or just someone on an extended holiday?'

Colin Caldwell, the liaison man with Cleave, said, 'I could see if anyone has moved away from the Camp in the last few weeks. But even if there is, I doubt they'd have needed house clearance. Most short-term staff rent one of our cottages nearby; we let them fully furnished. And we never sell. Management think it's important to have accommodation to hand, even if it's not always used.'

This was the longest statement Caldwell had made for some time. Maybe it was sufficiently removed from the technical work of the Camp that he could speak more freely. But it didn't move the discussion much further forward.

Joe Tremlitt had lived in Bude for many years. 'My wife usually gets her vegetables from Jake's dad's store. When we've finished I'll give her a ring, ask for a second opinion on Jake. But it sounds from what Jess says that he's reliable. We can't just ignore what he says.'

Jamie Sampson asked, 'Has Barry Fairclough got any sort of record? I mean, if he's dealing with used furniture and fittings and got a range of outlets, he'd be a useful person to get rid of stuff that had been burgled – maybe even stuff from another part of the country. Would that be a reason for him to disappear suddenly?'

Slightly irritated, Jess Holland replied. 'I checked that straight away. There's nothing at all – under the name Fairclough, at any rate.'

There was silence for a moment.

'It's a problem. Let's give it ten minutes thought,' said the sergeant encouragingly. 'Can we think of other people who would have regular contact with Barry? Who could confirm he's gone missing, or else tell us where he's gone? Does anyone know where he lives, for a start?'

'I've checked the phone books,' said Holland. 'He's in the

Yellow Pages both under "Sweep" and "House Clearance", but it's only a mobile.'

'And Jake didn't know his address,' she added. 'I asked him. Barry always rang the evening before he was wanted, he said, and then picked him up early in the morning.'

'But Jake's parents must have some way of contacting him,' protested Holly Berry. A new mother, she was learning a lot about parenting. 'There might be some sort of emergency while he was working with Barry.'

'Right,' said Travers. He wrote down an action on his notepad.

'When he clears a house, what does he do with the contents?' asked Caldwell. 'Even if he has a set of second hand shops that he sells things through, that can hardly all happen at once. He must have some sort of interim storage – perhaps on the industrial estate?'

'He must have a van,' added Tremlitt. 'DVLA in Swansea should be able to give us its description and number. We could put out a search for that, once we know what we're looking for. It'd not be the easiest thing to hide.'

Travers added other actions to his list.

'We can guess the sort of shops he'd sell through,' commented Holland. 'Second hand shops, say, maybe that antique shop up the road. They'd be mostly local; there can't be more than half a dozen outlets in Bude. It'd take us an hour on the phone to check them out. And that might give us a more recent sighting.'

'Or else information on where he's gone,' added Berry.

Travers added more actions. He would have thought of these

things himself but it was much better if it was the result of collective effort.

'The trouble is, it's very hard to get very far on a Missing Person enquiry without a picture of the bloke that's gone missing. I don't suppose Jake had a photo of the guy? Say the two of them together, humping a hideous piece of furniture round an awkward bend?'

'No,' replied Holland, 'I asked him. But he did better than you might expect on description.' She glanced down once again at her notes. 'He said Barry was "bald and tubby, with a massive beard. Aged, he thought, somewhere around forty. With tattoos down both arms." And one more detail: he always wore shorts and heavy boots.'

She added, 'He said Barry had a "strong Cornish accent". It must have been really strong for Jake to notice that; he's got quite an accent himself.'

'OK. Get that all written up, please.' The sergeant glanced round the room. 'Our first task is to see if there's more evidence, either that this bloke's disappeared or that he's moved to another location. This could go either way.'

Summarising, he said, 'We won't talk to the local press till we've made preliminary enquiries. So if you come across anyone who knew the guy, see if they can add anything more. Did he ever wear glasses, for example? Or have a limp? What shape was his face and what colour were his eyes? Was he tall or short? And let me know at once, please, if you find evidence that he's OK so I can take everyone off the case.'

There was a somewhat sullen silence from the team, grudging

acquiescence that this warranted police attention at all.

No doubt they would think of more questions to ask but there was plenty here to be going on with. Travers glanced round the room and made sure that, willing or not, each of his team knew what was expected of them.

A progress meeting was scheduled for the allegedly-missing man for the next day. The sergeant declared the meeting closed, stood up and returned to his office.

CHAPTER 4

The local doctor that George had called, Brian Southgate of Delabole, had said he would be call in and check on Maxine after his afternoon surgery. Her ordeal had left Maxine feeling extremely tired. It was agreed it would be best for her to try and catch up on her sleep for the afternoon.

George could ill afford to lose a whole day from her work schedule. After some thought she came to an agreement with Maxine.

'I've got to pop out to another meeting. I'll be back by five thirty,' she promised, 'in good time to let in the doctor.'

'What do you do, by the way?'

'I work for a country-wide consultancy. It specialises in computer-based models and statistics.'

'Where's it based?'

'London. But I have a deal: the firm will give me first refusal on projects in the southwest. That means I can keep an eye on this cottage and even use it for work.'

George noticed that Maxine was yawning repeatedly, not taking much notice. This conversation would need to be continued at a later date.

Her latest project was based in Bude, no more than half an hour away. George had been intending to start work straight after

31

her early morning visit to the antique dealer when Maxine had intervened. She had postponed one meeting but could still make another this afternoon.

The project was linked to a major exhibition taking place over the summer, one of a series across the country on "Innovation". Each show was linked to the work of inventors based in that area who had made a substantial impact with one or more inventions.

The exhibition in Bude was a tribute to the work of Sir Goldsworthy Gurney, a nineteenth century surgeon, inventor and entrepreneur. Gurney's most famous invention was a steam motor car – the first vehicle in the world to travel a substantial distance at speed – but he had also made significant contributions in other areas. He had discovered limelight and his oxygenated boosted lights had lit the Houses of Parliament for half a century. The Bude Exhibition was called "Limelight".

The exhibition included a tribute to the Bude Canal, which, with a link to the River Tamar, had been intended to link the Bristol and English channels. George had reflected that both items might have made more headway if they had not coincided with the development of the steam railway in the 1830s.

Even so there was still much that could be learned that might encourage young inventors today.

George's firm had been invited to find someone to go round the exhibitions for the summer, speaking at special sessions on the difficulties in moving from a bright idea to finding someone to make it work.

Even if it had not been based in the southwest, George would have seized the opportunity: it was right up her street.

She had prepared case studies for a wide range of inventions, including those covered by each exhibition. She could refer to the focus of each exhibition at all the others, making it an efficient overview. Some of the inventions were now seen as big successes and George had found it fascinating to delve into why these had occurred.

Others, like Gurney's steam car, were no longer remembered. These too offered lessons for future inventors.

Another aspect of George's remit was to review pricing at the various exhibitions. She had already held similar meetings in Bristol, Exeter and Plymouth. The exhibitions were all self-contained, designed to be visited in isolation, but one possibility was tickets allowing multiple show entries.

This afternoon's meeting was with the Sales Director in Bude. Sally Newcombe had a temporary office on waste land behind the long-term visitors' car park. It was two o'clock when George reached her office but she wasn't there. The business analyst sat down to wait in the small reception area and picked up a leaflet about Limelight.

The front cover showed a replica of the final version of the steam-driven cars produced by Gurney, as engineered by the exhibition's holding company. Inside she learned that more such vehicles were under construction. These would be available to purchase (price not specified). There was also a picture of Gurney's "Bude Light" and mention of experiments that visitors could conduct on light in the marquee.

At this point Sally Newcombe arrived, slightly embarrassed to see her official visitor waiting.

George introduced herself. 'I've been asked by your top management to analyse sales data from these Innovation Exhibitions, check we're making the most of the opportunities to maximise sales.'

'Ah yes, I had an email about that the other day.' Sally peered at various piles of paper on her desk, tried one or two but failed to find anything to aid the discussion. 'What sort of information were you after?'

'For a start I'd like data on, say, weekly ticket sales since the exhibition started. That was the beginning of June, I think?'

'Hm.' Sally frowned. 'That's highly confidential. We wouldn't want the local press to get hold of it.'

George managed to mask her irritation. 'Sally, I've been asked to do this work by your top management. Anything you give me will be treated in confidence. Now, do you have the data to hand or shall I come back for it, say, tomorrow morning?'

Sally looked upset but she could see that being even more awkward would make things worse. She headed for the filing cabinet and a moment later handed some papers over to George.

'That's a hard copy of my spreadsheet: visitors since the Exhibition began. That's adults, concessions, students and children.'

'How old are the children?'

'They're kids between the ages of six and sixteen. We don't charge anything for pre-schoolers.'

George looked at the table for a moment. 'How do these numbers compare with the ones you expected?'

'Are you here to help us or condemn us?' asked Sally. 'The numbers aren't exactly overwhelming, but they're more respectable now, I think.'

The Sales Director sounded defensive. George knew she had to make the woman realise they were on the same side.

'I've seen similar data from half a dozen other exhibitions from around the country. The overall pattern looks much the same. It's bound to take a while before folk take notice. It's probably made worse by the seaside. After all, visitors come to Bude for sand, cliffs and ice cream, not intellectual enrichment.'

Sally seemed to relax a little. 'Hey, would you like some coffee?'

Anything to smooth the conversation was worth trying. She continued to study visitor numbers as her host bustled around the reception area.

'What sort of offers have you tried so far?' she asked, once the interview resumed.

'How d'you mean?'

'Well, the numbers are well down at the start of every week. What about special rates for Mondays? It must be worth something to even out the visitor numbers. Where are you advertising?'

Once more Sally consulted the filing cabinet. 'These are the adverts we've been running so far. But there's plenty of budget left if needed.'

George took the bundle and leafed through them. 'They're striking enough. Who's seen them?'

Sally looked puzzled.

'For example, have you tried sending these to bed and breakfast houses in Bude?'

It seemed this was a new idea. The pair spent a few minutes discussing agencies that could do the delivery.

'I could take some to the Visitor Centres in Boscastle and Tintagel this evening,' offered George. 'I'll pass both on my way home.' The offer was gratefully received.

George asked for various other pieces of data. Daily income from the visitors so far was available, but there was nothing on repeat visitors. 'I'd need to do some work to get at that,' admitted Sally.

'It's important data to analyse,' commented George. 'We need to understand the people who come back, they're our best customers. Could we use them to bring in others?'

George left the office soon after four. It had been harder work than she had expected. Was this non-incisive thinking the kind of thing senior staff hoped she could expose?

CHAPTER 5

When George returned to her cottage in Treknow, just before five, she found her new guest was still asleep. That gave her chance to write up notes of the afternoon's meeting before Dr Brian Southgate arrived from Delabole.

It also gave George the chance to warn the doctor, 'There might be problems getting Maxine to talk.'

Brian could only smile. He had long reckoned that his bedside manner was one of his more successful attributes.

'I'll make you both a mug of tea then leave you to it,' said the analyst. Gently she coaxed Maxine awake then, once she was alert, left her to be checked by the doctor.

Half an hour later Brian gave George a call. 'Maxine thought you might as well be part of our wider discussion.'

George went into the guest bedroom and took the second chair.

'Dr Southgate – Brian – has given me a thorough examination. He reckons that though I'm bruised all over and very tired I've got no lasting injuries,' said Maxine. 'That's apart from a nasty scrape on my leg. Taking antibiotics for a week should sort me out – physically, at least. But he's been telling me – just like you did – that I really can't keep all this to myself.'

'The easiest thing, Maxine, you know, would be to talk to Peter Travers,' said Brian. 'He and I were at school together in Camelford: we've known each other all of our lives. Peter's the friendliest policeman you could ever meet – though he's hard enough with criminals. He's always lived in Delabole and the coast around here was his main patch. But he got transferred earlier this year, now he's in charge of Bude. So, insofar as the whole thing started there, he would be the right person to talk to.'

Maxine still looked uncertain.

'What I don't understand,' said George, 'is why you're so reluctant to report it. Oh, I can see it must be a strain to go over the whole thing one more time and answer loads of questions but I'd come with you if you liked. As it happens I know Peter Travers too.'

Maxine was silent and the analyst could see that more was needed.

George went on, 'These days the police are much better at handling victims than they used to be; and at keeping them out of the papers. I mean, surely you'd like the pair of villains tracked down before they try the same thing on someone else?'

Maxine gave a groan. 'It's all to do with my employers and the official, legally binding undertaking I've given them.'

'Look, Maxine, all three of us understand the constraints of keeping secrets, especially things that we learn as a result of our jobs.'

Brian suddenly had an idea of a possible cause of her coyness. 'Are you really saying that you ought to report all this first of all to your employer?'

There was a pause before Maxine replied.

'The trouble is, in their eyes I shouldn't have said anything to either of you. So I'll still be in trouble with them even if I go that way – probably get you two into trouble as well.

'I don't see how anyone can track down my kidnappers on what I know,' she continued. 'As I told you this morning, George, I didn't learn anything useful about where I was taken. I couldn't even give much of a description of the car I was taken off in. So I might as well pretend that nothing really happened at all.'

George looked across at Brian; the doctor shrugged his shoulders and shook his head.

'Maxine, I can hazily see that you don't want to tell anyone else because you don't think it will make any difference, other than getting yourself into some sort of procedural bother. If you really think that, why not tell the pair of us the whole story one more time and see if together we can spot any ways forward?'

Half an hour later Maxine had told her tale again. Her afternoon sleep had made her more lucid but the outline remained the same.

Even so George was left no wiser. Brian Southgate, though, had some different questions.

'I'm interested, Maxine, in your response to the drink you were offered. You were really thirsty – judging by the speed you drank the water given you in the antique shop – and yet you didn't take it. What did you think might be wrong with it?'

'I'd no idea. I was working on the principle that if they wanted me to do something it was better if I refused.'

'I'm not sure that's the whole story. You must have had some idea. What might have been wrong with it?

Maxine paused and then blurted out, 'It might have been poisonous.'

Brian gave a sigh. 'Maxine, what would be the logic in that? They'd got you tied up and hidden underground, away from anywhere you knew. If they really wanted to kill you they didn't need to use poison. Surely you were much more use to them alive than dead?'

'That's probably true,' Maxine conceded. 'Alright. What I really feared was that it was some sort of truth drug, given to me ahead of my being questioned.'

'Ah, that makes a lot more sense. So you know something about truth drugs. Was it covered on one of your courses?'

'I'm not allowed to say. For the same reason as I've given before.'

Brian did not look too surprised. Her answer confirmed the theory he had been developing in his mind.

'OK. We'll leave that for the time being. I'd like to ask a little more about your guesthouse – opposite the golf course, I think you said?'

'Tee-Side, it was called,' murmured Maxine absent-mindedly.

'How did you come to be staying there? Had you chosen the place? Maybe you'd been there before; or was it suggested to you?'

'My employer suggested it. He said they often used it for

short-term visitors. I hadn't been to Bude for years, I'd no idea where to look, so I was happy to take it. And the place was fine – at least, I thought it was.'

Brian could think of further questions about the guesthouse but he judged it better not to push Maxine into another refusal.

'OK. Suppose that you don't report this to anyone, pretend it didn't happen. How d'you think you can avoid being kidnapped again?'

Maxine blinked. The thought that she might be taken prisoner a second time had not occurred to her. She could see that next time escape might be a lot harder or even impossible.

'You can stay here as long as you like,' said George reassuringly. 'A day or two's rest after your ordeal won't do you any harm. But you'll probably want to go outside before long, maybe back to Bude. Do you think we should make a serious attempt at changing your appearance? For example, give you some glasses or tint your hair?'

Maxine gave a gasp. 'Glasses. That's what's wrong. I'm missing my reading glasses. They'll be somewhere deep in my handbag. No wonder I can't see too clearly.'

'I've some sunglasses. You could borrow them for a day or two. It wouldn't improve your vision but you'd look rather different. And tomorrow I'll slip into a chemist in Bude, get you some hair dye. Haven't you ever wanted to be a dusky brown?'

'Don't do that, George. I'll just tie my hair back. I don't do that often but when I do it makes quite a difference. Look.' She demonstrated.

'OK. I've plenty of spare jumpers you can borrow, anyway.

And I've got a hat. Taken all together that'll make quite a difference.'

She looked across to the doctor. 'Maybe, Brian, you could come over again later this week and we could take stock on the best way forward?'

He nodded. 'Sure. I need to make sure that Maxine's leg is on the mend, anyway. I'll come on Thursday. I'll bring you a sick note as well.'

Maxine smiled. 'OK. You're both being very kind, thank you. Now, if you don't mind, I think I'd like to go back to sleep.'

George closed Maxine's bedroom door carefully and followed the doctor down the stairs. He was heading for the main door but she beckoned him into the kitchen and closed the door. 'If we keep our voices down Maxine won't hear anything.'

'Are we being responsible by staying silent? If not what do you think we should do?' asked Brian.

'It has to be Maxine's decision on whether she reports the whole thing and who she tells. But there are one or things we could do in the meantime.

'Did you notice,' George went on, 'that she let slip the name of the bed and breakfast place where it all started? "Tee-Side." I could drop in tomorrow morning and pick up her belongings. I'm sure she'd be glad to be reunited with her reading glasses.'

'Mm, I have some anxieties about Tee-Side,' replied Brian. 'I'm not certain that the place is as innocent as Maxine seems to think. If you go there, whatever else, please don't give them your address.'

George looked at him, waiting for enlightenment. 'Are you going to tell me anymore?'

'I will when I've completed a few more enquiries. I won't give you any details at this stage. I think, though, that I might begin with a general conversation with Peter Travers.'

CHAPTER 6

Sergeant Peter Travers was expecting to spend Wednesday morning examining any new evidence on the "Case of the Elusive Chimney Sweep" when he arrived at Bude Police Station.

Instead he found his attention drawn to a notice from Regional Police Headquarters on his email.

From: Emergency Police Response Unit, Exeter
To: Sergeant Travers, Bude
Date: Wed Aug 7ᵗʰ 2013

Subject: Escaped Prisoner – heading for Bude?

Please note prisoner details and photograph on Attachment.
Christian Henry Holdsworth escaped from Dartmoor Prison on the morning of Aug 2ⁿᵈ 2013. He attacked and severely injured the driver of the Tesco Van on his regular Friday delivery of fish to the prison, then drove the van out of the courtyard in his place. An enquiry is now taking place on just how this could happen and whether Holdsworth had inside assistance.

On the evening of Aug 4ᵗʰ the Tesco van was found abandoned in Tavistock. It is suspected he has taken a blue saloon car in its place. There was a break-in around the same time at a local garage. We presume number plates have also been changed. The garage is still assessing the plates taken.

Also stolen was a set of clothes belonging to the car's owner. He lives alone and is in the early stages of dementia, so we are yet to identify the items that are missing.

Records show that Holdsworth originally came from Bude. The prison psychologist advises that he may return to the area.

We strongly urge a policy of caution plus targetted publicity. This man is dangerous. Regional Police will supply armed resources to recapture him once his location is known.

Travers put his head into his hands. Here was an item that would derail any search for a missing chimney sweep. Numbers on the Bude payroll were too small to do both. He read through the email again and then looked at the attachment.

There was a photograph alright but on it a swarthy-faced Holdsworth looked fresh and young. The policeman saw that he had been in prison for ten years. Probably the picture had been taken when he was first imprisoned – maybe even an earlier prison sentence? He probably didn't look much like that now. For example, did he still have a beard?

Holdsworth was said by the prison documentation to be "just over six foot tall and heavily built, with snake tattoos down both arms". That was something that was unlikely to have changed.

He recalled that Fairclough had tattoos as well. Was that the fashion for men of a certain age? All it meant for now, though, was that he wouldn't be going around in shirt sleeves.

What had the man been in prison for? Glancing down the

attachment, Travers saw that his latest spell inside followed a job as getaway driver in an armed bullion robbery near Heathrow. One of the guards had been killed and another badly injured. There was no evidence that Holdsworth had fired the fatal gun, but equally no evidence that he hadn't. He looked to be very dangerous indeed.

And now he would be desperate as well.

Travers read the email one more time, alert for sub-messages. Clearly something had gone badly wrong at the prison. Had Holdsworth devised the escape plan on his own – did he have some brain as well as plenty of brawn – or had he just been lucky?

Was the prison guard complement lower than it should be as too many were on their summer holidays?

The policeman noted the date specified and glanced at his desk calendar. Hell's bells, that was five days ago. Dartmoor wasn't far: Holdsworth could have been in Bude for a couple of days already. He hoped Exeter would be a lot faster at sending reinforcements (if needed) than they'd been at warning him of the problem.

The psychologist thought he "might have headed for Bude". It was an easy prediction to make but was there more behind it? Was that because he'd felt he had to say something or were there other facts pointing in this direction? If so it would be good to know what they were.

In particular, did Holdsworth still have relatives in the town? Maybe his parents still lived here? If so that would be one place to go looking. Was anything known of his acquaintances from ten or fifteen years ago? Was there anything he was noted for in his time here? For example, was he into the outdoor life, say surfing or sailing? It was hard to imagine but was he once a member of a local gym?

Travers went to the main office and told his team that there would be an important meeting in half an hour: they were to clear their desks, he wanted everyone there. Then he went back to his office and wrote a sharp email to Exeter, raising the most urgent questions he had thought of so far. He warned them that his team would come up with more questions later.

By the time he had finished this the half hour was up. The sergeant headed for the meeting room. This would be a test of his authority; and of whether the station could work together.

An hour later Travers felt somewhat reassured. His small team had responded to the news more constructively than he had feared.

Joe Tremlitt, the older policeman who'd lived in Bude for many years, actually remembered the court case.

'It involved a man from Bude, see. It was a long time ago, more than a decade I reckon. I don't recall all the details, but it would only be an hour or two's work to get the various police records from the archive.'

The WPC on duty today, Holly Berry, was similarly constructive. 'I could chase up a contact in the local newspaper, collect any old stories they had on the man.'

Travers had made copies of the email from the Region and distributed them to the team. It was dissected ferociously.

Jamie Sampson made a key observation: 'There is no evidence

from what they say that the man is armed. He's serially aggressive but it wouldn't be easy for him to get hold of a firearm.'

'Yes,' said Tremlitt, 'he might steal number plates from a garage but he wouldn't find a gun – at least, not in Tavistock.'

After further discussion Sampson was delegated to visit the only gunsmith in Bude and to make sure his premises were secure.

Travers decided to invite some open discussion on the best form of publicity to give the town.

'The trouble is,' he said, 'that if the publicity's too intense it could be counterproductive.'

'That's right,' said Tremlitt. 'We're only a small team. The time needed to reassure locals and visitors would make it impossible to resource the effort needed to search for Holdsworth. The publicity might also frighten him off to another part of the country.'

In the end, after much debate, it was decided that Travers would ask Exeter to handle the publicity. That would include dealing with the South West television services, pleading for a line that would apply across the southwest. 'If we widen the area declared to be at risk, we might avoid a wave of panic here in Bude.'

Of course, once there was hard evidence that the man was hiding in Bude – if that ever happened – then more focussed publicity would be needed.

The sergeant shrugged. 'The situation is unclear. It'll have to be re-assessed day by day.'

Travers did, though, decide that he would give the local media and the Bude Visitor Centre an off-the-record briefing. It was essential that he kept them onside for the days ahead.

Implementing actions took most of the day.

Some of the tasks, assembling records, were fairly straightforward. Tremlitt was a hoarder. He'd hung on to all his old work diaries, which included his observations and reflections; without much effort he could identify the date of Holdsworth's trial at the Old Bailey: July 2003.

From there it was a matter of assembling firstly the police's own record of the case and secondly the name of the key policeman involved.

The court case coverage showed that the escaped convict had been even more unpleasant in early life than Dartmoor had suggested.

The senior policeman on the case, Chief Inspector Reg Harvey, had since retired. That was not much of a problem. Joe Tremlitt had plenty of contacts with men of his own age throughout the police force and was able, eventually, to track him down.

Harvey had started his career in the South West. He had won promotion to London for most of his time and then, after he retired, had moved back to North Devon. He currently resided in Coombe Martin.

Tremlitt gave him a call. Soon the wily local policeman had established a rapport that would have been impossible using official channels. So far the escape had been kept from the media. Harvey was horrified to hear that Holdsworth had escaped and was keen help with his recapture.

Tremlitt arranged to visit the retired man the following day. It was not certain what would emerge but given the man's continuing interest something crucial might come to light.

Holly Berry was following a broadly similar path in the media as she rang her old friend Sarah. The journalist had worked at the Bude and Stratton Post for many years and was happy to meet for lunch in the Falcon Hotel.

Berry wondered how much she could divulge and checked with Peter Travers. 'Guv, did you say you were going to see the current editor of the Post this afternoon?'

'He's coming here. Along with a few others.'

After a moment's thought her boss gave her permission to share the whole story with Sarah on a confidential basis.

The Falcon Hotel was only ten minutes walk away, on the other side of the Bude Canal. Once salads and wine had been ordered Holly explained the reason for calling. Both women were too young to have taken any interest in Holdworth during his Old Bailey trial but Sarah could see how his escape was a cause for concern.

Holly made sure her friend understood that the man had a vicious nature. 'It'll probably be made even worse by him being on the run.'

'The trial happened in July 2003,' she added.

Sarah was sure her newspaper would have covered the trial: 'When all's said and done there are not that many well-known people from Bude – famous or otherwise.'

'I can also contact the other Cornish papers, get whatever they have. We use one another all the time, it's like a humanised Google. Don't worry, not everything needs to be explained.'

The most difficult meeting was hosted by Travers. He judged the most important thing was that the event happened today, so invited the key people to the police station.

After all, the policeman had no control over the regional media machine and when or how it might churn into life. It was vital that the locals heard the news from him rather than the Regional news.

The police station had one smart meeting room, used mainly for visits from senior policemen. Travers hadn't used it in his four months in charge but decided that this situation was a good place to start.

He had taken the trouble to meet all the people he'd invited today when he first moved to Bude. This did not guarantee bonhomie but it helped. Coffee was served, then the policeman began by outlining the contents of the regional email he had received that morning.

'You can see it makes for a fine mess,' he admitted. 'In the future no doubt heads will roll at the prison. But our problem – and by that I mean all of us here, not just me – is the tone of the warning we should give to the general public in the town.'

The Bude and Stratton Post editor saw the problem. 'If it was certain Holdsworth was around here – say, if he'd been sighted – then we could put out banner headlines. We're only a weekly paper, our next edition comes out tomorrow. But you can only do that once. If it turned out, by the next edition a week later, he'd gone on to Falmouth, say, then we'd look stupid. We're not aspiring to be the gutter press.'

The head of the Bude Visitor Centre was similarly cautious. 'This is the sort of publicity that takes minutes to issue and years to dispel. The threat of terrorism is everywhere; people are very nervous these days. Even a whisper could spoil many holidays – they wouldn't forget and they wouldn't come back.'

Others voiced similar reservations. In the end it was not too difficult for Peter Travers to persuade them to give him some room to act before anything more frightening was announced.

He had a few days – but he had to make the most of it. When the policeman had been put in charge of Bude Police Station he had been pleased that the staff team was so compact. They might give him some trouble but there weren't many to do so. Now he was not so sure.

He could only hope Holdsworth would keep a low profile – or preferably go somewhere else.

CHAPTER 7

"Tee-Side" was a smart looking bed and breakfast house directly opposite the Bude golf course club house. George found it without difficulty next morning, though it was a struggle to find anywhere to park her car: the resort was very crowded in the summer months.

She found the house bell inside the glass porch, alongside a plaque giving the name of the proprietors, John and Diana Murdoch. There was also a sign declaring that the place had a five-star rating from Visit Cornwall.

Mrs Murdoch took a few minutes to answer – glancing through the side window, George realised that she was still serving breakfast. Had she come too early? The analyst had been motivated primarily by the need to get on with her main project.

'Good morning. Mrs Murdoch? My name is George Gilbert. I'm an old university friend of one of your guests, Maxine Tavistock.'

Mrs Murdoch seemed familiar with the name, anyway. 'Oh, do come in Mrs Gilbert. If you wouldn't mind waiting five minutes, I'm still busy serving breakfast. Would you like a cup of coffee while you wait?'

All the rooms had been turned into guest rooms. There was no lounge, so George had to sit at a small chair in the hallway. The guests came out of the breakfast room in ones and twos. Most were casually dressed holidaymakers, often in shorts and sandals, on their way to the beach. One or two, in jackets or smart suits, were probably bound for the office.

Mrs Murdoch joined the curly, dark-haired analyst again a few minutes later. 'I've just been upstairs to check. Maxine Tavistock isn't here at the moment. She booked in for a month but she warned me that she might be away for one or two days during that time. So I'm very sorry . . .'

'Oh, I know she's not here. She's staying with me for a day or two. We met by chance in Bude yesterday and I offered to show her my cottage. We were having such a good time reminiscing that she ended up staying the night. The thing is, she's left all her spare clothes and belongings here. That's not much of a problem, she'll be back before long, but I wondered if I could collect her reading glasses?'

Mrs Murdoch looked doubtful. 'Mrs Gilbert, I'm sure you're who you say you are. But I have an obligation to look after guests' belongings while they're staying with us, especially if they've been sent here by a local employer. That does give us a rather special status.'

The landlady seemed to preen herself. Then a more disturbing thought struck. 'I do hope there was nothing wrong with the guesthouse that put her off? We haven't had any complaints for a long time. I don't suppose you have a note from Dr Tavistock, asking me to give you her glasses?'

'I'll get Maxine to write something when I see her later. I'm sure she'll confirm that she is perfectly happy staying here, there

54

are no problems and she'll be back in a day or two. All being well I'll come again tomorrow. I presume you'll be able to recognise her signature?'

George would have liked to know the name of the local employer and whether she had other guests who worked for the same one but it was clear that for now she would learn no more.

The analyst was shown to the door. She stood for a moment musing in the porch. Was there anything else she should have asked? Nothing came to mind. She was about to move on when the door opened behind her and a guest emerged. He was of the suited variety, presumably off to some local employment.

'Excuse me, I couldn't help overhearing some of your conversation in the hall. I'm a friend of Maxine, we work for the same people. Do I gather that she's staying with you?'

'Maxine and I are old college friends. She's staying with me for a couple of days. But she'll be back – I can't compete with this quality of breakfast. Tell your work people if you like. And can I give her your name?'

'Ah, it's Sam, Sam Hudson. Please give her my regards.'

'I will, Sam. I'm sorry, I've got to go now.'

George made no further reply and let herself out into the street. Deliberately, though, she turned left, to walk in the opposite direction from where she had parked her car.

The man was probably completely innocent but there was no need to let him see the make and colour of her latest vehicle.

Brian was also keen to learn as much as he could about Maxine's kidnapping before their next joint session in Treknow.

He phoned Peter Travers' home at six o'clock but there was no answer. Something must be causing him to work late. He left a message, tried again at seven and then seven thirty. Finally he made contact.

'Hi Peter. Is something brewing? You're not normally working as late as this.'

'Hi Brian. We may have trouble in Bude. But it's more serious than brewing. I've been flat out today and it'll be the same tomorrow, I expect.'

'You still need to eat. Would you like to come over for some of Alice's Beef Wellington? I'm afraid that she made too much. She's not used to our new diets yet.' Alice was Brian's wife and the local primary school head. Brian knew very well that Peter lived on his own and seldom ate more than a scratch meal cooked in a hurry.

'I can't come for long, Brian, but that does sound delicious.'

'Alice is out this evening, visiting her family. So there'd just be the two of us. Actually I've got something I wouldn't mind bouncing off you.'

The combination of a high class meal and an intriguing puzzle was irresistible. Peter arrived twenty minutes later.

Eating was the first priority and Brian could see, from the way he wolfed down first and second helpings, that his friend was very hungry.

'Didn't you get any lunch today?'

'You know, you're right. I had so much to do today that there was no time for it. No wonder I'm hungry.'

'I'm not prying or anything but if you need someone to

bounce ideas off I'm around at the moment.'

'Thanks. I will, but maybe not this evening.'

There was silence while the policeman finished his meal. Then he turned to his friend.

'Go on then. What did you want to run past me?'

'Well, I came across a yarn yesterday from a new patient that was rather disturbing. Of course I advised her to bring it to you but she wouldn't. George Gilbert was with me and heard the tale as well; she advised the same.'

'George was with you, was she? Bless her, she seems to have an attraction for trouble. Did this all happen in her cottage?'

'That's where the confession took place. But the patient wouldn't take it further. All we could get out of her was that her inhibitions arose from her employer. Reading between the lines I suspect it was our old friend the Official Secrets Act that made her fearful of who she should talk to.'

There was one local organisation that was more deeply awash with Official Secrets than anywhere else in Bude and both men knew it.

'Hm. So you think she works at Cleave Camp?'

Cleave Camp was the government listening station, a few miles up the coast. On a clear day its collection of white satellite dishes could be seen for miles. It had started after the Second World War. The role of the Camp today was shrouded in secrecy but was thought to be mainly monitoring and making sense of satellite signals from around the world.

'I suspect so. George told me that her friend was the top Cambridge maths student of her year: would that tie in, d'you

57

reckon?'

'Brian, mathematicians are often good at coding and decoding messages. Some of them were the key people at Bletchley Park during the war – Alan Turing, for example.'

'I guess there's a similar role for such people today.'

Peter nodded. 'OK, Brian. That's the background. Now let's hear the problem.'

The doctor smiled. 'It was a very dramatic tale as she told it. Course, I've no idea if it was true or simply the product of an overworked imagination. But her injuries matched her story.'

'Brian, I've had a very long day and I've got other ones ahead of me. I can't cope tonight with you stretching it all out. Just give me the edited highlights.'

The doctor could see his friend was very tired and switched to briefing mode.

'All right. This woman was called Maxine, by the way. I can't just keep saying "her". But I won't tell you her surname. She said she'd been abducted from her guesthouse in Bude. She was taken off to some derelict farm and dropped down a coal hatch. Next morning two men started questioning her but she said she would need her tablet. So one of them brought her back to Bude, parked the car and went to collect it.'

'This is intriguing,' said Peter Travers, smiling. 'Don't make the rest of the tale too condensed.'

'It gets better,' replied Brian. 'Maxine managed to escape from the car and into the nearest shop. George was the only customer. The two women recognised one another, they'd been at Cambridge together. George cut through her ropes, whisked her off and brought her back to Treknow. She's been here ever since.'

'That's quite a tale,' admitted the policeman. 'I wish more kidnap victims had that much pluck.'

'I'm seeing her again tomorrow evening to check her various scrapes and make sure they're healing. What might make the difference, in her willingness to talk to you, would be if I had any idea of how the case might be investigated if she did. Or rather, investigated with some chance of success. On the story so far d'you have any ideas?'

The policeman was silent for a few moments.

'It sounds serious. But I can't start to do anything till she tells me herself. I've got a vicious escaped prisoner who comes from Bude to worry about at the moment – and that's not just a yarn. I'm not starting a case on hearsay – even from you.'

He considered. 'All this took place, when, the day before yesterday? Once she talks to me, if her bedroom's been left locked ever since, I could get the Scene of Crime Officers to have a look. The villain might have left traces. Mind, that wouldn't be much use unless they already had a criminal record.'

'Peter, what about the clothes she was wearing? I gather that was just her bathrobe. She was about to have a shower when she was captured.'

'Ah. That might give us something. Make sure nothing happens to it. It'd be tragic if George put it in the washing machine in a moment of absent-minded hygiene.'

Peter Travers mused a little more. 'I'd ask more about motive. There must be a good chance that it's connected in some way with Cleave Camp, if that's really where Maxine works. She's around forty, you say?'

'All I said was that she was a contemporary of George at Cambridge. So you've inferred correctly that she's around forty. I'll find her exact date of birth if you like – tell her I need it for my records.'

'Someone that age would be quite senior at Cleave Camp. There would be a lot they could give away under duress. Entrance protocols at the camp, vulnerabilities, codes, emergency procedures and so on. To say nothing of current threats to Britain and what is known about them. It doesn't bear thinking about: she probably had a very lucky escape.'

'So is there anything I could tell her, to encourage her to come to you?'

'I'd want to know more about the car they took her about in. She only travelled in the boot, you say? Even so, she'd have heard the sound of the engine as it changed gear up and down the various hills. The girl wouldn't know it but the engine might have some distinctive sound patterns that went with the type of car. A skilled mechanic might get more out of her – though that still wouldn't give us the exact car, of course.'

There was a pause. The policemen had exhausted his immediate responses.

'I've one other question,' said the doctor. 'Is there any wider pattern? Has this sort of crime happened around here before?'

'Ah.' The policeman reflected for a moment.

'There's been nothing like this that I've handled, either at Delabole or at Bude. Mind, if it was someone who was associated with Cleave Camp they might not have involved the ordinary police at all.'

'Why ever not?'

'Well, we've got a Cleave Camp "specialist" who is linked to the station. Special Branch, I suspect. Colin Caldwell, he's called. He'd have hoovered up any crime linked directly to the Camp, solved it himself without telling the rest of us anything. He doesn't understand the concept of team. I'll ask him directly next time I see him.'

'Of course, he might not tell you the truth.'

'No, but I'm a policeman. If he lies I'll be able to tell.'

The two talked for a while longer and then the policeman announced that with his current workload he needed an early night.

Brian was pleased he'd taken the trouble to tap his friend's experience and feelings. He'd been left with several ideas that would be useful when he next talked to Maxine.

CHAPTER 8

Peter Travers wrestled with competing priorities as he drove in to Bude on Thursday morning.

Obviously, in the mind of his various bosses, his priority must be trying to track down Holdsworth. By now there should be information to hand on his relatives in the town, maybe a list of his old friends. They would all need to be visited and warned. For his small team that was a day or two's work in itself.

He was still exercised, though, by the missing Fairclough. There was no way he could put any resources onto tracing the house clearing chimney sweep ahead of the efforts on the escaped prisoner. He still had a feeling, though, that the man was important, it wasn't just a case of him taking an unexpected holiday break.

He gave a little thought to the doctor's tale from the previous evening. But he couldn't take action there until he was told the tale directly.

For now both Fairclough and Maxine would have to wait.

As usual Travers arrived at the Station ahead of his colleagues. Normally that wouldn't matter; today it bothered him a little. They would all need to up their game, at least until Holdsworth had been recaptured.

Quickly he checked his emails and then looked at the Regional website. No, there was no hard news: the man was still at large. Then he found the press release about him that had been issued to the television companies. He had been worried about starting a wave of panic in the southwest but there was no risk of overkill here: it was the most downbeat announcement he had seen for months.

Looking further through the press release, he saw that a non-illustrated version of the message had appeared on last night's Regional news, but appearing well down the order. Alert watchers in the southwest had been made aware of the escape but not in a way that would raise much alarm.

Given that there was no evidence yet to refute the idea that Holdsworth was hiding away on Dartmoor, that could be justified; but it was a different message to the warning he had been given about Bude.

At that moment Holly Berry arrived, and a few moments later his two police constables. Then to his surprise Jess Holland, walked in. That was an encouragement. Holly had rung her and she guessed she might be needed.

There was no sign yet of the Special Branch man, Colin, but there was no reason to think that Holdsworth would have any connection with Cleave Camp so that was more or less justified.

Using council and phone records, Berry had been assembling data on the escaped man's relatives still living around Bude.

'Both his parents have died,' she announced, 'since he was put away. There's still a sister and a younger brother here, plus a couple of aunts. There were others but they've died or moved away.'

Information on the man's old friends was harder to find. There was no data, for example, on his favourite drinking places. The police team had been told, however, that Holdsworth had been a snooker enthusiast and a fisherman. These were two areas now awaiting investigation.

Travers decided that top priority must be given to Holdsworth's relatives.

'Each family member that we know about needs a personal visit,' he declared. 'First we need to make sure that they understand that there is a real risk at the moment and they need to take extra care. This man is violent. Make sure they all understand that they have to lock their doors. And they ought not to go out on their own after dark until we give them the all clear.'

'We need to check that they've each got a mobile so they can alert us if they see or hear anything,' added Joe Tremlitt.

'Good idea,' said Travers. 'We've a pile of spare phones here in the station. Lend them one if they haven't got one – and make sure they can use it, at least to ring 999.'

'Are we just to give them a friendly warning?' asked Jamie Sampson.

'Much more than that. I want you to check if they've seen or heard anything of Holdsworth recently. When you go there and they come to the door, do they look surprised or is your visit half-expected? Ask when did they last hear from him? It'd be a relief if we could show that his escape was a complete shock in Bude. And while you're there, check if they know of any more relatives in the area.'

The final arrangements were made. Sergeant Travers insisted that they undertook the visits in pairs: 'Tremlitt and Berry together as one pair, please, and Sampson and Holland as the other.'

'What're you going to do, guv?' asked Holland.

'I thought I'd visit the snooker club. See if I can find anyone who remembers Holdsworth, maybe collect some names ready for another round of visits this afternoon. Then I'll contact Regional headquarters and see what progress they've made on stolen cars. But listen, I want to know at once if any of you learn anything specific.'

The snooker club was not immediately productive. A quick phone call told Travers that on weekdays it didn't open until eleven. He used the intervening time to bring his paperwork up to date.

When he arrived the club was fairly empty but there was an older man serving on the bar who seemed to be in overall charge.

'Have you been around here for long?' asked the policeman.

'Most of my working life,' he replied. 'I've only had the full time job in charge, though, for the last three years.'

'Right then, do you remember Christian Holdsworth?'

The man's face wrinkled in disgust. 'I remember him alright. Thank goodness he's not here anymore. Useless idiot, caused us endless grief. He started several fights and somehow or other he was never on the losing side. Why d'you want to know?'

'Routine police enquiry.' Travers had decided that he wasn't going to say any more at this stage. There was no point in starting a panic. 'Can you remember if he had any special mates that he hung out with while he was here?'

'Mates? You must be joking.' But he could see from the policeman's face that it wasn't a joke. He paused to give the question some thought.

'He didn't keep friends for long. He'd fall out with them over something or other. There was only one bloke that stuck by him through thick and thin, he was called Harry.'

'Full name?'

'Now you're pushing me. Harry hasn't been in here for years. But in his case it's cos he got married and started having kids. No longer allowed out, you might say. A triumph for feminism. Let me see . . . It was something like Harry Larwood. No, that's the old fast bowler. That's right, it was Harry Lockwood. He still lives around here, I reckon.'

The barman sounded unenthused. Travers decided that this was as much as he was going to get, it would be best to quit while he was ahead. There'd be other ways of finding out where Lockwood lived. It would be wise to warn him that his former friend was no longer safely behind bars.

Once back at the Station Peter Travers found that his team were still out, presumably dealing with the relatives. He decided to use the time till they returned checking up on progress at the regional level.

It took a while but eventually he was put through. He'd reached the woman who was holding the various strands of the Holdsworth case together. She sounded to be about his age, had a pleasant manner and was called Andrea. Travers made sure he had a note of her name and phone number, they might have more contact in the future.

'Have there been any developments since yesterday afternoon?' he began.

'You knew about the car, registration plates and clothes stealing in Tavistock?' Andrea began.

'Yes. Though I wasn't told the make of the car.'

'Well it's irrelevant now. That car was found in Okehampton this morning. We're still checking the DNA but the police there reckon he dumped it and took another in its place. It disappeared about the same time and place, anyway. The new one's a purple Ford Focus. The trouble is, Holdsworth's got a stock of registration numbers so we can't be sure of its number.'

'But you must be able to list the numbers stolen?'

'The trouble is, Peter, there were half a dozen break-ins at large garages near Okehampton overnight, with about ten sets of number plates taken from each. So it's not just one or two. He's being quite clever.'

'You've got the list of number plates stolen, though?'

Andrea sounded defensive. 'Almost. In every case but one, anyway.'

There was a stunned pause. 'Andrea, I can't believe I heard that right.'

'The trouble is, one of the garages happened to be in the process of being sold. The previous owner has disappeared and the new owners can't find any reference list of the plates that have gone missing. It must be there somewhere but the admin he's

67

acquired is a total muddle. So even if I give you my list it might not include his car.'

Travers was silent. There was no point, he told himself, in getting annoyed with Andrea. It wasn't her fault the previous garage owner had been sloppy.

'Right. Well here in Bude, given the unproven musings of the prison psychologist, my team are visiting all his relatives and friends to warn them he might appear. Fortunately he doesn't seem to have had many friends. I'm waiting for them to come back.

Andrea could see why he was frustrated. 'OK. I've got your number, Peter. I'll let you know when I have anything new. And can you do the same? If we don't all work together this whole thing could go horribly wrong.'

CHAPTER 9

Thursday evening: crunch time, thought George, as she drove back to Treknow from another day of interviews and demonstrations at Limelight. Her anxieties concerning its finances were building up. She had a vague sense that something was going on behind the scenes, but it would require a lot of energy to find out what it was.

Meantime Maxine had to be persuaded to take action of her own. Or if she wouldn't speak out to someone in authority, then she would need to take her chance and move out, perhaps back to Tee-Side.

George was relieved to find Maxine still in residence when she reached Ivy Cottage, looking much more alert than the day before. Her old college friend had made herself at home in the sitting room, doing something with a fresh notebook taken from George's stock. George had feared her guest might have done a bunk and moved away.

The analyst slipped upstairs, changed out of her business suit, had a quick shower and then returned, more relaxed, in jeans and a casual sweater. In the meantime her lodger made them both a large pot of tea.

Brian Southgate turned up a few minutes later. Nothing was said but all three could sense that the coming conversation was critical.

'Right,' said George. 'Time to catch up. Shall I go first?'

She took a swig from her tea and looked around. No one else was pushing to speak.

'Yesterday morning, when I got to Bude, I decided to take a short visit to Tee-Side.'

Maxine looked annoyed. 'I thought you said you would keep my affairs secret?'

'Maxine, I said nothing at all about your misadventure. I simply said that we'd known each other at college, happened to meet again in Bude and that I'd invited you to visit my cottage. Then you'd decided to stay with me for a night or two. Of course I didn't say where my cottage was.'

'So why did you say you were there?'

'Easy. I asked if I could pick up your reading glasses. The trouble was, the landlady was very conscious of guest-rights. She wouldn't give them to me without a signed note from you.' She shrugged. 'I could go back tomorrow and get them if you liked?'

'Hm.' Maxine pondered for a moment. She had known at the time that she'd let slip the name of her bed and breakfast house but hoped it hadn't been picked up. Could hardly complain that it had.

'The only other thing that happened,' said George, 'was that one of the guests followed me out. He said he'd overheard my conversation in the hallway and that he was a friend of yours. He claimed that you both had the same employer.'

'Did you get his name?'

'He said he was called Sam. Sam Hudson.'

'Sam. Oh yes, I remember him. He came to the guest house a couple of weeks ago. We used to meet over breakfast. But we didn't talk shop at all, except in his car. It wouldn't be right – or safe – in front of the other guests.'

Brian had been silent up to now but thought this was as good a time as any to nail the question of Maxine's employer.

'Maxine, I think we need to know more about your employer. I can believe that you're not empowered to tell people what you do. But if I guess, and guess correctly, then you wouldn't need to say. It would help, though, with our subsequent conversation.'

He paused. Maxine seemed to be trying to pick a way through the legal jungle.

'Go on, then, Brian. Try it. Who d'you think pays my wages?'

'The only employer I know around here that's into Official Secrets on an industrial scale is Cleave Camp – you know, the government listening station up near Morwenstow. There must be millions of secrets they hold there, from all that they pick up with their satellite dishes.'

Maxine did not confirm his suggestion but nodded slowly.

'The sort of thing they might do, that would make use of a top-class mathematician,' he added, 'would be decoding the encrypted messages.'

Maxine did not confirm he was correct but neither did she dismiss the idea as wrong.

All this prompted further thoughts from George. 'You know, Maxine, I wondered why you'd dropped below the parapet after finishing your PhD. I wrote to you once or twice but you never replied. Did you get my letters? Were you embargoed from contact with the outside world? Have you been hidden away ever since? If you've been living here it's amazing we've not run into one another in Bude.'

'I was only transferred to Bude a month ago. Before that I was based in Cheltenham. I can drive but don't currently own a car. The management found me somewhere to live on site for a couple of weeks and then Sam appeared. That meant they could pack the two of us off to Tee-Side. It was comfortable and convenient, he could give me a lift in on most days.'

'What about coming home?' asked George.

'The Camp runs a late bus into Bude every evening, you see, for when any of us are working overtime.'

'It makes more sense why you were so wary of telling us too much,' admitted George. 'But all this secrecy stuff cuts both ways. If you had a duty to stay silent, your employers had a duty of care to protect you. They're the ones who have failed, not you.'

This was a new angle. Maxine did not immediately respond.

'It stretches belief to think that your abduction had nothing to do with your job,' continued Brian remorselessly. 'You must accept that?'

'I resisted the idea at first, but I've been thinking more clearly today. You're right, there's no other reason I can think of why anyone should be interested in me. I mean, I don't have a rich uncle who would pay a ransom to get me back – not a big one, anyway. That's the ransom, I mean, not the uncle.'

Maxine turned to Brian. 'What put you on to the Camp, can you say?'

'George has said how she took up one strand of your story. I decided to pursue another – without giving anything away, of course.'

Maxine looked at him quizzically. 'Go on.'

'As I told you, I've known Peter Travers since our school days. He lives the other side of Delabole. Last night my wife was out so I invited him for supper. He lives on his own, you see, so he's always glad of a decent meal.'

Maxine could see where this account was going. 'And you told him my story. Despite telling me it was all in confidence. That's despicable.' She looked angry.

'Hey, take it easy. As I say, Peter and I are close. Fifteen years ago he was best man at my wedding. He often bounces ideas and issues from his work off on me and I sometimes do the same with him. We never give names or operational details, just enough to allow a wide ranging discussion. He won't – can't – do anything unless you take the initiative and go and see him. He's got far too much on at the moment anyway.'

'And it was Peter that suggested I might have connections with Cleave Camp?'

'To be honest, I can't remember which of us said it first. But we kicked it around a bit and we couldn't think of any alternative. I mean, you talked about a local employer and there aren't any other government offices around here. What I was really after was some idea of what he might do to push the case forwards. I thought that, if there was something tangible, that might encourage you to speak out.'

'So what would this latter day Sherlock Holmes do?'

73

'Don't mock, he's an up-to-date copper. There were two areas he picked on that we didn't mention two days ago. The most urgent, I guess, was to get a Scene of Crime team in to examine your bedroom and shower at Tee-Side. If your assailant spent much time in there and then had to get you away there's a good chance that he left traces.'

'Ah, the distinctive right thumbprint?'

'I had more hope from traces of DNA. Can you remember, was he wearing gloves when he seized you?'

'I'm not sure. I wasn't aware of anything like that at the time. But it was all over in a few seconds.'

'Hey, wait a minute,' interjected George. 'There's something else that might help. He must have touched your bathrobe. And you've still got that – you were wearing it when you escaped.'

'What happened to it?' asked Brian.

'When I took it off I put it in the linen basket in the bathroom,' Maxine admitted. So where was it now? She looked at George inquiringly.

'Goodness me, I haven't had time to wash it yet – I'm a working woman.' George replied,' I only do clothes washing at weekends.'

The mood level across the room rose. There might be ways out of the maze after all.

'Brian, you talked about DNA in the shower,' said Maxine. 'What was the other strand Peter suggested?'

Privately Brian felt relief that she no longer sounded so angry. 'Peter thought that there might be something to be learned from what you heard in the car. He said the police had access to transport experts. Every type of car is subtly different. They might be able to glean something from the sound of the engine, say as it changed gear.'

'The thing is, Maxine, if anything is going to be done to find your assailants, every day that goes by makes it a lot harder.' George sensed that Maxine was far less negative this evening than she had been before.

'Before we discuss that, can I share my new ideas and findings too?'

This was a surprise. George looked across to Brian. What on earth could her old friend have found?

'Can you pass the notebook, please?'

George reached over to the table and handed it over. Maxine took the book and opened it to her jottings of the day.

'When we talked two days ago I think I was suffering from delayed shock.' She looked across to Brian who nodded that this was a possibility.

'I mean, I didn't know why I had been taken but I could see my job was the most likely cause. I started to recollect all the things I knew and realised what an enemy power might do to make me share them. It wouldn't be just a matter of dying but dying in a slow and painful way. I don't know how well I'd cope with that.'

She paused for a moment.

'Anyway, today I found I had much sharper recall of the whole thing, in particular the journey from the farmhouse back to Bude. I told you, didn't I, that John Humphrys was announcing the time on the car radio every few minutes. Well, I've always been good at remembering numbers. I found that, if I forced myself, I could link several of those times to changes in car speed.'

'Go on,' urged Brian. This was better than he had dared hope.

'In particular, I remembered Humphrys giving a time just as we came up to the rush hour traffic jam. I think that's what it must have been. The speed dropped from a steady forty or fifty down to no more than a jittery twenty miles per hour. It happened at eight forty four.'

Maxine paused for effect and then continued. 'After that the journey was repeated stops and starts. We finally stopped for good – outside the antique shop – at the start of the nine of clock news. So that would give just under quarter of an hour to traverse the rush hour traffic. Do you reckon that could be useful?'

'Maxine, that's brilliant. We know it was Tuesday when you were brought to the antique shop. Traffic around here will have a different pattern in August because of tourists and school holidays. But it'll be much the same for each weekday over the whole month. We could experiment. Crucially, it might be possible to deduce whether you were driven in to the town from the south or from the north.'

Maxine looked pleased to have earned some praise. She had spent far too long telling herself that in some way she must have failed.

'There was one more thing I remembered,' Maxine added. 'Near the start of the journey, no more than five minutes in, I heard a splashing of water outside the car. What on earth d'you think that was?'

A moment of silence while they each tried to imagine.

'It couldn't possibly be a car wash, could it?' asked Brian. 'Mind, I can't see why he'd have needed to wash the car on this journey – unless he was a very upmarket villain.'

'Could it have been a burst water main?' asked George.

'Might the clever policeman be able to tell us?' wondered Maxine.

It sounded that, at long last, she was agreeing to tell her story to Travers. Brian, though, had an alternative idea.

'Maxine, there was one more thing I learned from Peter. That is, he mentioned that one of his colleagues was on the payroll of Cleave Camp: Colin, I think he was called. Would it be easier for you to tell your story to him?'

For a moment doubts flooded across Maxine's face. In her enthusiasm to take the case forward she had forgotten her worries about the Official Secrets Act.

It did sound, though, that talking to the Cleave Camp security officer might offer her the best way forward.

CHAPTER 10

Friday morning saw Peter Travers once more battling to recapture, or at least keep track of, Christian Holdsworth, as he trawled through his messages in the Bude Police Station.

Colin was not there – Travers assumed he was working on some security issue or other in Cleave Camp – but the rest of his team were all present. That was good: working on an important case seemed to be drawing them closer together.

At nine thirty the sergeant began their daily progress meeting on the hunt for Holdsworth by summarising the latest news from Regional HQ – i.e. Andrea. He had rung her as soon as he got in but there had been no further hard news since yesterday.

'She believes, and I accept her evidence, that Holdsworth stole a purple Ford Focus from Okehampton and then refitted number plates. Unfortunately, for technical reasons, we can't be sure of the new number.'

'Purple isn't such a popular colour for cars these days,' observed Sampson. 'Someone needs to check the traffic cameras. There'll be less purple ones than red, black or silver.'

'Can you distinguish purple on a black and white screen?' Travers had some doubts.

'Our troubles will really start when the bloke starts using a bicycle,' observed Tremlitt. 'People don't even bother to report when one's been stolen.'

That was a miserable thought, mused Travers.

'As long as he's using cars, the crucial thing will be to see where the Focus is dumped and the next one is taken,' responded Berry. 'Is he heading for Bude or the opposite direction? Exeter, say or even back towards London. After all, that's where he was living before his latest arrest.'

'Yes, Okehampton is more or less due north of Dartmoor,' agreed Travers. 'It'd be good to have something better than a psychologist's hunch to guide us on his direction of travel.'

'So where've we got to with his local relatives?" he asked, after it was clear no one had anything to add on vehicles.

'Between us we've seen all the relatives on yesterday's list,' summarised Tremlitt. 'They all seemed shocked he'd escaped and rather frightened. They'll lock their doors from now on. We had no sense that any of them knew more.'

'And we didn't hear mention of anyone else in the family either,' added Holland. 'We've covered the field. So what about friends?'

'The snooker club wouldn't be pleased to see him back,' said Travers. I talked to the man behind the bar, he runs the place these days. He could only think of one person who had stood by him in all his troubles, a chap called Harry Lockwood.'

'And did you find him?' asked Sampson.

'I tried to see him yesterday afternoon. He lives up near the golf course. He wasn't at home, his wife said he was at work – he's a taxi driver. But he normally comes home for lunch and to see his toddler. I told her one of us would try again this lunchtime. But he's settled down now. No reason to think he's part of any escape plot. We have to make sure he knows Holdsworth is no longer inside, so he's ready in case he appears.'

'So for now there's nothing more we can do?'

'The only other clue we've been given on friends is that he used to go sea fishing.'

'I fish on my days off,' said Sampson. 'When the weather's not too rough, anyway. D'you want me to chase that one, guv?'

'That'd be great, Jamie. OK on your own?'

'Feminism is still a work in progress in the fishing community. It's mostly a male preserve. I'm happy to go on my own.'

Fifteen minutes later Travers' team were back at their desks, catching up with the jobs they'd been doing before Holdsworth took all their attention.

The Sergeant's thoughts turned once more to Barry Fairclough. Only three days ago the man had been his top concern. They'd been starting to collect various items of data: how much was now available?

'We had a return call from the Visitor Centre,' said Holly Berry, once the question was raised.

'What did that tell us?'

'I'd rung them yesterday morning you see, guv. They rang back to say they'd checked their recent records. Fairclough's name had been mentioned by a complainant who rang from Crackington Haven.'

'A recent Fairclough customer, you mean?'

'Well, sort of. He'd booked Fairclough to come and clear his mother's house. He'd even paid a deposit but the man hadn't turned up.'

'How long ago was that?'

'Three weeks. So if that was soon after he disappeared it's consistent with what Jake said.'

It was information of a sort. 'Was there anything else?'

'We've had another reply from the DVLA,' replied Holland. 'We'd given them a headache. They're used to identifying vehicles from the name and address of the owner; and identifying the owner from the make and number of a vehicle. Our question fell somewhere between the two.'

'It must be possible. That's what computers are good at. Tell them it's urgent.'

'I did, guv. Or rather, I told them it was a murder inquiry – well, it might be. They've now checked their records. They've got two vehicles registered to Barry Fairclough: one's a small green estate, a Vauxhall Astra, the other's a medium-sized white van. Neither of them is very new. They've given us both their numbers.' She looked further down her notes. 'They've also given us his address.'

'At last,' said the sergeant. 'Where is it? One visit should be enough to tell us whether he's gone off on holiday, or else had some sort of accident.'

'And now we've got his registration numbers, guv, we might see if either vehicle has been caught on the traffic monitoring cameras,' added Sampson.

Jess Holland looked at the address then stood up to study the large scale map of the area which hung on one wall. 'It's as we thought on Tuesday, he lives in the middle of nowhere: a mile from the nearest hamlet and about five miles from Bude. The nearest town is Holsworthy.'

The name triggered an idea. 'Hey guv,' said Joe Tremlitt, 'isn't that the sort of place Holdsworth might hide up in? He'd pass that way if was heading from Okehampton to Bude but staying off the A30.'

It sounded a good excuse to visit sooner rather than later.

Half an hour later Peter Travers set out in one of the station's police cars, accompanied by Holly Berry. Travers drove while Berry navigated.

The journey didn't take long. Fairclough's cottage was off the road, down a bendy lane which ran through a dense wood. There was a gate into the yard which needed opening but it wasn't locked.

The officers studied the building carefully for a few minutes before getting out of the car. It was a small, thatched cottage in reasonable condition. The walls were whitewashed and the paint on the windows looked to be recent. There was no sign of any vehicles.

'No reason to think it's been abandoned, anyway,' observed Berry. 'Let's see if anyone's at home.'

Both officers got out and strolled over to the main door. Peter Travers gave it a solid knock but there was no answer, even after he knocked a second time. The policeman gave a shrug.

'There's no car so it's no surprise he's not here, Holly. The question is what was he planning when he went away? Let's have a look round the back.'

Both officers scanned the windows as they struggled through the garden to reach the kitchen at the rear, but they were all firmly locked. The kitchen doorway too was firmly shut.

'Hold on a minute,' said the sergeant. He leaned down and picked up the doormat. Beneath it nestled a Yale key.

'Looks like Fairclough didn't feel the need for top grade security. Probably thought he was safe enough, living out in the country. We'd better have a look inside.'

He leant forward and tried the key. The kitchen door swung open and the pair stepped inside.

'Try not to touch anything, Holly. This might turn out to be a crime scene. We don't want to give the Scene of Crime team the excuse that we've corrupted it.'

The pair walked slowly through the cottage. It was reasonably tidy: there was no evidence that there had been violence or any other disruption.

'It looks like I would expect for a working man who'd gone out to do a day's work,' said Holly. 'If he'd gone off on a long holiday he'd surely have left it in less of a muddle?'

Travers tried one or two drawers. There was a spare key in one and he slipped it into his pocket for later examination.

'Can you see any sort of calendar or diary?'

They wandered round downstairs but nothing caught their eye.

'OK, let's try upstairs.'

The cottage was compact; the staircase ran up the side of the living room. Travers led the way, though he didn't expect to find anything odd. Gently he opened the first door on the landing and peered round it.

'There's no one here, anyway.' He stepped inside and Holly followed him into the room.

A scruffily made-up double bed stood on the far side. A modest amount of furniture – a wardrobe and a chest of drawers – had been placed against the other walls. There were no signs of books or diaries.

'Doesn't look like he hangs onto the furniture he takes in his clearances,' observed Holly. 'None of this lot is worth very much.'

'He needs the money more than the furniture. I bet he's not home all that often. Come on, let's go.'

'It looks unlikely that he's gone off on holiday,' said Travers as the pair made their way downstairs. 'Which makes it more likely that something's happened to him while he was on a job.'

'The houses he clears are empty, so he'd be there on his own. Might he have fallen down the stairs?'

'It's possible, I suppose. And broken his phone in the fall?'

'Trouble is, guv, we've no clue where he was working. There are plenty of empty houses in the area. And they might not be revisited for ages.'

'Hm. Our best hope is the white van. That should be easy to spot. Let's get back and see if Jess Holland's turned up anything from traffic control.'

The pair relocked the door, headed back to the police car and set off back to the road.

As they drove away a tall, heavily built man watched them

from the woods.

There had been a massive reel of green twine in the kitchen, no doubt for bundling up items collected. It was as well, he thought, that he had arranged the string across the lane. That had given him some warning of when to expect visitors.

He had slipped out of the kitchen door and into the woods just as the police officers had been knocking at the front.

CHAPTER 11

That same Friday morning, George Gilbert drove Maxine up the A39 towards Bude and Cleave Camp. Maxine had had one or two moments of doubt the previous evening but had finally confirmed that, whatever the complications, she would go and report her story to security staff at the Camp. In practice that meant Colin Caldwell.

George had offered her a lift all the way to the Camp to make sure she got there and her resolve didn't falter.

But even on the journey Maxine was starting to worry again.

'For goodness sake, don't look so guilty,' advised George, glancing across to her passenger as she drove along a straight bit of road. 'You've not done anything wrong. You're the victim, not the assailant. It's down to you that you got away. Just tell 'em your story, same as you told me. And if they start to bully you, ask them if it's ever happened before.'

Maxine looked puzzled. 'What difference would that make?'

'If you're not the first person from Camp that's been attacked, that'd reveal a huge gap in their security. I mean, if you're carrying secrets in your head for them, secrets which others would value, they've got a strong duty to make sure you're kept safe. In this day and age I'd have thought some sort of tracking devices could be fitted to all their staff. Security can't be just about

86

guarding barbed wire fences.'

Maxine looked moderately reassured.

'Won't you need a security pass or something?' asked George as they drew close to the turnoff into Bude.

'Crumbs, in all my worries that'd completely slipped my mind.' Maxine thought for a second. 'That'll still be in my handbag in Tee-Side, along with my reading glasses. Would you mind dropping in there on the way?'

'I'll come in with you if you like. Prove to Mrs Murdoch that you and I really do know one another.'

There was the usual struggle to find parking – it was only eight thirty, most tourists were enjoying breakfast while many workers hadn't yet left home – but eventually George found somewhere. 'We shouldn't need to be more than a few minutes,' she observed.

Mrs Murdoch was pleased to see Maxine and relieved to see her and George together.

'Your room's been double locked all the time since I found you weren't here on Tuesday morning,' she said. 'It was a pity you didn't give me advanced warning – but then it was a nice surprise for you two to meet one another. When will you be back here properly?'

'I'll let you know later today,' replied Maxine. She'd already decided that would depend on what happened at the Camp.

She followed the landlady upstairs and watched as she produced a bunch of keys and used two of them to open her room. 'I won't be a minute,' she said. 'Would you mind double locking it again when I leave?'

She entered the room and claimed her handbag, checking the security pass and her reading glasses were still present. Remembering last night's conversation with George and Brian on crime scenes, she decided not even to open the door of the shower. Soon she was back downstairs.

Meanwhile George, waiting downstairs, had once more bumped into Sam Hudson as he came out from the breakfast room.

'Oh, hello Sam. Maxine's with me this time.'

'Ah, does she want a lift?'

'Ask her yourself. She'll be back down in a minute.'

Maxine seemed pleased to see Sam again and grateful to be offered a lift. George reflected that psychologically it would be good for her friend to revert to her normal Camp routine.

And she would avoid the extra journey. The Camp was off the beaten track; going there and back might take an hour. Today she had a busy morning planned in the Bude office and later her first weekly talk to visitors at Limelight. She also wanted to cross-check various details. Maxine was not the only enigma in this part of the world.

Maxine shared the story of her last few days with Sam as they drove to Cleave camp. There was no need for secrecy, he too was an insider.

It was a useful rehearsal. Wary of gossip, she asked him not to pass on the story to anyone else until she had also shared it with Camp security.

An hour later she was in Colin Caldwell's office and telling her tale again.

Caldwell did not interrupt, listened carefully and made occasional notes on his laptop. Maxine finished with her escape from the car and into the antique shop, culminating with her rescue by an old college friend. 'And that's where I've been ever since.'

Caldwell was obviously shaken. His first concern, though, was with possible threats to the Camp rather than with offering sympathy to Maxine. But at least he didn't raise the spectre of the Official Secrets Act.

'Would you mind waiting here for a few minutes, Maxine? There are one or two things I need to check. I'll get Samantha to bring you some coffee.'

He took his laptop with him. Half an hour had elapsed before he returned, looking slightly harassed.

'It's as I feared. You're staying at Tee-Side? I've just been checking the Personnel records. That was where the last analyst was staying before she went missing. That's the one thing I can find that you both have in common. Somehow or other, I fear, they've latched onto the place as a Camp vulnerability.'

Maxine felt a deep sense of betrayal that it had happened before but she managed to hide the emotion; Caldwell might not know how to respond. Instead she considered what he'd said. This was telling her a lot more than she'd expected. 'How long ago did this happen, then?'

'Oh, not long. It was earlier this year: end of June.'

'So what happened to her?'

Caldwell looked like he was about to start on his "need to

know" homily and then puffed his cheeks and relented. The fact that Maxine was here, free, that she had outwitted her captors and could tell her story, was a golden opportunity. He was wise enough not to let it slip.

'Last time, Maxine, we were never sure what really happened. It was a trainee analyst called Colette. She was an Irish girl, this was her first trip to Bude and we heard from several colleagues that she seemed homesick. And she'd recently lost her latest boyfriend. That might have affected her more than she had let on.

'The first we knew that anything was amiss was when she didn't come into Camp. We checked with Cheltenham, of course, but she wasn't there either. But for several days we had no reason to suspect foul play. She was owed some leave and had been talking to colleagues about using it to explore other parts of Cornwall. It might just have been a muddle as to how she took time off.

'After a week or so she hadn't reappeared. One of my colleagues went to Tee-Side to check but her room was locked and empty. The landlady assumed she'd left. It was as if Colette had decided to give up working here.

'Then my colleague was given a handwritten note addressed to the Camp Commander. We checked: it was Colette's handwriting. It asked for special leave: said she'd heard that her mother had been taken ill and she'd gone back to Northern Ireland.'

'But you've got everyone's family details on file. You must have checked?'

'Of course. But it turned out Colette's records were slightly out of date. Her mother had moved home a year before and we didn't have her new address. Further investigation showed the mother had also remarried and changed her name. It took a couple of weeks to track her down; she was perfectly well and living in a Belfast suburb.'

'But wasn't she concerned?'

'She hadn't heard from Colette but she wasn't worried. Her daughter had told her that she might "disappear" from time to time.

'The trouble was, three weeks had now elapsed and we didn't know where to start looking. There was no reason why she should disappear from her lodgings, for example, she might have gone walking on the cliffs. Her letter might just have been a way of swinging some free time. By now she might have reached Lands End.' He shrugged, 'Equally, she might be fine and living in another part of the UK.'

'So you did nothing?' Maxine did her best to keep a level tone but it was not an encouraging account.

'It was a unique problem. There was nothing else happening to make us think that the Camp was under attack. I wasn't certain that it mattered. We only have limited resources here so we put it on the back burner. Now you've come with a similar tale, of course, we'll have to take it much more seriously.'

There was silence. Maxine wondered what "taking it seriously" would actually involve and what difference it might make. Caldwell looked to be asking himself much the same question.

After a pause Maxine decided to push her ideas (which had mostly come from George or Brian, though she wouldn't admit that) as far as she could.

'In terms of evidence, Mr Caldwell, I've still got the bathrobe they took me away in. I put it in a plastic bag. They man-handled me several times so that might carry some DNA traces. And my room at Tee-Side has been locked ever since I was abducted. There might be traces of my assailant inside the shower.'

'In other words, you think we should involve the local police and treat it as a crime?'

Maxine was incensed. 'It is a crime, surely? Abduction is a violent crime. It must be against the law. And goodness knows what might have happened to me next if I hadn't got away.'

Caldwell's instinct for secrecy battled against the common sense wisdom of involving the local police. 'You may be right. I'm worried about how we keep control on the local police once they're involved. Who will do the interviews when someone is arrested? I'll give it more thought.' Another idea came to him. 'By the way, where are you staying this weekend? It'd be best to keep away from Tee-Side until we've had a chance to check it over. I'll let you know when it's had the all-clear.'

Maxine wandered back to check new material at her desk. At least there'd been no mention of the Official Secrets Act. She'd have to stay a few more days with George. That'd give the two of them more time to think around the underlying problem.

CHAPTER 12

After she had dropped Maxine off at Tee-Side, George walked through the town to the Exhibition offices behind the Visitor Centre.

While she was keen to know the effect of Maxine's tale on the security staff at Cleave, her priority for today was to spend longer with the sales data collected by Sally Newcombe. The first task was to compare this with the data she had obtained from other Innovation Exhibitions.

That afternoon she was scheduled to give her first talk in Bude on "*Inventing Triumphs and Disasters*", based around the life of Sir Goldsworthy Gurney. Although this was similar to talks she had given elsewhere, it would require a final run-through later in the morning.

George was pleased to find Sally already at her desk when she arrived. Not too surprising: it was already nine thirty. It was an improvement, though, on the woman's slackness earlier in the week.

The first challenge was to negotiate some working space within the office block. After some debate George was allowed to hot-desk in an adjacent office normally used by the Operations Manager.

'Nick's on duty at the main desk today,' said Sally. 'He won't need his office till Monday.'

George gave a quiet sigh of relief and unpacked her tablet. Then she used the machine to download the data she'd been shown by Sally two days before. This comprised daily ticket sales since the exhibition began in June.

George added this to the data collected earlier from Exeter and Plymouth and then set out to make comparisons.

First she arranged the data for each exhibition into weekly totals. Attendance rose steadily for several weeks but levelled out once the exhibition was established.

What about attendance variation over the week? In all cases there were more visitors at weekends. Bude was unusual in having low figures on Mondays, compared with the rest of the week. Was that due to Bude being a seaside location? Maybe tourists wouldn't take much notice of any exhibition until they had exhausted the pleasures of beach and sea.

Sally had given George daily revenue totals as well as actual numbers coming in. The analyst checked that the same broad patterns were evident and found that this was the case.

Then, for no good reason except mathematical curiosity, she worked out the average price paid in Bude for each ticket on each day. The average was fairly steady from one day to another but seemed rather low.

George hadn't been told the entry charges but Sally must have them. She stood up and went next door.

'We charge adults £12 each, concessions £10 and youngsters £5,' said the Sales Director. 'And we don't do anything complicated like family tickets. You might be able to advise us what we should try.'

'Do you have any more data? Does your team ask visitors if they've been here before? Or anything else about them – for example, the ratio of men to women? Have you any estimate of their ages?'

Sally started to look defensive. George realised she wasn't helping by asking so many questions at once. 'Never mind. I'll start with what you've given me.'

George returned to her office and compared the numbers she'd just been given with the average prices she had worked out earlier.

That was odd. They must have a huge proportion of young-sters for the two sources to tally up.

It would be interesting to see the ratio of young people in the audience when she gave her talk that afternoon.

Glancing up, the analyst noted that it was already eleven o'clock. Her talk required attention. She'd better spend the rest of the morning checking her facts and running through her conclusions.

Late that afternoon a slightly weary George left the end of the large marquee where she had been talking, in search of a cup of tea.

There was a café within the exhibition but right now that would be full of her recent audience, thirsty and noisy after a stimulating session. For a few moments she was in need of some peace and calm.

They had asked lots of questions – there'd been no lack of

interest in the issue of innovation, past or present. Some of her listeners were very knowledgeable and knew more about Gurney than she did. That had exposed several areas where more research was needed for the next talk. But right now she needed a break and a cup of tea.

George knew of another café, a part of the Castle which had once been Gurney's home. (He had wanted to prove that with care you could build on sand.) With a bit of luck she wouldn't be recognised there at all.

Soon the analyst was seated with a pot of tea and slice of cake at a table facing onto the beach and the afternoon sun.

George jotted down the questions she hadn't been able to answer properly. Could she tackle these from the resources within the Museum?

Then she thought about wider questions and how these might be addressed. Would Gurney have been helped, for example, if he operated in a more cooperative style or deliberately sought partners with the skills that he patently lacked? Or were all inventors primarily loners?

Reflecting on her first talk took some time. It was a while before George remembered the question of the mixture of adults and youngsters.

There was no doubt her audience were predominantly adults. Perhaps a quarter were young students, but not more. She consulted her earlier notes and scribbled some calculations. That meant . . . the exhibition income here was around twenty percent below the amount she would have expected, from the numbers said to be attending.

Was this the problem that she was supposed to be looking for? Or at least a symptom of some underlying corruption?

For a start, did the phenomenon arise elsewhere? George hauled out her tablet and checked the data she'd downloaded elsewhere. No one else had given her revenue data in the same form so she couldn't be sure.

This might be a scam that occurred only at Bude.

Assuming her calculations were correct, was the real problem here exaggerating the number of visitors, routinely failing to take payment from some of them or siphoning off the income?

The only person whom George could imagine might benefit from expanded numbers was the Sales Director. Her contract might include an incentive bonus linked to exhibition attendance. Could she just scale the visitor numbers up by twenty percent before they were passed on to headquarters?

This was a fair-sized business, could that really happen? Sally wasn't working seven days a week; what happened when she wasn't there? Or did some other senior manager, the Operations Director, say, carry out an independent check?

What if not all the money received was properly collected? This Exhibition had been put together by an engineering team. Could they design tills where some of the takings were hidden from view? Might a screen come down, that would hide some of the takings from the routine nightly collection?

As she mused, George realised that it could be any of them. In truth, she had not acquired much grasp of the mechanics of the process.

It was now five thirty. George consulted one of the publicity leaflets and confirmed that on weekdays the exhibition closed at six. Was there anything else she could do in the time remaining?

She had agreed to meet Maxine at seven. Then she could either give her a lift back to Ivy Cottage, or find out what had happened to her at the Camp over a meal at the Falcon Hotel.

Before that there might still be enough time to find a place in the exhibition marquee from which she could observe the emptying of tills. It would be good to ask further questions next week from a position of strength rather than weakness.

CHAPTER 13

It was two o'clock before Peter Travers and Holly Berry returned to the police station, each armed with the pasty needed for a late lunch.

In the open-plan office Travers found his team hard at work, making sure their responsibilities for keeping order in the town – less urgent but no less important – were not being neglected.

There was no more news on Holdsworth. Sampson had returned from a chat with his fishing contacts to report that none of them had heard of the wanted man in years. That exhausted their list of Holdsworth's known contacts and the work they could do to chase him.

While eating his lunch the sergeant phoned his Regional contact but Andrea had nothing new to report either.

'We're still waiting for someone to spot an abandoned purple Ford Focus,' she said. 'If it has a trace of his DNA in it, the location should give us a clue on which direction he's heading.'

'One of my team spent the morning looking through traffic camera footage,' replied Travers. 'A dead loss. We've not seen any of that make and colour here in Bude over the last forty eight hours.'

'Trouble is, Peter, he must know we're on the lookout. If he's got any sense he'll be keeping well away from anywhere civilised.'

Once he and Holly had had their lunches, Travers called a meeting to give his team a report on their visit to Fairclough's cottage.

'It looked like he'd been in there till recently,' he admitted.

'The main bed had recently been slept in,' added Berry. 'The duvet was just thrown off. If he'd gone off on holiday he would have at least made the bed. And I saw a bottle of milk in his fridge. It smelt alright, anyway.'

'That doesn't explain why he's no longer answering his phone,' commented Jess Holland. She'd been the first one involved in this problem and recalled the anguish of young Jake.

'He might just have lost it. Then got a new number,' suggested Joe Tremlitt.

'But this is the way he gets asked to do house clearance,' Holland replied. 'Surely he'd need to find a way of hanging on to his number – or else make sure any call to his old phone is redirected. I talked to Jake's parents, remember, they used to call Fairclough regularly. They tell me that his old phone hasn't worked for weeks.'

'You know, we didn't see either of his vehicles,' mused Berry. 'Fairclough lives right out in the country, no bus service nearby. I could see why he'd take one or the other, the van or the estate, depending on the size of the job, but where was the other? I'd have expected it to be left at his cottage.'

'When it was all in focus I put in a call to the traffic people,' said Holland. 'Admittedly there aren't many cameras here in Bude. They ran a check, but they've no record of either vehicle over the last few weeks.'

It was less and less clear what was happening. Travers felt annoyed with himself for not nailing it down more firmly.

He grimaced. 'I wish we'd left an official message in the cottage. Asked him to get in touch, confirm all was well.'

A further thought struck him. 'The thing is, if someone else is living there – not Fairclough – we need to know who it is; and to ask, did Fairclough invite him to stay? If so, how long's he been there and when's he expecting Fairclough back? That might help us know what is going on.'

There was still a mystery, but it wasn't clear if it was one the police should be trying to solve.

At the end of the afternoon, as Travers was about to go home, there came a development on Holdsworth. Andrea from Regional HQ called the policeman with an update.

'Peter, glad I caught you. You can relax for the weekend. We've found the purple Ford Focus.'

Travers remembered the comments from his team. This might not be good news at all. 'So what's Holdsworth taken instead?'

'Nothing. The place the car was found is the bottom of a lake near Exmoor – Lake Wibbleball. It looks as though he skidded, came off road and plunged straight in. '

Peter didn't wish anyone ill but Holdsworth was a very unpleasant character, he wouldn't be greatly missed. 'Sounds good. And you've found the body?'

'Give us a chance, Peter. It's a remote spot. The car was only noticed this lunchtime. We managed to get a diver down this afternoon but there was no one inside. The lake is too big to search properly; we'll have to wait for his body to come to the surface.'

Travers wasn't completely convinced. But at least the man had been heading away from Bude when the accident happened. The town was no longer in the firing line.

He breathed a sigh of relief and closed his office door.

CHAPTER 14

George reached the exhibition marquee at five thirty, just as it was closing to further entry. A proper tour would take at least an hour, so that made sense. There were still plenty of visitors from earlier in the afternoon but they were being herded gradually towards the exit.

The analyst had hoped that the process of emptying the cash from the tills might begin as soon as transactions were over and she could watch unobtrusively from the crowd. But it appeared the process would not even start until all the visitors had gone. She recalled from her analysis earlier in the day that the typical daily revenue might total several thousand pounds. To handle this amount without people around was sensible from a security viewpoint, anyway.

It did, though, pose a question: where she might hide to watch it being done? The space around the tills was no use, it was just wide open. In search of something better George slipped into the main exhibition area.

The exhibition was housed in a huge marquee, broken into halls. In the first there were plenty of engineering pieces to pore over, starting with a full-scale, modern-day replica of Gurney's steam car. The car's engine wasn't fired up now but the piece was still a massive attraction. Visitors were taking it in turn to sit in the driving seat or else occupy one of the seats built precariously over the boiler at the back.

There was no obvious place to hide here. George continued on to the next hall, which was dealing with a series of inventions to do with infrastructure and communications. These included a variety of cables, trenches and pipes, geared to handling phones, internet links and water. None were invented in Bude but George remembered reading that Bude and Widemouth were points where a few internet cables came ashore. So there were some direct links with the cables being used. Maybe there was also expertise on how they were brought ashore?

At this point, though, the analyst's main interest was in finding somewhere that she could hide, so she passed on.

The next hall was a quiet area, a library with comfortable chairs and plenty of material on the engineering history of Cornwall. Beyond that came the café, now starting to wind down.

Alongside was the hall where George had given her talk earlier. When this wasn't hosting some live talk from an inventor, industrialist or academic, it was used for a variety of other events, including dramatic reconstructions of Gurney's life by the local drama college. At other times the hall offered video recordings of talks given earlier.

After that came the Light Hall, furthest from the main entrance and now clear of visitors. Another of Gurney's areas of invention was novel ways of exploiting lighting. George reminded herself that the inventor lived before the discovery of electricity.

Gurney's inventions had included a clever way of amplifying

the effect of carbide lamps. The exhaust outflow was arranged to heat the pipe of air on its way into the combustion chamber, giving a hotter and brighter flame. Gurney used this idea in various forms, including making the steam engines on his cars more powerful.

Gurney had also managed to light his own home in Bude, using a series of mirrors to share one bright, limelight through every room in the house. George reflected that "Smoke and Mirrors" might also have made a good Exhibition title

A similar arrangement demonstrated this around the internal walls of the exhibition marquee, powered by a powerful lamp housed in a small, waist-high cupboard in the Light Hall.

Suddenly George had an idea. How close were the trajectories of the mirrors to the tills in the entrance?

She stepped over to examine the cupboard. It was locked but the key was still in the door. Yes, she could manage to get in. Without much thought she crouched inside and peered through the hole in the side wall, from which the light would project.

The lamp wasn't on but she could still see along the line of mirrors. And to her joy she found she had a good view of one of the tills in the entrance.

The exhibition was much emptier now. Quietly George pulled the cupboard door closed from the inside and pulled out her pocket torch to give a little light. Then she settled down to wait.

Fifteen minutes later the analyst saw movement around the tills. A man in a dark suit, holding a large rucksack, came up to the till she had in focus and fished out a bunch of keys. He chose one, leaned over the till, unlocked it and opened the cash drawer. Then he glanced around before plunging his hands in and drawing out a huge number of notes, which he transferred to his rucksack.

After a few moments he closed the drawer and relocked the till. Then disappeared from view.

George remained in her cupboard. She wanted to see if the man would reappear at another till. Then she heard a shuffling noise just outside her hiding place.

Followed by the sound of the cupboard key turning in the lock.

George was still for some time. How had she been detected? After a while she reflected that her mistake had been the use of her torch. She was an idiot. If she could see the man, he could look the other way and see her – or at least her torch.

But what did he intend to do next? Had he gone for help? Did he suspect she was a burglar, hoping to remove the takings or some other valuables? Or would he be content to come back for further action next morning?

This was ridiculous. George was loosely attached to the staff at the exhibition. It might be embarrassing but she could explain, more or less, what she was doing.

But how innocent had the man been? If what he was doing was part of a scam, then he might not want input on his actions at all. Perhaps he just wanted to confine her while he made his getaway.

Whatever the truth was, she did not want to stay here all night.

She was already feeling uncomfortable – the cupboard was not that large.

She had her phone still with her in her handbag. But who on earth should she ring?

Half an hour later George heard noises in the Light Hall. Whoever it was, she had to catch their attention.

'Help,' she shouted, 'help!'

There was the sound of someone – maybe two – coming towards her and then a female voice said, 'Blast, the key is missing.'

'Don't worry, I have a complete set,' said a second voice. This one was male.

There was a pause while various keys were tried and rejected. Then the correct one was identified.

A moment later the cupboard door swung open and George slowly rose from her knees and prised herself out. Her half hour's captivity was enough to leave her feeling very stiff.

Maxine was standing there, together with one of the security guards she had chatted with earlier.

'Thank you very much indeed,' said George.

'That's all right, Ma'm,' replied the guard. 'Your friend showed us the text message you sent. It's time though, I let you both out. Then I can lock up for the night.'

Ten minutes later the two women had made their way down the canal, over the bridge and into the Falcon Hotel. They both had plenty to talk about but first food and a drink were needed.

107

'What on earth were you doing, locking yourself in that tiny cupboard?' asked Maxine, when each had obtained a glass of local cider, placed their meal orders and they were seated at an unobtrusive table at the back of the restaurant.

Several replies came to mind. George might have retorted that it was top secret and she could say nothing; but that would hardly build up trust.

'I guess that makes it "one all" for rescuing one another in Bude,' was the reply she chose. 'Thank you, Maxine. I was very glad to be let out.'

'Yes, but why were you in there?' Once her curiosity was aroused Maxine was not easy to fob off.

George gave a brief explanation of the inconsistencies in the sales data and the recorded revenue which she'd found that morning, and which had led her to take a look at how the tills were emptied.

Maxine was sceptical. 'George, what makes you think you've got the full story? Some expenses might be paid at once – daily expenses in the café, for example, or costs of an outsourced security operation. You might not have the full revenue costs at all.'

George did not immediately reply. She had investigated in too much of a hurry. 'And now I think about it, some entrance fees will have been paid by direct debit. Those wouldn't appear in the cash tills either. You're right, it wasn't properly thought out.'

There was a pause, then Maxine made another comment.

'Even so, the fact that you were locked in that cupboard is suspicious. If there was nothing to hide why should they bother?'

By now George was in a mood of self-criticism. 'The cleaner doing her final tidy up? Could be part of her job to lock up and take away the key.' Glorious certainties were starting to cloud over.

Two large helpings of chicken tikka masala arrived at that moment and provided a welcome distraction.

CHAPTER 15

The meal had been delicious. Chicken had been followed by Black Forest Gateau, then coffee plus mints. As the pair walked back through Bude, George decided that it would be best to tell Maxine the full story: why she'd been looking for a scam in the first place.

Apart from Maxine's "terror twins", she had no idea how many villains lived in Bude, but two heads might chase them better than one.

'While we drive back, Maxine, I'd like to tell you why I was looking for something odd. Having you staying with me for the next few days, as you've been told to do, is a real bonus.'

Maxine seemed pleased at the accolade. 'OK, I'm ready to listen. We've spent enough time on my troubles, they'll wait at least till we get home.'

The women got into the car. 'We'll take the main road way home at this time of night,' said George. Soon they were out of Bude and onto the A39.

'The thing is, Maxine, there are several strands to my remit here. I have to give regular illustrated talks linked to innovation and what makes it work. Also to look for any ways of boosting exhibition ticket sales, for example by reducing prices for repeat visits.'

'But neither of those would make you look for skulduggery?'

'No. But before I started I had a chat with the chairman of the parent company. He's an old friend of my boss – to be honest, that's probably how we got the contract. He took me out to dinner in his club. Then told me that something was going wrong in this corner of his company – something was twisted.'

'Did he suspect anyone in particular?'

'It's a large firm. Most Directors have been in post for a long time. The part that deals with Engineering Innovation is relatively small, below the level where he knows any of them well. He'd be glad, he said, of any insight on what's going wrong. That's why I'm on the lookout for scams.'

Maxine didn't seem shocked by the revelation. Maybe her work in security had hardened her to what went on below the surface in the commercial world.

'You're talking about a major engineering company, George, with suspicion being voiced about actions at Director level. If something is going on, it won't be easy to spot. It must be more than pinching some of the day's takings, surely? This company must be audited regularly. It must have internal checks about what goes on?'

George sighed. 'You're probably right.'

'Back in the restaurant you mentioned direct debits. That's probably worth much more than the direct income. Well, would it be possible for someone to fiddle with one of the card machines so that for one of the tills the money was paid into a different account altogether? Maybe a holding account for the parent company? It would look OK at first glance, but would be one a

Director could have later access?'

'That could be spotted by auditors too.'

'If they were alert and honest. But someone at Director level might have influence on who did the auditing – and what they reported.'

'Alright, Maxine, that's one idea. I might be able to check that myself. How else might money be siphoned out?

Maxine was silent for a moment. 'Let's start by assuming this is some sort of financial racket. That might not be the case but it's the easiest place to start.'

'Hm. If it's as well-hidden as you suggest, might it be something to do with a subsidiary, rather than the main event?'

'Well, George, from what you've told me, these Exhibitions cover a lot of ground. A lot of costs will fall on suppliers. With a tame auditor, could someone double charge?'

'You mean, send in duplicate bills to different parts of the company – say one to the Finance Department here in Bude and another to Headquarters?'

'That sort of thing. Why, does any particular operation come to mind?'

George thought for a moment. 'One feature of this show is that you can buy a replica steam car – full sized and ready to drive. These aren't made by the company itself. They're made in Wolverhampton and brought down one by one on a lorry.'

Maxine mused for a few seconds. 'Are they popular? How much does one cost?'

'The sales figures are secret but I believe they've sold a dozen so far. The price is also commercially sensitive, but I know they're handmade, rivet by rivet. They're each a lot better than the originals; there was no Health and Safety in those days. You're probably looking at upwards of thirty five thousand pounds each.'

Maxine did the maths. 'So that's income for the Exhibition of what, four hundred thousand pounds. Huge.'

'That's right. And I can tell you, that part of the business is kept very low profile indeed.'

By now they had almost reached the point where they had to turn off the A39 down the side road that led home. There was one more point which needed clarification.

'Maxine, if this isn't a financial racket, have you any idea what else might steer it?'

'I don't know enough about the Exhibition. Are there any highlights still to come?'

'There's supposed to be a Very Important Person coming down in a couple of weeks – either here or Exeter.'

'A politician, maybe, coming to show they care?'

'Exactly. Perhaps there's someone in the firm with a deep-seated grudge. They might want to take advantage of the potential bad publicity if something were to go wrong.'

CHAPTER 16

Colin Caldwell awoke on Saturday morning with a headache. He had had a rough night and decided he had no choice but to check out the Tee-Side guest house in person – and to do so right away.

With embarrassment he remembered the previous day's encounter.

Late on the previous afternoon he had what turned out to be an awkward meeting with the Head of Security at Cleave Camp, Geoff McAndrew. McAndrew was a dour Scotsman who had been in overall charge of security at the Camp for decades. He wasn't really a process man, his declared specialty was the wider security climate. Caldwell had asked for the meeting to bring the man up to date with the tale he'd heard that morning from Maxine Tavistock.

It had turned out to be one of those meetings which started badly and got steadily worse.

Caldwell had booked the meeting at short notice with McAndrew's secretary. She had tried to fob him off with a session sometime in the week after next but he could sense that might be far too late. If there was anything afoot that might disrupt the Camp then it needed urgent, high-level attention.

When he arrived at the senior man's office he could see that

McAndrew already had several matters claiming his time. His intray was piled high with documents requiring approval. More puzzlingly, his desk was littered with quality broadsheets, including the Times and the Daily Telegraph. Caldwell saw he was currently engrossed in a leading article from the Guardian.

'Caldwell. Sit down. Hope this won't take long, I'm rather pressed this afternoon.'

That was the point at which Caldwell later realised he'd made his key mistake. Out of politeness he showed a natural interest in his boss's problems rather than pressing on at once with his own.

'And it's all in the Guardian, sir?' He tried to take the tone of derision out of his voice. If his boss had been reading the Times it might make some sort of sense but the Guardian could never be classed as the authentic voice of the establishment. If McAndrew had time to read that, not just skim the headlines, he could hardly declare he was overworked.

'Caldwell, it's this lunatic leaker. Snowden. More of his material has appeared in the Guardian this week. Have you seen it? It's very serious.'

Caldwell had heard the name, read it in standard security briefings, but didn't usually bother with the Guardian. He didn't think it was an issue with resonance in back-of-beyond Cleave. 'Isn't he American, sir?'

'That's right. An American contractor with full security clearance. He's been given access to all the US government's surveillance computers. Like a million others, it says here. Trouble is, he's copied files containing all their darkest secrets onto his laptop. And then disappeared.'

'Won't that teach 'em to be more frugal with their clearances in future, sir? A million is a hell of a lot. I mean, it must be impossible to keep watch on that many. And who's doing the checking? There must be at least another million of those. Who checks them?' He paused for a moment. 'But that's not our problem, is it, sir?'

McAndrew blew out his ruddy cheeks in frustration. These days the younger generation seemed so naïve. 'The problem, Caldwell, is that these leaks undermine the status of security – here as well as across the pond.'

Caldwell hadn't noticed angry crowds heading up towards the Camp to protest. 'How d'you mean, sir?'

'Well, I'll give you an example. In these latest leaks, Snowden shows that governments are capable of intercepting emails written by pretty well anyone – and regularly do so. No need to get permission, they pick them up first and see who they're written to. Track the linkages from one internet site to another. Then decide which ones they need to look at. So you see, the whole notion of confidential emails is illusory.'

'But Snowden isn't lying, sir. That's currently how it is. It's not that bad, though. There are billions of emails sent every day. They – we – can't possibly read more than a tiny fraction of them. Not with the resources the government has decided to give us, anyway. Judged as a whole it's a sensible system. Just needs to be well explained by the politicians, now Snowden has let the cat out of the bag.'

McAndrew sighed. 'Caldwell, do you realise how lowly the ratings of politicians are, in the view of the public these days?

Putting the words "politicians" and "explained" in the same sentence is a contradiction.'

The younger man (he was aged nearly forty) still could not see the scale of the problem. 'It's August, sir. The public don't bother with newspapers this month. It's the silly season. The whole thing might just blow over.'

There was a short pause. McAndrew was deciding whether to bother trying to explain any more. Caldwell decided he might as well try and make headway on what he perceived as a more urgent problem that had brought him here in the first place.

'What I wanted to see you for, sir, was to share something rather worrying that I learned this morning. It's about one of our analysts, Maxine Tavistock.'

'I don't think I know her. Is she under thirty?'

'I doubt it, sir. I'd put her more in her late thirties.'

'No doubt she's emotionally overcharged. What did she want?'

'She brought a bizarre tale. Apparently she had been kidnapped from her lodgings on Monday evening and taken off to a remote farmhouse.'

'Where she was, no doubt, stripped naked, hung from the rafters and given electric shock treatment. Some of these women have far more imagination that intelligence. I hope you didn't take it seriously?'

'She seemed very clear, sir. Explained that she had escaped from the car when her captors brought her back into Bude to pick up her laptop.'

McAndrew gave a bellow of laughter. 'Wonderful. And no doubt now she wants permission to write the whole thing up for the monthly Camp newsletter.'

Caldwell could see he wasn't being taken seriously. Maybe this was payback for his earlier indifference to McAndrew's concerns over leaks from Snowden.

'I did some checking. This is the second time this year that a woman has disappeared from these particular lodgings, sir. Last time it was a new graduate from Northern Ireland. There was a hint from her colleagues that she'd been homesick and her mother was ill, so in the end we did nothing. But if Maxine's tale is genuine, there might be someone out there who is aiming to disrupt the Camp. This woman is fairly senior. Heaven knows what they might have done to her, what she might have let slip, if she had not managed to get away.'

McAndrew put down the Guardian and thought for a moment. 'Before we take her story seriously, Caldwell, we need to check that it really happened. Why don't you start with a visit to her lodgings? Exactly which room was she taken from? How did they get in and out again without being seen? You need to ask, can anyone back up any part of her story? Do we know she was there earlier in the Monday evening? Was she actually missing from breakfast on the Tuesday morning?'

Caldwell was about to respond but McAndrew continued remorselessly. 'And if all that stacks up, why not call her in and give her a really tough interview. Does she stick to her story or change it in some way? The oddest part to me is that she managed to get away. Maybe, though, that was intended? Had the kidnapper inserted some sort of location tag into her body so they could find her again?'

McAndrew smiled. 'She might need a full examination from our medical people, to check that nothing's been put inside her. Which could be an incentive, you see, for her to bother us less in the future.'

Caldwell had gone away from the meeting feeling depressed. It had never once crossed his mind that Maxine could have been misleading him. Far more likely was that McAndrew was transferring his annoyance with Snowden onto someone more local. Which might be understandable but was hardly fair.

Caldwell had rechecked Maxine's record. This was an experienced GCHQ analyst who had worked for the government, here and in Cheltenham, for fifteen years. Surely his responsibility – his duty of care – was to assume her tale was true until some inconsistency emerged?

Caldwell had assumed, as he left the Camp on Friday evening, that he would visit Tee-Side to check on Maxine's story on the Monday. But the more he thought about it the angrier he was with McAndrew's attitude. That made him desperate to confirm her tale as soon as possible.

Consequently, when he awoke on the Saturday morning, he resolved to visit the place that day. It helped that his wife did her weekly shopping in Bude on Saturdays. He could leave the car in Sainsbury's while his wife did the family shop and he walked round to Tee-Side.

Caldwell had visited Tee-Side just once before, several years ago, when the place was being added to the Camp's list of recommended accommodation. But on that occasion he had dealt with Mrs Murdoch. This time he encountered her husband. Caldwell discovered that a place specially chosen because of the tightness of its guest security was not so easy to handle as he had presumed.

For a start, on an August Saturday, the place was humming with guests moving in and out. The breakfast room was still being used for coffee and there was no lounge so Caldwell found himself ushered into the kitchen.

'Mrs Murdoch is busy with guestroom changeovers,' explained her husband. 'Half a dozen guests are leaving this morning and they'll be replaced by others later in the day. We mostly take weekly bookings in high season, you see, Saturday's our busiest day. How can I help you?'

'I believe you have a guest staying here called Maxine Tavistock?' began the oh-so-innocent Colin Caldwell.

'I couldn't possibly say, sir,' returned Mr Murdoch smoothly. 'Our guest list is covered by data protection and I won't be revealing it to you.'

'The thing is, I work at the same place as she does.'

'Indeed sir? A happy coincidence for you both. If you work together all week why d'you need to see her on Saturday as well?'

Caldwell ground his teeth in frustration. 'The thing is, Maxine told me that she was kidnapped from this guest house last Monday evening.'

'Indeed sir? We don't have many abductions these days but I may have missed it. Since I'm not going to confirm that Ms Tavistock has ever stayed here I can hardly confirm or deny the allegation that she's gone.'

'I don't suppose you'd let me check her room?'

'Which room, sir? I've not yet admitted she has one.'

There was silence as Caldwell tried to work out a way through Murdoch's obstructiveness. He had heard colleagues claim that security could be overdone but this was the first time he had observed it for himself.

'Look, would it help if I gave you the phone number of my employer. He could confirm who I am then maybe you'd be a bit more cooperative.'

'What would be the point sir? You might just have an accomplice at that number, ready to lie on your behalf.'

Caldwell made a sound halfway between a cry and a howl. Murdoch looked at him with anatomical interest. 'It doesn't really matter who you are, sir, or what sound you make. You won't be shown any of our guestrooms unless the guest is here alongside you. Perhaps you could make suitable arrangements when you meet her again on Monday?'

CHAPTER 17

The Port William was the only pub in Trebarwith Strand, just down the hill from Ivy Cottage. It was in an idyllic location, popular with beach-lovers and surfers. George and Maxine had just settled in the far corner of the main bar when the mobile bleeped.

They had just each ordered a pint of cider and a plate of sea bass and chips. George had declared over a late breakfast that, after the week they'd just had, they both deserved a Saturday treat. In any case, what was the point of owning a cottage that overlooked a famous beach if she didn't make some use of the local facilities?

'Get them to ring back later,' she urged.

Maxine glanced at her phone. 'It's a work call.'

'No one's that essential. It's the weekend, for goodness sake.'

Maxine shrugged, picked up her phone and wandered off to the ladies to take the call.

George was only mildly irritated. Over the years she'd had enough meals spoilt by work calls of her own. Normally the service in the Port William was quick. She hoped that on this occasion it would be slower.

It was ten minutes before Maxine returned, looking angry even before she saw that the food had already been served.

George remembered to smile. They didn't both need to be cross.

'The food only arrived a few seconds ago,' she said.

'Huh,' was the reply.

For a few moments, settling themselves to eat, with generous portions of tartar sauce, took their attention. George disciplined herself not to ask the first question. The women were friends but not intimates. If Maxine wanted to tell her what was going on it was best she did it in her own time.

Maxine fumed silently for a few moments. Then, giving a sigh, she decided that she needed to share her frustrations with someone.

'What an imbecile!'

'Are you thinking of anyone in particular?'

A pause, while more mouthfuls of food were consumed.

'He's second in command of security at one of the most vital places in the country, yet he has no understanding of people. You might as well replace him with a robot. At least that could be trained.'

'I take it you're talking about your recent phone call? I told you to ignore it.'

'Wouldn't you think, if you ran up a work colleague on a work matter on a Saturday lunchtime, you'd at least check, as an opening line, that it was a convenient time to ring?'

'Well, you and I would. But then we're women,' said George, making the most of their shared gender. 'Mind you, plenty of men would think of that as well. If you're allowed to tell me, what did he want?'

Maxine took another sip of her cider and considered.

'You know, Caldwell didn't ask me, at my interview yesterday, who I had talked to; or warn me not to tell them more. No mention of the Official Secrets Act, anyway. So I guess I can continue talking to you on the same confidential basis.'

'That's fine with me. So what was he after?'

'Well, one thing I learned yesterday was that I wasn't the first woman that had disappeared from the Camp. . .'

George put her hand over her mouth. 'Maxine, that's dreadful. What happened to the last one?'

'Security didn't take it seriously. It was generally assumed she was homesick and had gone back to her mum, at an unknown address in Northern Ireland. The thing is, Caldwell told me that she had also been staying in Tee-Side.'

George was even more shocked by this detail. 'That can't just be a coincidence.'

'No. That's what he thought. So this morning, without any preliminary phone call to anyone, Caldwell turns up at Tee-Side and asks to see my room.'

George gave a laugh. 'They were very fussy when I tried that. Wouldn't let me in there, even with the hostess standing beside me, to pick up your reading glasses. Muttered data protection or something. Don't you remember, I asked you that evening to give me an introductory letter?'

'That's exactly what happened to Caldwell. I mean, he hit a brick wall. Except he was trying to argue with the host, so got even less traction than you did. Well done Mr Murdoch.' She gave a laugh. 'It's rather funny in a way, a security man being thwarted by proper security.'

'And he rang you because . . . '

'He wanted me to turn up this afternoon at Tee-Side and vouch for him so he could interview them all at great length. What an idiot. Like you say, it's the weekend – the worst possible time to start an inquiry in a guest house. If he bothered to look he could see – it's on my record – that I don't have a car here and I'm certainly not dragging you all the way back to Bude to take me. I told him we could discuss it at Camp next week.'

The thought occurred to George that Peter Travers would not behave in this way. But maybe now was not the time to say so.

They chomped on in silence for a few moments. The sea bass was delicious.

'If you're disillusioned with Camp Security, Maxine, maybe you and I need to give it more thought, see if we can advance the rate of progress. What was Caldwell hoping to find out? And can we find it out for him? That'd squash his arrogance a little.'

Squashing Caldwell was an attractive option; Maxine smiled.

'If two of us were abducted from the same place, one big question is, how on earth was that done? I mean, the Tee-Side front door was locked every time I arrived back there. And I never heard any talk of a break in.'

'Yes. And someone as careful as Murdoch would never leave downstairs windows or the back door open either.'

The women paused for a moment, both thinking hard.

'Maxine, you say you let yourself in. So . . . does that mean you had a copy of the house key?'

'Yes . . .'

'There'd be nothing to stop you taking that key to a local locksmith and getting a copy, would there?'

'Suppose not. Taking its distinctive Tee-Side label off first, of course. I bet they don't change the front door lock that often.'

'Well, doesn't that mean the protagonist probably stayed there as a guest in the fairly recent past?'

'Hey, yes.' For a moment she looked thrilled and then doubts assailed her. 'Though not necessarily under their own name. I mean, this isn't Russia. You don't have to show Mr Murdoch your passport.'

'But you have to pay. You'd need a credit card in the name you'd chosen to use. That'd take a bit of effort.'

'All of which proves that they were very serious about it. Which my experience bears out.'

Another silence.

'They'd also need a key to your bedroom. I suppose they could get that at the same time.'

'Provided they'd managed to be assigned the right bedroom. That might mean they came several times, each time staying in a different room. They might come as a couple, of course, bringing a wife or girlfriend.'

'In any case,' said George, 'if they did let themselves in this time with a copied key, wouldn't a stranger wandering about be spotted?'

'Most of the time. In mid-evening it's pretty quiet; they might not be noticed. In any case, most guests don't stay for long. Unless you'd had a leisurely breakfast there for a day or two and looked carefully at everyone else eating you wouldn't know who else was staying.'

George considered strategy. 'We know this location was used at least twice – maybe more. The whole thing must have been well planned.'

'Yes?'

'The villain would also need advance intelligence. For a start, they'd need to know that Tee-Side regularly took in analysts from the Camp. How would they know that?' She frowned. 'I don't like the thought, but doesn't that suggest there's been a leak of data from the Camp?'

'That'd be hard to achieve, George. Carswell's inept with people but he's got a lot of procedures in place.' She paused, looking for other solutions.

'I reckon, you know, that the Murdochs have been security vetted. That would mean interviews with friends. Bude is a close community. Other bed and breakfast hosts will know – it might be source of jest, or a cause of jealousy. I bet Tee-Side isn't the only guest house taking guests from Cleave Camp. So staying around here and asking casual questions of your hosts might be all you'd need.'

'But once you'd got that, you'd also need to know which guests were associated with the Camp, which room they slept in and what time they went to bed. How would you manage that?

Maxine was starting to appreciate George's forensic insight. The questions were awkward but not impossible. She thought for a moment.

'There's no lounge in Tee-Side, you know. My room is on the first floor, at the front, overlooking the golf course. So if I'd been followed home – and the late Cleave bus drops everyone in the Strand, I'd be easy enough to follow in the dark – then they could watch for a bedroom light going on, just a few minutes after I went in.'

'That link's not certain,' mused George. 'Someone else with that room might be going to bed at the wrong time.'

'True. But if they kept watching and the same thing happened regularly, then they would be pretty sure.'

'OK, Maxine. Let's push it a bit further. Where would they stand to watch as they waited for you to arrive?'

'That's easy. They'd sit in their car. There's plenty of parking nearby. Then once they were certain, one of them would let themselves in at, say, nine pm, go to my room and wait till I arrived.'

It might not have been exactly as they surmised. But it was good to have a working theory. And there were other enquiries which this could lead on to.

After lunch, George took Maxine for a walk up the steep hill behind the Port William and south along the cliffs. Once they were away from Trebarwith Strand the crowds disappeared rapidly.

Two rugged miles further on Maxine found herself looking down onto a deserted beach.

'That's Tregardock. It's more or less the local beach for Delabole.   You can see a lot more of it at low tide,' George promised her. 'Would you fancy a swim?'

'Only if you've got a spare swimming costume. It looks deserted down there but I don't fancy skinny dipping.'

'I don't suppose your man, Caldwell, would want you exposing yourself anyway.'

'Stuff Caldwell. But my costume's not even in Bude. I assumed swimming was off the agenda, left it in Cheltenham.'

'We're a similar size, Maxine. I'll lend you one of mine. Tomorrow morning, maybe?'

'Provided it's not raining.'

When the pair got home and Maxine was preparing omelettes for supper, George took the chance to ring Brian Southgate from her room.

'Hi, Brian. Maxine's talked to Camp security. Without much effect, I think. And she and I are a bit further on with our ideas of where to go next. Is there any chance we could bounce them off you?'

'George. Thanks for ringing. I was about to call you anyway. Alice insists that we invite you for Sunday lunch tomorrow. She thinks it's important that Maxine meets normal people, long-term Cornish residents, not just tourists in a guest house. She's told me to invite Peter Travers as well.'

'Thank you. We'll come after our morning dip at Tregardock. D'you think, though, that without being dishonest we could try to gloss over Peter being a policeman? For as long as possible, anyway.'

It wasn't clear that Maxine would talk to a policeman, even one she met out of uniform, but George reckoned this might be the best chance of making it happen.

CHAPTER 18

When Maxine looked out of her window on Sunday morning she could see that she had been over-enthusiastic and over-committed. True, it was not raining – yet. But the weather looked cloudy and very windy. If it did happen this was going to be a cold swim.

She hoped that George might postpone the excursion, but conversation over breakfast showed her friend had no inhibitions. For her this was a treat: she didn't often have time for a swim when she was working from her cottage. Swimming on your own wasn't much fun either.

'It'll be a bit cold standing on the beach in our bathing costumes. But once we're in the sea and splashing about the wind won't make much difference. We'll just have to keep moving to keep warm.'

Maxine had expected that they would repeat their walk from the day before, starting down the narrow footpath from Treknow to the beach. However, this time they set off in George's car.

'I want to drive as close to Tregardock beach as I can,' she explained. 'We'll still have to walk down the cliffs and back up again afterwards, but at least we'll be on the way to Delabole for lunch.' A thought struck her. 'I don't intend to come back here first, by the way. Bring anything you might need for discussing the case in the afternoon.'

Maxine did not know this bit of Cornwall at all. It was a maze of minor roads. She was surprised when George turned left almost at once, went down a very steep, winding hill and then up an even steeper gradient on the far side.

'I hope we don't meet anyone on this stretch,' Maxine said. The road was extremely narrow and had stone walls on either side. She was glad no one else was coming the other way.

'This is Trebarwith village,' explained George, when they reached the top of the hill. 'Look, over there you can see the coast. This place is even smaller than Trebarwith Strand, where we had lunch yesterday.'

But they weren't stopping here. They continued along and eventually emerged on a main road. 'This is the road from Delabole to Polzeath. We'll turn off again in a minute.'

They turned off following a sign to Treligga, another village Maxine had never heard of. But ten minutes later they took an even narrower road that George declared led to Tregardock. She pulled in at a slightly wider point where there was a verge, just before an isolated farmhouse.

Seizing their rucksacks with swimming gear and towels, the women headed down the road.

'Hey, we're back where we were yesterday,' said Maxine as they crossed over the South West Coast Path. She still felt cold, buffeted in the wind, but had resolved not to complain. She was, after all, George's guest; and she didn't want to talk herself out of borrowing that spare costume.

The pair plunged down a zig-zag path towards the beach, which she could see stretched much further than the day before. It was still deserted. At the bottom Maxine was amazed to find that she was expected to scramble down the final twenty feet while hanging on to a rope.

'Like I said, it's a very local beach,' commented George. 'It's even more of a challenge to climb back up again.' Maxine decided not to worry about that until she had to.

Soon they had changed into their swimming costumes and started to walk down to the sea. There was no protection now from the wind. Maxine couldn't help shivering and was relieved when she saw that, ahead of her, George was doing the same. The sea was choppy; striding out into the incoming waves was even more of a shock. Maxine gritted her teeth and resolved not to moan. It was slightly less arctic once she was fully immersed and starting to swim.

After half an hour George suggest they got out. She produced a Frisbee from the rucksack and tossed it to her friend. 'This is how Robbie and I would warm ourselves, the few times we came here.'

'Who's Robbie?'

'An old friend of mine. He's a regional journalist in the southwest for a top UK newspaper. But he's working abroad at the moment.'

Maxine looked horrified. 'George, I hope you wouldn't in-volve him in any way with my concerns. He'd have a professional interest in broadcasting it to the world. Even a casual mention could be catastrophic.'

George realised that she had been seriously undiplomatic. 'As I say, Robbie's abroad at the moment – in Spain, I think. He's there for the summer, looking at their renewable energy programme and asking if any parts would transfer here. But I wouldn't dream of talking to him about you, by phone or by email, unless you'd given me permission first.'

Maxine relaxed a little. 'OK, I accept that. But you gave me a bit of a shock. Here, let's have a go with the Frisbee. I'm very cold indeed.'

It was half past eleven by the time they gave up, got dressed and headed back for the car. The walk back, up the rock using the rope and then the steep hill, certainly helped warm them up.

It was just after twelve when they reached the Southgate's house in Delabole. 'Aren't we a bit early?' asked Maxine.

'They're both time sticklers at work but entirely different at home. Don't worry, it'll be fine.'

As of course it was. They found Brian busy in the kitchen, grappling with a special dessert involving double cream which he had never made before, while Alice was tidying the lounge. George introduced her old college friend to the local primary school teacher and the two seemed to hit it off immediately.

George decided that she wasn't needed to cement the new friendship and headed off to see if Brian wanted help. She was no expert on desserts but she might help steady his nerves and stop him drinking too much of the Cointreau. At least she could sample the product as it emerged and make encouraging noises.

They were so engrossed that neither noticed the sound from

Peter Travers as he knocked at the front door and a minute later joined the pair in the lounge.

'Peter, you're welcome,' gushed Alice. She remembered being told that Maxine was allergic to policemen, though she'd not been told why.

In turn the policeman was enjoying his first day off duty for a couple of weeks. He wasn't going to spoil it by admitting that he was a copper, least of all to the slim, attractive girl on the settee beside him.

'Peter, this is Maxine. She's a friend of George Gilbert, staying with her for a few days at Ivy Cottage. Hardy women, they've just come back from a dip at Tregardock.'

'Pleased to meet you, Maxine.' Travers rose slightly and shook her hand. He was by no mean indifferent to the opposite sex but normally, apart from his work colleagues, he came across them mostly as victims.

Not much younger than himself, and far less worn down by life, he could see Maxine was in a different category altogether.

'So how d'you know George?' he began.

'We were maths students together at Cambridge. We both dozed through the same lectures. Anyway, that was a long time ago. How about you?'

'I first met George just after she bought Ivy Cottage. She was starting to think the place was haunted.'

'Gosh. She didn't mention that to me. Tell me more.' She gave him a smile that shook his insides and her blue eyes stared at him intensely.

'I'm sorry to say, Maxine, the solution turned out a little more prosaic. The previous owner had been murdered in the bath.'

There had been no time, over the last few days, for George to go over any of this ground. In any case it was now all a few years ago.

'My, oh, my. And here was me thinking George had nothing more in her back story than searching out financial scandals.'

Peter noticed that her eyes had started to sparkle. That was enough almost to throw himself off his stride. Focus, boy, he told himself. 'George not only worked out what had happened, Maxine, she managed to identify the killer. A good piece of work. Anyway, tell me about yourself. Are you down here on holiday?'

Alice interrupted. 'I'm just going to see how the meat is doing.' She disappeared into the kitchen.

Maxine considered her response. Like Peter, she didn't want to talk about her job on a day off.

'Most of the time I live in Cheltenham. I'm just down here for a few weeks. George and I met by chance in Bude a few days ago. She invited me to come and stay with her. Apart from terrifying me on the first day by a bath with a mind of its own, we're having a grand time. I never knew this bit of Cornwall was so interesting.'

'Yes, I remember her telling me about the bath. I've never tried it myself. That's where the murder took place, you know. She never thought to warn you?'

'I might have been alright but I was in a bad place to start with.'

'Oh? Her driving can be a bit erratic. Especially if she comes the back way, near to the cliffs. There are lots of very steep hills.'

135

She grabbed his arm. 'No, Peter, it wasn't that. I'd just got away from an attempted kidnap, you see. In fact, George had helped with my rescue.'

Peter gave a laugh. 'Sounds like you two are competing to be the most dare-devil woman in Delabole. That's a tight competition, you know. There's a farmer's daughter I know near Treligga . . .'

Alice rejoined them at that moment. 'I don't want to interrupt,' she said, 'but I came to tell you that lunch is served.'

Afterwards, Maxine reflected that it was the most riotous lunch she had enjoyed for months. She contrived to be sitting next to Peter, with Brian on her other side and George and Alice seated opposite. Though two of the five round the table were brand new acquaintances, it quickly felt that they had all been friends for years.

The Merlot flowed freely. Brian and Alice were not intending to go out anywhere this afternoon. Peter had walked round from his house on the other side of Delabole. George did not intend to drive away for some time and Maxine was under no alcoholic restriction at all.

'Don't worry, the lunch will absorb the alcohol,' pronounced Brian. The professional medical advice gave their consciences some cover.

'I don't want to pry, Maxine,' said Peter at one point. George glanced quickly at Brian and held her breath. What was coming next?

'I reckon that, just below the surface, I can hear a suppressed

Cornish accent. Is that right – and if so why in the world are you suppressing it? I may be biased, but seems to me it's the best accent on the planet.'

Maxine gave a giggle. Brian had been refilling her glass of Merlot more frequently than she was used to. She wasn't drunk but was feeling light headed.

'Peter, you must have an amazing ear. That's right. My parents now live at Lands End but they come from Helston. I was brought up in Cornwall until I was eighteen, the last two years at Truro College. Trouble is, the posh folk at Cambridge squashed most of it. I didn't want to sound like a country cousin, you see, so I started mimicking the rest. And once I left there I was based in Cheltenham. Plenty of public school types there, that killed off what was left.'

'You need to spend longer in Cornwall, Maxine. Given you've lived here that long, the lilt would come back. Make you sound like a local.'

He sounded a little wistful. There weren't many bright, unattached women around these parts. Mind, he had no hard evidence that Maxine was even single. For all he knew she might have a long-term boyfriend tucked away in Cheltenham.

The conversation moved on. George wondered to herself how on earth Brian planned to get them to reflect on Maxine's adventure. How could her case be pursued and ideas shared once lunch was over? It looked as though Maxine would not have many inhibitions talking to Peter, anyway.

Once the main course had been finished and cleared, Brian's dessert was brought in and was much appreciated on all sides.

George guessed that the doctor didn't try to cook very often. That would be why Alice did her best to praise his efforts on the few times he did.

It was as George came back from helping Alice clear the table of dessert plates and preparing to serve coffee that it dawned on her there might be another solution.

Peter was extolling the virtues of the area. 'Even Delabole has got its significant charms,' he boasted. 'Have you heard of our famous Slate Quarry? It's been here since the thirteenth century. Supposed to be one of the biggest in Europe.'

'Don't bore the poor girl,' urged Brian.

But his warning wasn't needed or else wasn't heeded.

'It's near here?' asked Maxine. 'Not too far? Once we've finished lunch could you show me?'

So with no contrivance from Brian or George, that was that.

As soon as coffee was over the pair set out for a long walk round the Slate Quarry.

CHAPTER 19

At nine o'clock on Monday morning a casual passer-by in Treknow might have been surprised to see a small police car pull up outside Ivy Cottage. A cheerful-looking policeman got out and made his way to the door. A few minutes later he returned, accompanied by an elegantly-dressed woman clutching a notebook. They got into the car, which immediately drove off.

'Did you sleep OK?' asked Peter Travers. One of the many things he had learned on their long walk the afternoon before was that Maxine was still suffering anxiety attacks from her experience the week earlier.

'Much better, thank you Peter,' replied Maxine. 'The fact that you'd promised to support me from now on made a huge difference – far more than I'd ever thought possible. I'm sorry, I was stupid not to come to you earlier.'

'You'd had a dreadful experience. For some people that could lead to post-traumatic stress. That sort of thing is not easy to talk about. It was only your own wit that got you away. George and Brian are wise and did their best but Caldwell is hopeless. He doesn't relate or empathise with anyone. He comes in for staff meetings, never stays on for a chat afterwards. Thank goodness you took an interest in the Slate Quarry. At least that gave you and I time to talk.'

'Wasn't it huge? Are you sure Brian hadn't tipped you off beforehand?'

'If you remember, it was you that suggested the walk. Brian had given me a broad outline of what you'd told him a few nights ago, without mentioning names. I had no idea when I met you that the person was you. He didn't tell me, you see, that he'd invited you to Sunday lunch as well. That was just a wonderful surprise. The best thing that's happened to me for months.'

The policeman smiled with pleasure. He'd been feeling upbeat all day.

'You don't want me to start telling you about my adventure as we're driving into Bude?'

'I'm happy to have a preliminary chat, Maxine, if you want, but what I'm really after is a formal, recorded interview that I can start the case from. In my opinion policing needs to be well-organised and thorough.'

That seemed fair enough. She didn't mind being cross-questioned by Peter, however long it took. There was a short silence.

'Are you very busy in the police station at the moment?' asked Maxine. 'Will you have time to process me? Or are the rest just watching errant tourists?'

'Chance'd be a fine thing, Maxine. I can't give you details, of course. This conversation is entirely private, yes?'

Maxine nodded.

'Two cases began last week that have both taken a lot of time. Firstly a local man whose summer job is to clear houses has gone missing. That might or might not be serious, we can't even be sure he's not just gone on holiday. Then a day later we were warned that a convict who'd grown up in Bude had escaped from Dartmoor, clobbering one of the wardens as he did so. He's a habitually violent man. We were asked to check if he'd been seen by any of his old friends.'

'Do you often get overloaded like that?'

'To be honest, hardly ever. But then, I've only been in charge at Bude since Easter. Before that I was the community policeman in the area round Delabole. That was almost entirely minding the tourists.'

'Apart from responding to George's observations at Ivy Cottage,' said Maxine. She told me the tale last night. What an eye opener! You guys sometimes have to dig down a really long way.'

Maxine was glad to see that Bude Police Station was not hidebound, either in its attitudes or its processes. There was a small team of uniformed officers who all seemed to be busy, but they said 'Hi' in a friendly manner as Peter Travers took her through the open-plan area and into his office.

For twenty minutes he dealt with the most urgent emails and made a few phone calls. Then, having made sure they each had a mug of coffee in their hands, he led her down to the interview room on the floor below.

For the first hour Maxine was invited to tell the whole story in her own words.

'Make yourself comfortable and take as long as you like,' said the policeman. 'I'll come back on the details afterwards but first I want to hear it from your side.'

It helped, of course, that she had told the tale twice before, once to George and then to Brian. But this time she really wanted to please. Having the sturdy policeman watching her carefully and listening to her every word added to her resolve to recall the detail.

Forty minutes later she stopped.

'You've got amazing recall,' said the policeman. 'I wish even one in a hundred of the witnesses I talk to in here could do that well.'

He paused to arrange the list of odd words he had noted down into a logical sequence; then he began.

'I'll begin at the beginning. You came off the late Camp bus at half past nine and walked steadily up the slope to Tee-Side. Looking back, did you notice anyone following you?'

Maxine paused and then shook her head.

'For the data recorder, please,' instructed Travers, nodding to the machine on the side.

'No. Though, to be honest, I wasn't particularly looking.'

'And after you'd gone into the guest-house, did you stop in the dining room for a drink of hot chocolate or anything before you went upstairs?'

'No. There was a kettle in my room if I needed it. But I don't tend to drink after eight in the evening anyway.'

'OK. So you got into your room. Did you have any sense that there was anyone else there?'

'Not in the bedroom. Nothing had been disturbed.'

'But had anything been added?'

Maxine paused, mentally examining the room. She had not

been in there for a week.

Then she gave a start. 'Now I think about it, there was a paperback at an odd angle on the bedside table. I would always leave the pile tidy.'

'I don't suppose you can remember the title?'

She frowned. 'It wasn't one of mine. The cover was rather violent. It looked foreign . . . maybe Dutch or Danish? I'm sorry, the title wasn't in English.'

'Maybe the abductor had been reading it as they waited for you?'

'Perhaps. It was on the side of the bed nearest the shower.' Maxine was silent now, kicking herself that she had missed a warning clue. She had nothing to add.

'So you decided to have a shower. Took off all your clothes, including your shoes. Stuck the items you'd use again in the wardrobe and the rest in the linen basket. Then headed for the en suite bathroom.'

'That's correct.'

'Where you found the light not working. It was a cord switch, I assume?'

'It was. I wasn't suspicious, every bulb wears out sometime.'

'Then someone grabbed you from behind, held your arms and shoved some sort of chemical pad over your face. Was there any warning at all?'

'No. I realised they wanted to make me unconscious. I held my breath for as long as I could. But in the end I had to breathe in and I blacked out.'

There was a pause. For Maxine, reliving the moment must

have been hard. And what had happened to her made Peter Travers very angry. But there was one more question he had to ask.

'Maxine, when you escaped next morning you say you were wearing a bathrobe. Did you have that on when you went into the shower? Or was it something the assailant threw over you before carrying you downstairs?'

'The latter. I was completely naked when I went into the shower.' She paused as the gravity of the whole thing hit her afresh. Her eyes filled with tears. 'He could have done anything with me – anything at all.'

Travers decided that at this point they each needed a few minutes respite. 'You wait here, Maxine. Or go for a stroll round the station. I'll go and fetch us more coffee.'

When they resumed he could see Maxine was in control once more. He sat opposite her and turned on the recorder again.

'I'd like to move on now to the next morning. See if I can prompt any more memories from the trip back to Bude. By now, I understand, you were fully conscious?'

'That's right.'

'What I'd like you to focus on for a few moments is smell. The smell of the kitchen, say, or the smell of the farmyard.'

'I wasn't taking much notice of smells inside the kitchen. I was scared to death of what they might be going to do to me.'

'I can understand that. But relax for a moment, shut your eyes and take your time. Was there any smell there at all?'

Silence for a moment.

'You know, there was a smell. It was . . . floor polish. That's right, someone had recently polished the kitchen floor. What on earth can we make of that?'

More silence but no more smells came to light.

'OK, Maxine, how about the farm yard?'

There was another silence.

'There was a smell there, too. It was a chlorine sort of smell. As though the whole yard had been given a strong flush of disinfectant.'

'Right, we'll come back to that. But while you're still there in your mind, can you hear anything – either in the farm or on the journey?'

Silence again, but this time a more potent silence. Maxine wasn't just going through the motions she was earnestly dredging her memories. What else had she heard or seen?

'They dragged me rather roughly across the yard. But I wasn't blindfolded or anything. One thing I can recall, flying over the farm yard, is a flight of large birds. They were in formation. Geese, I think. They were honking away like everything was right with the world.'

The policeman smiled, 'In their world it probably was.'

Another pause as Maxine let subconscious thoughts emerge.

'Once they'd put me in the boot of the car I couldn't see very much. But there was a short gap before they slammed the lid. In the far distance I could hear the noise of machinery.'

'Can you narrow that down?'

Maxine concentrated even harder. 'It was like. . . like something being winched up. There was a screeching, sounded like

145

machinery needing more oil.' A pause while she thought some more. 'Followed a moment later by what sounded like the noise of a large vehicle, revving up and then starting to move. They put the boot lid down on me then, I don't know what happened after that.'

'Right. We'll come back to that. Now, have you anything on the journey into Bude?'

Maxine reached down for her notebook. 'I made progress on this when I was talking to George. I've got the notes here.' She proceeded to astonish the policeman by the extent to which she could remember John Humphrys' announcements of time on the car radio and their associations in her memory with driving speed.

'That's remarkable,' admitted the policeman when she had finished. 'If we're smart that should tell us whether the farmhouse they kept you in is located north or the south of where we are now. Holly Berry drives in from Stratton and I drive up, as you saw, from the south. We can try it tomorrow morning – that's exactly a week on.'

'There was just one more thing, Peter. Early on it sounded like we'd gone through a huge puddle. There was a splash of water hitting the car, followed by a burst of acceleration.'

The policeman smiled again. 'It's been a dry few weeks, Maxine. Not many puddles out there now. But is it possible . . . it was a ford?'

CHAPTER 20

Later that morning, after a preliminary phone call to pave the way, the policeman and Maxine walked through Bude up to Tee-Side.

Monday was certainly a better day for a visit than Saturday. Only a couple of guests had left on Monday morning. They found Mr and Mrs Murdoch relaxing in the kitchen, enjoying a cup of coffee.

The sight of the policeman alongside their guest made the point without a word being spoken that there were questions needing answers. But Travers let the couple settle – even gave them a moment's small talk – before starting his questions.

'I've been talking to Dr Tavistock here about what happened to her a week ago. Right now I need your input to take the case forward.'

'We'll help any way we can,' began Mr Murdoch. 'We knew there was something wrong from when your friend came to pick up your reading glasses. But she didn't leave an address so we had no way of contacting you. Then that dreadful man on Saturday . . .'

His wife took over. 'He seemed to think he could barge in here and tell us all what to do, see. My husband, he wasn't havin' that. If anything was wrong we wanted a real policeman.'

'I'm real, all right, Mrs Murdoch. The thing is, I'm sorry to tell you, Dr Tavistock was abducted from here last Monday evening. I've only just got to hear of it so I want to make enquiries as soon as possible.'

The couple looked at one another, both clearly shocked that anything like this had happened to one of their guests. This was far from a normal occurrence. 'Are you alright, m'dear?' asked Mrs Murdoch.

'I'm getting over it,' Maxine replied. 'That's why I moved away for a few days to stay with my old friend. I expect I'll be back here soon. But before I do that I'd like to be sure it couldn't happen again.'

'What happened to Maxine after she was taken from here is not up for discussion at this point,' observed Travers. 'But we've had a long chat and we've got some ideas about how the whole thing might have been arranged.'

'We don't want it ever to happen again,' said Mr Murdoch, shaking his head. 'Please carry on.'

The policeman continued. 'Maxine came back here last Monday evening just before ten pm. There was a man (or possibly a strong woman) in her room, hiding in the shower. We don't know how long they'd been there but it was perhaps half an hour. They'd taken out the shower light bulb so it was dark when Maxine went in. They put a swab of chloroform over her face, knocking her out. Then carried her downstairs and out to a car.'

The guesthouse owners looked horrified.

'But Sergeant Travers, this is Bude,' said Mrs Murdoch. 'How on earth could such a series of events happen in this town, in this respectable guest house?'

'That's what I'm here to find out, madam. First of all, to narrow things down, have you had any break-ins in recent months?'

'We were burgled soon after we started,' admitted Mr Murdoch.

Travers attention heightened. 'Was that recently?'

'No. It was, what, fifteen years ago. After that we fitted better locks and put alarms on all downstairs windows. We've had no trouble since.'

'But Maxine tells me all of your guests have a front door key lent to them during their stay. Have you ever lost any of these?'

'One or two over the years. People forget to hand them in, see. But we change the lock barrel every winter. If someone had kept an old key it wouldn't do them any good later on.'

'And we haven't lost any this year, have we?' added Mrs Murdoch.

'Right. So given all that, the most likely thing is that one of this year's guests borrowed the key and made themselves a copy. Probably they also did the same thing to obtain a second key to Maxine's bedroom.'

Mr Murdoch nodded. 'We always knew that was a risk if someone planned to come back later. So as a safeguard we had a deal with the local locksmith down in the Strand, that's Sandy Jenkins. We asked him to make sure he took the name of anyone who came in asking him to copy a key.'

'Excellent,' said Travers. 'I'll go and see him as soon as I've finished here. And to match it, would you be able to give me a full list of this year's guests, please? I'll return it, of course, once the investigation's over.'

That had gone better than he dared hope. He glanced down his list, what else was needed?

'Now sir, if you wouldn't mind, I'd like to take a look at Maxine's guestroom. Am I right that no one has been in there since last Monday?'

Mrs Murdoch took up the story. 'Maxine's colleague, Sam Hudson, noticed she wasn't having breakfast on Tuesday morning – they usually share a table and travel to work together. I went to check and he was right. I didn't know why she'd gone but I double locked her room straight away. That'd be about eight thirty. So I'm sure no one's been inside since then.'

'No chance this key was copied as well, madam?'

'None at all.' She pulled a bunch of keys from her apron pocket and selected one. 'It's this one, see. A special key we don't lend to anyone.'

'Very impressive, madam. So could we see the room now, please?'

Travers, Maxine and Mrs Murdoch tramped up the stairs, Mr Murdoch evidently deciding he wasn't needed. Two keys were applied and the door swung open.

'Remember, ladies, this is almost certainly a crime scene. I don't want any of us to touch anything. But I do want any comments on anything that looks out of place.'

Mrs Murdoch knew how the room normally looked between guests and gave it a rapid appraisal from the doorway. 'Well, there's a lot of dust gathered here over the last week. But that's not down to criminals. I guess it's what you'd expect.'

Maxine took longer. 'That book I told you about has gone. But I don't think they took away anything of mine. Can we look in the shower?'

The door was still ajar. Maxine took care not to touch it and peered inside, Travers standing just behind her.

'He must have been standing over there.' She pointed over to the far wall, which was tiled.

'I doubt he'd leave much trace on that,' observed Travers.

'But look. He didn't bother to replace the light bulb,' said Maxine. 'It's down here in the bin.'

'Might be a chance of fingerprints or DNA from that, then. Unless he wore gloves the whole time he was in here. In which case, I'm sorry to say, we'd be stymied.'

He turned to Mrs Murdoch. 'What I'd like you to do, please, is to double lock this room again for the time being. I'll send round the Scene of Crime team for a full inspection as soon as I can. They'll probably come this afternoon.'

CHAPTER 21

By the time Travers and Maxine left Tee-Side, the girl could see it was almost lunch time.

'D'you have a canteen in the police station?'

'That's what they call it. But it's not intended for use by witnesses. I doubt it'd pass Health and Safety.' Travers hesitated and then asked, 'Could I take you for lunch at the Falcon?'

'Is that in the role of witness or victim?'

The policeman wasn't sure quite how to answer. Then he saw Maxine was smiling in a roguish manner. He responded, 'How about simply as friends – or maybe co-workers?'

It didn't take long to walk down the hill and across the canal to the hotel. Bude was a very small town. In her relief – whether because her interview was over or because she was enjoying the company – Maxine found herself chattering about anything and everything. Later she found she could remember nothing of the route they had taken. Peter Travers had an instinctive grasp of the route but seemed almost equally afflicted.

It took something of an effort, once they'd reached the hotel and taken their places in the furthest corner of the restaurant, to remember that they had promised themselves a working lunch.

'Right,' said the policeman, extracting his notebook as the waitress disappeared with their order. 'To business. Let's start with Tee-Side.'

'One thing that might help us is if we can find a common name for customers of the locksmith and the guesthouse.' Maxine paused. 'How many keys d'you reckon get copied in a place like this?'

'Dunno. We'll see after lunch. Maybe one a week; fifty a year?'

'And how many guests stay in Tee-Side?'

'Judging by the size of Murdoch's hard copy file, a lot. The host was saying that the place can take a dozen families at a time. And so far there've been, what, 210 days this year. Even if it's no more than half full that's a few hundred names.' He gave a sigh. 'Good job the list Murdoch gave us was digital.'

Maxine noted with pleasure the way he was talking about "us" and not just "me" but made no comment. 'So finding one name that's common to both lists could take us some time?'

'Hm. It sounds almost a mathematical problem. If you're volunteering, Maxine .. ?'

'That'd keep me busy for the afternoon, anyway.'

'Great. Now I've got various items that emerged in your interview that, put together, might narrow down the location of the farm where they took you. Plus some things to look for, once we're at a possible farm, to check if we're in the right place.'

The policeman scowled in concentration at his list. It was more of a jumble than he had expected, his thoughts must have been confused. The process was disrupted for a minute by the arrival of their sweet and sour chicken.

Maxine realised the stress of the morning had made her very hungry.

The policeman said, 'Listen. What I've got here is: a flock of geese; a puddle that might be a ford; and a piece of noisy machinery. There are also some slow-traffic timings, but we can't do anything with them till tomorrow. Where shall we start?'

'I'm not certain they were geese but they were big birds and certainly flying together. Doesn't that mean they were heading for open water?'

'It's only August: they wouldn't be migrating. Not yet, anyway. The fact that they were all honking might tell us something. What we need is an expert on local birds. I'll look up some names once we're back at the station.'

He paused to eat some of his lunch.

'I don't suppose you've any idea which direction they were travelling?'

This was a new line of questioning. Maxine's first instinct was to rebel: what on earth was her companion thinking of? But she had seen enough, now, of Peter Travers to give him the benefit of the doubt.

She paused, thinking hard. 'They were almost at right angles to the direction the car was facing.'

'Good. And have you any idea what direction that might be?'

A longer pause. Maxine screwed up her eyes, trying to recall the detail. 'It clouded over later on, but when they carried me out of the farmhouse the sun was shining. They didn't bring me far though, the building kept us in the shade.'

Another pause as the geometry was computed. Travers recalled that she had studied maths at Cambridge. Probably just as well.

'Yes, that's right. The car must have been facing more or less due south. Hence the birds were flying due east.'

'Excellent. I wish more witnesses had this depth of recall. Let's have more of our lunch.'

Later Travers took up the analysis again. 'If the splashing you heard was just a big puddle, I don't see how we can take it any further. I mean, no one keeps a database of puddles.'

'I have the impression, you know, that the splashing was on both sides; which makes a ford more likely. Do the police have any list of local fords? Are there many round here?'

'Quite a few, on the minor roads. I don't think the small ones are even marked on Ordnance Survey maps. But the Council might have compiled a list of their own to help with traffic control. If there was bad flooding, for example, you wouldn't want to divert traffic over a second ford. That might be even worse. We'll check when we get back.'

He glanced again at his list. 'That leaves us with the noisy machinery. Can you think of what that might have been?'

'It's a puzzle. I don't think it was much before eight o'clock. But surely not much machinery gets used that early in the day?'

'Not in Cheltenham, perhaps. But out in the country folk are up with the lark. You say . . . it sounded like something being lifted. There's only one thing I can think of that might need lifting up that early.'

Maxine was silent, trying to match her companion. But she was less familiar with life in Cornwall. 'Go on then, tell me.'

'Well, how about milk? I bet the tankers collect that from early on, so it's as fresh as possible.'

'Could be. But how does that help? Won't their collection be a random process?'

'The farmers can't be expected to supply at random. There must be a schedule for milk tankers to do the collecting.'

'OK. I can see that farmers would know when their collection was expected. But who would know the overall pattern?'

'You'd need to ask the Milk Supplies middlemen. If I can find the right person I'm sure they would be happy to oblige. That could be the vital clue: where were all the North Cornwall milk tankers at eight o'clock on Tuesday morning?'

The policeman saw that they'd both finished their main course. 'Do you want a pudding? Or coffee? If not, then we could go and have a chat with Sandy Jenkins. After that maybe you could come back to the station, sit in the office and try and help us with some matching.'

CHAPTER 22

Peter Travers wondered whether it was right to involve Maxine so closely in the case. Had he lost his detachment? But a clear-thinking abduction survivor is a rare type of victim. Everyone in the open-plan office would be chasing one or other aspect of her case. It could be useful, he thought, to have her as a primary source of reference alongside them.

So for most of Monday afternoon, Maxine hot-desked in the open plan outside Peter Travers' office as a special, albeit temporary member of his team. It might be frowned on but the sergeant knew he needed her help. He introduced her briefly and then left them all to it.

Maxine knew the case far better than anyone else and, he remembered, had a high level of security clearance – at least as much as Caldwell. And the abduction had happened a week ago: time was of the essence.

When Travers had first introduced her the team had invited her to share her story. They were gobsmacked. She had outlined her recent ordeal and had received a very sympathetic hearing.

Maxine couldn't help noticing that at least one of the team was pursuing ideas that had come up during her lunch. At least, she assumed that must the reason for a series of calls from Holly Berry to Milk Supplies middlemen. It seemed to be a long slog –

no doubt most policing was like that. It was very similar to working in security.

Earlier she had accompanied Peter to the locksmith; the Strand was on the route back to the station. The interview with Sandy Jenkins had gone well. Maxine inferred that the policeman must know the locksmith from some previous encounter. That must have gone well too, for the man was highly cooperative.

Eventually a memory stick holding a computerised list of his 67 key-copying customers in 2013, including their declared home addresses, had been handed over for analysis.

Maxine had been assigned a spare police computer. Now she could use her wiles to find matching names from the two lists.

She first imported the lists from Tee-Side and Sandy Jenkins onto a spreadsheet. Then she wrote a macro which took each Jenkins name in turn and looked for matches in the longer list.

'While you're waiting, could you get us all a coffee?' asked Jess Holland. That made Maxine feel she was part of the team.

When she returned to her desk ten minutes later she was initially amazed to find that there were no less than a dozen matches.

As she examined these in detail, though, her amazement rapidly declined. In most cases, although the surnames were the same, the first names were different. In one or two cases a full name had been provided in one place but only an initial in the other.

But in one case at least, the initial at least matched the name. "J. Smith" had stayed at Tee-Side from May 6th to 8th. And "Jan Smith" had copied two keys at Sandy Jenkins on the day in between.

Now she had a possible name for the thug that had taken her. The name, though, was probably counterfeit – Smith was far too common. But Maxine knew that before she took this any further every detail had to be checked.

Her first algorithm hadn't looked at dates at all. The macro was now refined so that it only considered links where the copying happened during the time the guest was staying at Tee-Side.

"Jan Smith" again plopped out. That at least showed the procedure was working.

Now Maxine relaxed the algorithm. Capital letters had not always been used so she first reduced all the names to lower case. Then she dealt with the name-matching procedure. On this latest version surnames did not need to be exactly the same but could differ by one or two letters. This would allow for accidental or even deliberate misspellings at each location.

But still, given the requirement imposed on interleaved dates, "Jan Smith" emerged as the only contender.

Was there anything else could go wrong? Maxine sat still for twenty minutes, thinking hard.

Finally, for completeness, she set any two names to be picked out as a match if either one was a subset of the other. It was possible that someone had clocked in as, say, "Nick Harvey Jones" at Tee-Side but simply "Nick Jones" at the locksmith.

The computer whirred once again. This time there was a second name. And this one looked even more interesting. At least, it did to someone who happened to know the names of other short-term visitors that summer at Cleave Camp.

By now it was half past five and her new, unofficial colleagues were ready to go home. Maxine was head down, starting to double-check her results before announcing them, as Travers emerged from his office.

'Right, team. What I need for tomorrow morning is one of you – more if you want – who can set off in their car from north of Bude, intending to get themselves here bang on nine. You'll need to work back from when you normally get here and then make an adjustment.

'I'm going to do the same,' he went on, 'but coming from the south.'

'Why has it to be exactly nine?' asked Jess Holland.

'That's the time Maxine was delivered by her captors, a week ago tomorrow, to the antique shop just up the road.'

'What're we looking for, guv?' asked Holly.

'I want everyone who's doing the trip to note the first time at which you are seriously slowed by traffic. It's unlikely, I hope, that north and south cars will be slowed at exactly the same time.'

He paused to check they were with him and then continued.

'Once we're all here we'll compare those times with the time Maxine remembers her car first coming to a halt. Even from the boot she could hear John Humphrys announcing the time every few minutes on the car radio, you see. With a bit of luck that should give us a steer on whether she'd been held north or south of Bude. That's the start we need. After that we can start pulling together all the other clues, see if we can pick out the hideaway farm.'

160

It all sounded promising, a game of hide and seek that they might for once be able to win. There was a buzz of anticipation as the team tidied their desks and made their way to the door.

When they had all gone, the sergeant turned to Maxine. 'Can I offer you a lift home? I should be going in a few minutes. I promise you I won't talk shop.'

The promise was kept. But though they left without much delay, he didn't deliver Maxine to Ivy Cottage for good until late in the evening.

'I'd like to take you to a restaurant not far from Delabole,' he said, 'which I think is rather special.'

He dropped her for an hour at Ivy Cottage to freshen up. Then he called again to take her out to the Riverside Restaurant in Boscastle.

'It's a five-star restaurant at affordable prices,' he said as they drove along the coast road in the evening sunshine.

At the restaurant the two were warmly welcomed. Then they were served two magnificent grilled rump steaks. Later there followed Eton Mess for Peter and fruit salad for Maxine. Without either of them referring to the current case a great deal of personal history was shared.

Peter learned that Maxine lived on her own in Cheltenham, been there for years, had no "significant other". Her main hobby was playing the flute.

'Ah, you mean in a local orchestra?'

'I'm afraid not. I'm in a band that performs in local ceilidhs.'

'Sounds cultural enough for me. I strum a guitar, but not very well.'

'What else d'you do, Peter?'

'Work keeps me pretty busy. When I'm off duty I do some bird watching and photography. I've a brother in Padstow. He and I share a sailing boat that's moored in Rock. He uses it much more than I do.'

This was the first time for years that Peter Travers had found a companion who seemed on his wavelength, with an interest in crime and a shared interest in Cornwall; one, moreover, who was also unattached.

At the end of their evening, as he dropped her back at Ivy Cottage, Peter took the chance to offer his new friend a lift to Bude next morning. 'I reckon we need to leave Delabole about eight fifteen. I'll come for you just before eight.'

Next morning, Tuesday, the embargo on the case was over. The policeman clearly regarded his journey to work as a chance to review the developments so far. Maxine was happy to do so. There was time for a short conversation before they reached the Bude traffic queues.

'Did you find any link between the two lists yesterday?' he asked.

'It took a while,' replied Maxine, 'but in the end I did. I've got two names that overlapped and the dates interleaved, between Tee-Side and the locksmith.'

'Sounds good. Can you remember the names?'

'One of them was a "Jan Smith", came in May. With a name like that I couldn't be certain if it was a man or a woman.'

'Presumably Tee-Side can give us their address – which might or might not be genuine, of course. When we get into the station we can see if we can find anyone with a criminal record under that name.' He sighed. 'Trouble is, Smith is the sort of name you'd use as cover if you didn't want to be picked up. Who was the second?'

'A "Gina Hartley Brown". That was the name she gave at Tee-Side, anyway. Sandy Jenkins had her down simply as Gina Brown. It took me a while to match the two. But the dates in each place matched exactly as you'd expect. She was there in mid June.'

'That's a sophisticated name to adopt – might even be real.'

Maxine seemed distressed. 'Trouble is, Peter, I know a Gina Hartley Brown from Cheltenham. She came for a short visit to Cleave Camp in June – and that would account for her stay at Tee-Side. She's a senior Personnel Officer in GCHQ.'

'Hm. That needs a lot more thought. Maybe even a chat with Caldwell.' The policeman gazed at the road ahead. 'But we're getting close to Bude now, Maxine. Watch the time, please, and write down exactly when we hit the first proper traffic hold-up.'

Twenty minutes later they had reached the police station, parked in the yard and a moment later joined Jess Holland and some of the others in the open plan. After a few opening pleasantries the analysis began.

'I hit a solid holdup when I got as far as Stratton,' said Jess Holland. 'That was at eight forty two. And I'd timed it pretty well, I think. I got to the station at eight fifty nine.'

'We didn't have to queue for the Bude turn-off until eight fifty,' said Peter Travers. 'That's ten minutes later, we got here just before nine as well.' He turned to Maxine. 'Can I have your diary, please?'

Maxine handed over her notebook, which she'd already opened at the relevant page. The policeman examined it for a moment.

'A week ago, Maxine recalls, the car that brought her in hit its first big holdup at eight forty. Hm. It's looking pretty likely that she was coming from the north.'

It was the final narrowing down that they needed. For an hour there was intense activity. Jamie Sampson took a spare, large-scale map of the area north of Bude, laid it out on a side table and, using a compass, pencilled the smallest and largest diameter circles centred on Bude that made sense. 'Those are the furthest you could reach at twenty and forty mph respectively.' Between the two circles showed where the hideaway farmhouse might be expected.

Overnight Peter Travers had been sent the latest milk tanker pickup schedules from the Milk Supplies middle men. He sent them on to Holly and then retreated to his office to handle the day's correspondence.

Holly and Maxine carefully highlighted each route onto Sampson's map, then picked out where each of the tankers should be at around seven forty five.

Meanwhile Joe Tremlitt started the task of marking the locations of all fords listed by Cornwall and Devon Councils in the area north of Bude.

Just before ten Peter Travers joined them. Maxine had just made them all mugs of coffee and they stood around the map cogitating.

The sergeant took a different coloured highlighter pen and started systematically working down the map, aiming to put question marks wherever the milk tankers and fords were adjacent.

After a careful search he stopped. 'I reckon, you know, there are only two places where our sources come anywhere close to coinciding. And in both cases they're shown as being near to a farm. That's here . . . and here. "Keldrake Farm" and "Titchcombe Lodge". So is there anything else we know that can help us decide one is more likely than the other; or should we visit them both?'

Silence as the team pondered.

'Hey, what about the direction of flight of the geese?' asked Maxine. She looked around the room. 'Has anyone managed to find a bird expert?'

Most of the team hadn't been told this nugget. The idea that the birds were flying either to or from a large stretch of water seemed plausible.

Jamie Sampson was nearest to the map and swiftly looked at the possibilities. 'Look,' he said, 'east of this farm, Keldrake, takes us, after a mile or two, to Tamar Lake. The birds might well be heading there. That's the one I'd try first, anyway.'

The sergeant had been thinking about how they should proceed.

'You know, this is all quite tricky,' he began. 'What sort of operation is this? I mean, let's assume for a moment that this is the hideaway – or at least it was, a week ago.'

'I'd say,' said Jess Holland, 'that the abductors will have moved on.'

'There's a chance they're still there,' replied Jamie Sampson. 'Not one victim in a million would remember the details Maxine did. They probably think they're perfectly safe. Might even be planning the next abduction.'

That thought confirmed Travers' own feelings.

'Right. We've no choice but to get there as soon as we can. With two cars, just in case there's a struggle.'

He turned to Maxine. 'You'd better stay here in the station, please, out of danger.'

'But don't you need me with you to check this is the right place? How else will you know?'

It didn't take much to change his mind. 'You're right,' he admitted. OK, you'd better come with me. Jamie Sampson and Joe Tremlitt can come in the second car. But stay out of sight, please, until I call you.'

Just ten minutes later they were on their way.

Travers did not use his siren but nor he did hang about. His Sat Nav guided him expertly and they reached the end of the muddy lane leading up to Keldrake Farm within forty minutes. Jamie Sampson and Joe Tremlitt were not far behind.

The sergeant had been mentally refining his tactics as they drove. He could not be sure what they would be up against, had to prepare for the worst.

'Right. I'm going to drive in and I want Joe Tremlitt beside me. Maxine, can you swap to the second car, please. Which can stay on the road until called.'

There was no argument. This was a police raid.

Travers and Tremlitt drove slowly up the lane. Keldrake Farm itself was a further half-mile. He'd seen no sign by the roadside and there wasn't one next to the farm either. That fitted with Maxine's memories, at any rate.

The metal gate was firmly locked. Beyond they could see a small farmyard.

'Hey, look,' said Travers, pointing. 'There's a hatch down to a coal cellar or something over there. That might be where they hid Maxine.'

Just at that moment they heard an engine noise behind them. Turning, the policemen saw a rather battered green Citroen Estate, now unable to pass their police car in the single-track lane and in consequence stuck in the lane.

An elderly farmer unpeeled himself from behind the wheel, got out slowly and came towards them.

'Good morning, gentlemen. Is there anything I can help you with?'

167

CHAPTER 23

George Gilbert had been too busy to miss her current guest much on Monday.

Monday was the day for her weekly visit to the Innovation Exhibition in Bristol. There she would give her weekly talk, based here around the prodigious engineer Isambard Kingdom Brunel. There was no shortage of success that she could talk about here, at any rate.

It had become her policy to make this a full day visit. Bristol was two and a half hours drive from her home in Cornwall and once there she wanted to make the most of the day. Before she gave her talk in the afternoon, George would meet staff at various organisational levels. Amongst other things she would collect the latest data on sales and revenue.

She had also developed the habit of having an evening meal in Bristol with one of the staff before starting her return journey to Cornwall. She learned more about behind the scenes details over dinner than she ever learned in the office. As a result it was after ten before she was back at Ivy Cottage, tired from a long day.

She had received a text from Maxine to say that Peter Travers would be giving her a lift home from Bude. It sounded as though any inhibitions about her spending time with the policeman had been not just broken so much as smashed to smithereens. George was pleased for her friend but hoped she was not being reckless.

She was slightly surprised that Maxine was not asking for a lift into Bude when they met at the breakfast table on Tuesday morning, but gathered that some sort of timing trial was to take place at the edge of Bude. Maxine was tight-lipped on the details. She would miss her friend's company on the drive in but assumed they could catch up with one another in the evening.

Today, Tuesday, George had to make the most of the first of a series of interviews she had arranged this week with the senior management for the Bude Exhibition, starting with the Operations Manager, Nicholas Judd.

Once in Bude, George parked near the Exhibition Office and made her way inside. She knew which was Judd's office, she had used it on Friday. But first she had to pass through reception. She saw a sparky young woman behind the desk today.

'Hullo. I haven't met you before? I'm George Gilbert, I help with the talks here,' George greeted her.

'I'm Jacqui Francis. I've been on one of the tills for the last two weeks, facing the customers. But they're very good, the management here, they swap us round over the summer. To give us as wide a range of experience as possible. At least, that's what they say.'

'Great. I've got an appointment to see Mr Judd at ten.'

Jess consulted the desk diary. 'Ah yes. I'll give him a ring.' Five minutes later George was in Mr Judd's office, making her introductions.

Judd was a short, dynamic-looking man with dark hair and a

tidy beard. This certainly wasn't the man she had seen on Friday evening emptying exhibition tills. But if she didn't recognise him, there was no reason for him to recognise her. At least she wouldn't have to justify her unusual behaviour to him from the week before.

'Pleased to meet you, Ms Gilbert,' Judd began, shaking her hand.

'Call me George.'

'Fine. And I'm Nick. I sat in on your talk on Friday, by the way. Very clear and challenging. Exactly what did you want to talk to me about?'

'As part of my role here, your Chairman asked me to take an overview of the exhibition processes. See if, coming here as an outsider, I could spot any ways they might be improved. But if I'm going to do that, I first of all need to know what the processes are.'

She was glad to see that the Operations Manager did not look unduly put out. George thought that the Chairman might have hinted to the senior staff that that some tricky questions had been raised.

'Personally, I reckon we've got it working fairly well. There were a few teething troubles, of course. But it never does any harm to have a fresh look. Where d'you want to start? Or do you want me to take you on a guided tour?'

'Let's talk first, anyway.' George consulted the list of topics in her notebook, looking for a safe place to start. 'How do you manage the security and the safety of the site?'

Judd looked fairly confident. 'We use an independent security firm, Mattersons. They do lots of work with us all over the country. Here we have much the same scheme as on our other sites. Mattersons hire the staff and arrange the shifts: they have a couple of men keeping watch over the site every night, armed with the latest communication gizmos. There are some in the daytime too – more in fact.'

'And you reckon that's enough?'

Judd considered. 'If there is any trouble, the men have a direct line to the police station so they can call for reinforcements. But we've not had any problems and I don't expect any. I mean, Bude's a holiday town, it's not the docks of Amsterdam. And the more valuable bits of kit here have extra protection.'

'You have no say in the staff recruited?'

'None at all. Mattersons do the adverts and the vetting. They have contracts which they apply "without exception". They normally take on local staff who want to hang on to their jobs. It's not been a problem here, anyway.'

'Good. Can I ask about the layout of the Exhibition? Was this your design?'

'Goodness me, no. That's a different sort of skill entirely. The place has a part-time Research Director, appointed a couple of years ago. That's a professor from Plymouth University, Joe Nuffield. He's a very charismatic figure, you may have seen him on television. We funded his course at the University so he could take a year's sabbatical to help us.'

'What did Nuffield do?'

'His remit was to make contacts with museums all over Corn-wall and to identify unusual exhibit items on the theme of Innovation. Then he had to form a team of advisors who would pull the best ideas together. They were also charged with spotting engineering pieces that could act as highlights. That's how we got the steam car here, and Gurney's special lighting effects. That gave us the name "Limelight".'

'I'm most interested in the steam cars. Those aren't made down here, are they?'

'Don't ask for the impossible, George. Our parent company has a subsidiary in Wolverhampton that has the gear to build specialist items like that. One at a time, I might say. They're pretty expensive – but that doesn't stop wealthy people wanting to bid for them.'

'Are they road-worthy?'

'The boilers on Gurney's originals exploded regularly. It was an exciting ride for his passengers.'

'Ah. So it wasn't just competition with the railway that made him fail. There were safety issues.'

'Not just that, Nuffield said. They've done the experiments. The frictional effort to go along a road is ten times the amount needed to go along a smooth set of rails. Rail transport is so much more efficient.'

'Wow.' Here was something else to go in her next talk.

'Today's models are much stronger,' Judd went on. 'They won't explode, but no, they're not licensed for the road. But the people rich enough to afford them usually have large estates with private roads which they can drive round. Enough to show off to neighbours, anyway.'

'How many have you sold? And where d'you keep them till

they sell?'

'There's not much room here on site, that's for sure. The marquee takes up most of the space we've leased for the summer. There's an industrial estate round the back of Bude. We've leased a unit for equipment storage – and that includes two or three steam cars at any one time. We bring them down as needed on a large trailer. It's good publicity as they pass slowly through the town. Or sometimes the buyer will arrange to collect them direct from the storage unit.'

'They're impressive-looking vehicles, Nick. I imagine they make a good profit?'

'They do. But exactly how much is a closely guarded secret. Even I don't know the production cost. And the selling price is the highest bid made by a customer each week, so that varies. You'd have to ask the Finance Director about the overall profit, though I'm not sure he'd tell you.'

'I'll ask him anyway. I'm hoping to see him later this week.'

There was a pause while George consulted her list. 'As Operations Manager, d'you have anything to do with the exhibition catering?'

'That's another outsourced item, George. A firm called Mayfield Catering do all the work here and give us a fixed amount for the privilege.'

'Do you know the size of their profit?'

'Ah, that's their commercial secret.'

'So how d'you know what to charge them?'

'There's a standard charge per table that we make at all our exhibitions. To a host of different caterers.' A shadow of doubt passed over Judd's face. 'I suppose the fact that we never have any difficulty finding catering partners might mean that we're not charging them enough.'

'But if you charge more and the caterer charges more, your customers might not be so keen to come. So overall revenue could be down.'

'That's true.' The conversation continued across other operational items, many of which Judd batted off to someone else.

If George wanted to know about insurance she would need to talk to the Finance Director.

'There's personal liability, of course, to cover the chance of something going wrong with the steam car. Also fire and theft cover for the whole site. We even have storm protection. That marquee is pretty strong but I doubt it'd stand a hurricane.'

'And who decided the layout details? Was that . . . Nuffield's team?

'I did have a part in that. It's partly a matter of trial and error. Once the items had been chosen, you see, it's a matter of logic how they're best arranged.'

The interview drew to a close. George still had a sense there was something amiss somewhere but she had no idea what it might be. Judd seemed straightforward enough, anyway.

Maybe one of the other senior managers might give more away?

CHAPTER 24

It was Tuesday evening before George and Maxine finally had enough time for a catch up on their stories from their last two days.

George was back at Ivy Cottage first. She'd conducted another interview in the afternoon with the Exhibition's Commercial Manager, Jerry Scott. She would need to look over her notes but on first hearing it had not been particularly enlightening.

She decided that both of the day's interviews, with Judd and Scott, could as well be written up at home as perched at a table in the Castle's café. That was the task she had in hand when Peter Travers dropped back Maxine just before six. George was slightly surprised that the policeman did not drop in as well.

'Everything alright?' she asked once Maxine had returned from the kitchen with a tea tray. 'You look a bit miserable.'

'Huh. It's been one of those days. Peter and I started this morning timing where the traffic hold-up began from here into Bude. It's Tuesday, exactly a week since it all happened. It was clear from the times we'd noted between us that the hideaway farm must be north of Bude.'

'Right. And then ...?'

'Peter was very gentle yesterday in his interview, made me feel very special. After I'd told my story he moved me on to sounds and smells. It's amazing, you know, how much you pick up. After a while I remembered a mechanical noise, not far away, that I'd heard in the farmyard. At that time of day, Peter declared, it must be milk being collected. So he'd got hold of all the collection schedules from the milk distributors for North Cornwall.'

'Clever. Assuming the schedules were up to date.'

'Yes. And d'you remember the splash on the way into Bude? He said that was probably the car going through a ford. So he got the whole of his team putting all the data together. In the end they identified two possible farms, both well off the beaten track, where I might have been taken.'

By now George was sitting on the edge of her chair. 'What happened next?'

'We organised raids on them both. Or to be exact, Peter did.'

George looked at her in some disbelief. 'And of course you had to go with them? You had the security clearance, I suppose.'

'I happen to be the victim. I had to go with the police, George, to see if they'd found the right place. I had things about the farm in my head but I couldn't explain them all. It wasn't that dangerous, I stayed in the second car as the first went in. We couldn't be sure, you see, if the villains were still in there, planning their next abduction.'

George decided she'd had enough for now of Maxine the heroine. 'So were either of them the right place?'

'No. One was a farm run by an old codger while his family were off on holiday in Spain. Peter was very suspicious of him at first. The story sounded thin and he looked fairly disreputable. So he called the second car and brought me in to the kitchen. I could see at once that it couldn't be where I was held.'

'Your memory was that good, eh?'

'One way and another I'd thought about my captivity very hard. At first it was promising. There was even what looked like a bunker accessed from the yard. But it turned out to be where the farmer stored the heating oil for the winter. No solid fuel in there, anyway. And the kitchen was entirely the wrong shape.'

For some reason George didn't feel as sympathetic as she would have expected. Was she feeling a little jealous? Out of the loop? Peter Travers had never taken her on any of his raids.

'So what happened at the second farm?'

'It was afternoon by the time we got there. There was a massive puddle on the entrance lane which might have accounted for the splashing. Again Peter and one of his colleagues went in first. This time they found the place empty.'

'More farmers on vacation, maybe? So once again you were brought in with your expertise?'

'I was. But I could see, even before I was inside, that this one was no good. There was no hatch in the yard at all.'

'Come, come. They'd had a week to move on, Maxine. Could the cellar not have been cemented over before they went away?'

Maxine didn't spot the heavy sarcasm. 'Worth considering if that was the only thing about the place that was wrong. But the kitchen wasn't right either. This one was long and thin, whereas the room where I'd been questioned was almost square.'

She sighed. 'Yes, it was very disappointing. Everyone was down. They'd been gung-ho when they started out. I think, somehow or other, they reckoned Peter had let them down.

177

Which was very unfair.'

'There might have been other explanations of your noise memories. Even if you'd remembered them precisely.'

Maxine bristled. 'Why shouldn't I remember them?'

'You were under a tremendous stress, Maxine. All I'm saying is — '

'All you're saying is that Peter Travers is not infallible.'

'None of us are. Even Sherlock Holmes got things wrong.'

'Huh. He was fiction. Conan Doyle did that to add drama – and sell more books.' She mused for a moment. 'All right then, George. Peter thinks you're a genius. Give me some other explanation of what I heard.'

There was silence for a moment. George felt uncomfortable that she had upset Maxine. But maybe some scales did need pulling from her eyes. Even her new hero, Peter Travers, could get things wrong.

'OK. You say that Peter says that the early morning lifting noise must have been a tanker collecting milk.'

'Right.'

'But could it not have been a dustbin lorry, collecting waste? Every property has a visit every week or fortnight.'

'No it couldn't. Because . . .'

Maxine pondered for a moment. 'I suppose it just could.'

Identifying sources of operational data was a routine activity for George. 'It'd be easier to get hold of dustbin lorry routes than those for milk tankers, you know. The Council must hold them – people will ask about them, say, when they move house.'

Her enthusiasm grew. 'They'll be weekly schedules, too. With

178

each day showing a different route. That's much easier to interpret than daily patterns. So all you need to know – or, to be precise, all that Peter needs to know – is the route each one takes on Tuesdays.'

'George, I hate to admit it, but that's a very good idea. D'you mind if I make a call to share it with Peter at once?'

The call seemed to take an inordinately long time. However the pair juggled it, the idea wouldn't take that long to share, either to impart or to absorb. What else were they talking about? After a while George decided she'd go for a shower and change into her out-of-work clothes.

When she came downstairs again, Maxine was waiting, looking very smug.

'Peter's decided that between us we've made a good suggestion. He checked online while we were talking and found all the routes are available. He's requested the dustbin lorry routes for North Cornwall to be sent at once. He'll do some work on them later this evening.'

'A fresh mind offers a new way forward,' murmured George. 'Isn't cooperation wonderful?' But Maxine wasn't listening.

'If any of the Tuesday dustbin locations at seven forty five are close to a ford, he says, he's prepared to try another raid tomorrow morning. And since that's likely to happen, George, he's offered me a lift to the police station. If he's got anywhere to look at, I'll be on hand ready to assess it.'

'You don't seem to need my lifts any more,' observed George a little sadly. It appeared that Maxine now owed more loyalty to the police than to Cleave Camp.

'Your friend Dr Southgate signed me off work till the end of this week. Using the time to help the police on my case is the least I can do.'

'I guess so. Right now I've got another suggestion,' said George. 'I think that, after today's disappointments, we need to cheer ourselves up. It sounds like Peter is busy for the evening. So why don't you and I walk down to the Port William for our evening meal? The fresh air will do us good. It'll also give me a chance to tell you about my conversations at Limelight. This'd be your chance to add your fresh ideas to mine.'

CHAPTER 25

Despite the new set of council data on dustbin collection, Peter Travers had more trouble motivating his team for another raid on Wednesday morning than he'd had the day before.

Two successive visits to remote farms where, for all they knew, they might be shot at or otherwise resisted had stressed them out – even though no shots had come. Bude did not give them much practice at coping with violence. Travers had noted their fears and pointed out that there was not a shred of evidence of guns being used on Maxine but that had little traction.

'They didn't need to use guns, guv. The girl was already unconscious. '

'And in the morning trip she was locked away in the boot.'

Travers took a deep breath. 'The thing is, guys, Maxine heard machinery heaving and a vehicle starting early in the morning. Two events together, interlinked. We've found it wasn't a milk lorry. A dustbin lorry is a plausible alternative. I spent half of last night with the schedules. There's only one anywhere near to a ford at that time on a Tuesday morning. Sure, it might not be the place but we need to try. Either to catch the villains or at least give ourselves chance to grab evidence on who on earth they are.'

They arranged themselves as they had the day before. The

women police constables were left in charge of the base. Until they reached the location, Maxine travelled with Peter Travers. She didn't understand her feelings but he was tender and protective towards her. Was he like this with every victim, she wondered?

The new target location was close to Tamar Lake, which was consistent with the flight of honking geese. Encouragingly, both police cars found they had to traverse a deep ford with a fast-flowing stream, no more than a mile away.

Once they reached the muddy lane leading off the road to the farm there was no name-sign visible. The team rearranged themselves, Joe Tremlitt sitting beside Travers, and the car headed quietly up the lane.

Once again they came up to a locked gate outside a farmyard. But Travers could see a wooden hatch set into the yard within, beside the farmhouse. There was no sign of life inside the farm, even when Travers gave them a loud call demanding access.

A few minutes later the second police car was called to join them. Maxine got out and peered over the farm gate.

'You know, guys, this looks very promising. The yard is about the size I remember and that hatch is right beside the farm wall.'

It wasn't clear that further delay would do them much good. 'Right,' said the sergeant. 'I'm climbing over to knock on the door and if that has no effect I'll have a closer look through the windows. You lot stay here and warn me if there are any signs of life. If a shotgun appears at a window please let me know. The gate's got no barbed wire on it, anyway.'

Silently he climbed over the farm gate and advanced towards

the door. Every eye behind him scanned the building for any movement within but it was frozen in its stillness. Was no one there or was this a trap?

Travers reached the door, seized the knocker and gave it a massive bang. He held his breath and waited for a response.

Sound came there none. He waited a full minute and tried again. Still there was nothing.

The policeman eased himself away from the door and looked through the kitchen window. He could see no movement inside.

Then he started walking slowly round the farmhouse, peering into one window after another. He wouldn't be able to see anyone, say, hidden behind a sofa. But as far as he could tell the farm was deserted.

Greatly relieved but outwardly calm, he walked steadily back to the team. 'As far as I can tell there's no one there. Maxine, would you be brave enough to come over with me? There's a good view through the kitchen window. If the place is the wrong shape then we've been misled – again. But if it's correct . . .'

Maxine was quivering inside but tried to look as confident as possible to hold up morale. Steadily the pair went back towards the farmhouse. Maxine stood on tiptoe and stared inside. Then she gulped.

'Peter, I'm almost certain that this is the place they brought me. The kitchen's exactly the right size and shape, anyway. Is there any way we can get in?'

Breaking into a property was not an approved police procedure but Travers told himself that this was almost certainly a crime scene. His witness would not be able to say for certain until she was inside.

One option would be to return to Bude and start the process of obtaining a warrant but that would lose them at least another day. He was aware that well over a week had already elapsed since the abduction; time was crucial here.

Half an hour later the team had forced their way in by breaking one of the leaded panes on the utility room door and then reaching in to twist the key and undo the bolt.

'Don't touch anything,' Travers warned them. 'The SOCO lads will kill us if anything is contaminated.' He handed out three pairs of protective plastic galoshes which he had had the foresight to bring with him and put on a fourth pair himself. Then they all put on blue plastic gloves.

Maxine took the lead in heading for the kitchen, Peter Travers just behind her. She stood for a moment at the doorway and then turned to him.

'This is the place, Peter. They sat me at the kitchen table, just over there. Hands and ankles tied together. I remember: I was sore, thirsty and very cold.'

She looked around further. 'And look at the floor. D'you remember? I told you there was a smell of polish. It's almost as if the place is about to be sold.'

Travers looked around for a moment in silence, taking in as much as he could. The place was not well furnished and the walls were bare. It could well be a farm in the process of being sold or re-let.

'Right guys,' said the sergeant. 'I'm going to call for the Scene of Crime lads. They come from Bodmin, won't be here for at least an hour. Before they get here we're going to walk carefully through the place and see what's been going on.'

He continued, 'Remember, stay on your toes. We've done well to find this place, the villains didn't expect that, it should give us an edge. Let's make sure we make the most of it.'

He glanced around. 'I've got my camera, give me a shout if you see something worth photographing. And watch out especially for any remnants of clothing that could give us DNA, or documents that might tell us what they're about.

'But first I'll ring our colleagues in Bude and bring them up to date. At last we can report solid progress.'

CHAPTER 26.

Fred Taylor and Geraldine Norris had lived in Boscastle for many years: they ran an outdoor clothing shop. It was a good line to be in, waterproof clothing was always needed in Cornwall, and it made a profit throughout the year. Business was especially brisk at weekends. Mondays were mostly taken up with checking and reordering stock. Tuesdays were the time for new deliveries to be placed around the store.

As with most other shops in Boscastle, Wednesday was a day for early closing. Consequently on these days they handed the shop over to the care of Fred's dad, took the whole day off and set out to explore lesser known parts of North Cornwall.

Today their target was the Bude Canal, built in the early nineteenth century. The canal's purpose had been twofold: to carry sand to farmers inland from the coast; and, more strategically, to link Bude to the River Tamar and hence the sea at Plymouth. The goal was a passage from the English to the Bristol Channel that avoided the long and hazardous voyage round the rock-strewn cliffs at Lands End.

The canal in Bude, passing the Visitor Centre and impounded by huge sea-lock gates, was a well-known tourist landmark. As well as being available for fresh-water angling, visitors could hire a rowing boat to explore its first two miles. It also formed the final part of a popular walk that led along the high cliffs from Bude to Widemouth, cut a mile inland across fields and then returned to Bude via the canal towpath.

Fred and Geraldine had walked the section near Bude many times, it was a favourite winter walk. But there was also a more obscure part of the canal, linked to Tamar Lake, about six miles east of the town. Intriguingly an "aqueduct" was marked on Explorer maps along part of this route, together with a towpath. It was off the beaten path, well inland, and Geri was keen to investigate.

'We'll encounter fewer tourists,' she told Fred, 'than if we walk along the Coast Path. And it's August. At this time of the year we should be able to collect some early blackberries.'

Fred was less interested in the prospect of fresh fruit but he knew his partner would use it to make jam so he was happy with the overall plan.

By mid-morning they had driven on the A39 up as far as Kilkhampton and then across country to a small car park just below Upper Tamar Lake. Geri was pleased to see theirs was the only car present.

'See, I told you this trip would avoid the crowds,' she said with a grin.

Soon they had changed their shoes for walking boots, picked up the lunch rucksack and their walking poles and were on their way. Geri was pleased to see that their route was officially recognised, with a footpath sign at the gate leading off the road.

'This bit of the canal is narrower than the main stretch in Bude,' noted Fred as they started on their path. Even at the

187

widest point it was barely fifteen feet across, at some points even narrower. In places it was almost overgrown by shrubs and bushes.

There would be no way of rowing or kayaking this section. The best that could be said of the colour of the canal was that it was murky. The flow rate was negligible and, with the bottom lost to view, the depth hard to determine.

The towpath ran alongside, mostly through trees. The canal followed the contours of the valley as it bent around a gentle curve, heading eventually for Bude. 'Think about it,' said Fred. 'In 1800 they only had manual tools. So they had to make the most of the natural contours.'

He kept consulting their map. 'Hey, this is the point marked as an aqueduct.' He looked at the gentle drops on either side of the path and canal. 'I'm afraid it's not as dramatic as we'd hoped.'

As they walked further Geraldine kept her eyes peeled for blackberries. They weren't as plentiful as she'd hoped either.

Every so often they passed isolated buildings. The most interesting place looked like a small mill. No one else, though, was walking this section of path.

Then Geri spotted several blackberry bushes, growing on the far side of the canal. A gap in the trees meant that they had regularly caught the sunshine, which in turn had speeded up their growth.

'The best lot so far. Pity they're out of reach,' commented Fred.

'No, look, there's a bridge over the canal into that field. I guess it's to let the farmer get to those cows.'

What was good enough for cows would do for them. Soon the couple were on the far side of the canal and heading back towards the blackberries. There was no path on this side; progress was more difficult.

Fred stopped to take off the rucksack. Then he removed a large plastic container, an ice cream tub in an earlier life, and handed it over. 'Sorry, Geri, I'm not going any further. But if you are, I think you'll need this.'

This bank of the canal was swampy mud, virtually overflowing his boots. Fred had no wish to sink in any deeper.

But having set her mind to the task, his partner was desperate to collect some fruit. Step by step she inched her way forward, relying on her walking pole to keep her vertical. Then she leaned into the bushes to start picking. For a few minutes her mission was a total success.

'These are really large and juicy, Fred. And there are masses of them. I bet not many people come this way.'

Then, overconfident, she reached too far. Her walking pole hit a low point in the canal bed and sank even more deeply into the mud. Then she keeled over and fell head first into the canal.

Fred had feared that something like this might happen, which was one reason why he had hung back. He wasn't that worried: his partner could swim and in any case, now that she'd stood up, he could see the water reached only up to her waist. He managed to suppress his laughter. She would be alright, he thought, as long as she didn't drink the stuff. On this stretch of water being poisoned was a bigger risk than being drowned.

He could see, though, that helping her to get out again might be a little tricky.

'Fred, yuk, the floor of this canal is disgusting. It's a two-foot depth of slime. It's . . . it's like walking through treacle,' Geri complained.

'Maybe that's why no one else has been picking blackberries here?'

'Huh.' Geri tried to take a step towards the bank, failed to extract her back foot from the deep mud, lost her balance and fell over once more into the water. Now she was covered in mud up to her neck. By the time she had scrambled up again she had lost one of her boots in the mire.

Fred stopped laughing and reached out to her with his pole. 'Hang onto this, love. I'll try and pull you out.'

It was a good idea and might even have worked if Fred had been sturdier or his wife a little lighter. As it was, gravity triumphed and Fred ended up alongside his wife in the canal.

It took half an hour before the two had managed to extract themselves from the muddy water and make their sodden way back onto the path.

'And the worst thing of all,' said Geri crossly, 'is that I dropped that box of blackberries somewhere in the canal as I went in. Here we are, we're both soaked to the skin in filthy water. My jeans and shirt are ruined, I've lost one of my boots, I'll have to walk back to the car in my socks: and we've got nothing to show for it.'

Fred could see that Geri was really upset. There was little prospect of finding the missing boot, which was more or less the same colour as the mud. Though they ran an outdoor clothing shop, she could at least get a replacement pair at a discount –

maybe a newer model?

But perhaps, Fred thought, there was some hope for the blackberries. 'It's a plastic box. It'll float, won't it? Look, there's no one else around. Why don't you slip your shirt and jeans off and rinse them in one of the cleaner sections of water? Then try and clean yourself up a bit. I'll do my best to fish the box out with my pole.'

Matching action to words he started to wander along the canal. It didn't take long to spot the container. It was drifting slowly towards the bridge they had used earlier. A minute later he was kneeling on the bridge, with his pole poised to stop the box as it passed and manoeuvre it towards the side.

And that was the point at which he glanced down; and saw directly below him what looked like a body, lying trapped below the surface.

CHAPTER 27

It was just after noon when the call came through to the Bude Police Station. The receptionist listened for a minute and then quickly passed it on to the most senior policeman around. On the station rota that should be Sergeant Peter Travers. She tried but was told he wasn't there. Instead the call was put through to the only police officer in the station at this moment, WPC Jess Holland.

The call might be a hoax but to her experienced ear it sounded genuine.

'Good afternoon, sir. Yes, Bude Police here. How can I help you?'

She listened to the panic-stricken account being poured out. As the caller eventually paused to take breath she took the chance to intervene.

'Let me get this straight, sir. You've just seen what you believe is a body, submerged in the Bude Canal? Up near Tamar Lake?'

And up near the hideaway farm to which Travers and her colleagues had gone searching, she thought, though of course she did not say. 'Are you on your own or is anyone else with you?'

It seemed the man was with his partner, Geraldine. 'She's in the car here beside me. But she's not thinking clearly. I fear she's in a state of shock.'

Holland noted their names and other contact details. Then she concluded, 'Right, sir. We'll get someone to you as soon as we can. You're slightly out in the wild from here. It might take us half an hour to reach you. Will you both please stay in the car park, keeping your doors locked, till we're with you?'

A moment later, Jess Holland rang Peter Travers and told him of the call.

'It sounded like someone needed to be there quickly, guv. I mean, the bloke – Fred – might have got confused by a moving shadow or something but a body's hard to mistake. And he said his woman – that's Geraldine – was in a state of shock.'

It was a headache. In truth his small force was not equipped to deal with two crises at once. Then Travers consulted the map. The car park he was being called to was only a mile or so from his current location.

His team was still waiting for the Scene of Crime team from Bodmin. So far they'd walked slowly through every room in the farm, including the cellar, but seen nothing much of interest. But they weren't all needed to bring the specialist searchers up to speed.

Then the thought came to him, prompted by the geography: could this body be one of the kidnappers? The one, maybe, that had let Maxine get away in Bude? Had that event gone on to trigger a suicide? Or worse?

In normal circumstances Peter Travers would never have dreamed of taking Maxine with him to answer an official call. But there was just a chance, he told himself, that she might be able to recognise the victim.

More legitimately, he'd been told that a woman was needed to look after Geraldine. Given the urgency of the call and the limits on his choice, Maxine was a viable option. She'd be as good as anyone to stay with Geraldine while he took Fred to look for the alleged body.

Until he had seen and confirmed it for himself he was reluctant to take Jamie Sampson as well, or to call out other emergency services.

In case it was needed, he checked the boot of his police car: yes, it held a pair of waders and some rescue tackle. He had recently been involved in rescuing a teenager from the mouth of Boscastle Harbour at high tide.

So how would Maxine feel? He could at least pop the question.

He beckoned his friend over to the privacy of the utility room. 'Maxine, something's just come up. I need a female with me to look after a woman with shock, while I go with her partner to look at a dead body.'

Maxine didn't need to think too hard. 'If I can help, Peter, I'll be glad to come. I've done a First Aid course at the Camp.'

'Great. Thank you very much. I'll leave Joe Tremlitt and Jamie Sampson to liaise with the Crime Scene lads when they turn up.'

'The man who phoned in, Fred Taylor, might just have been mistaken,' the policeman observed, as the pair bumped down the lane and out onto the road. 'It could be some article of clothing, overalls say, that had been dumped or fallen in.'

'So you think this'll be a false alarm?'

'I didn't say that, Maxine. Fred had managed to convince himself that he'd seen someone in the canal. And his partner had no doubt either. There must have been something there to put her in shock.'

Given their searches the previous week, he had some thoughts on who the dead person might turn out to be. Be he must hold these in check. Speculation was a waste of energy without some basic facts to start from.

For a moment there was silence. The car park had no postcode so Sat Nav wouldn't work. Maxine took some maps out of the glove compartment and struggled to match the northern edge of the Bude map with the southern edge of Hartland, which covered the area further north. Like all emergencies and battles, this was taking place on the edge of two maps. After a minute she worked out where they were going.

'Is it worth using your siren, Peter?'

He shook his head. 'Not justified at this stage. It's a dead body we've been called about, not someone injured who needs urgent help.' He could see no traffic holdups ahead anyway.

Ten minutes later they reached the car park, which lay on a footpath between Upper and Lower Tamar Lake. Travers saw that only a single car was parked there. A tense-looking couple, probably in their thirties, were occupying the front seats.

'Let's be thankful,' he remarked to Maxine, as they parked alongside, 'For the time being, at least, the media aren't aware of the issue.' They both got out.

'Mr Taylor and Ms Norris?' asked Travers as the car window

opened in response. The pair nodded.

The policeman introduced himself and showed them his warrant card. Then he introduced them to Maxine Tavistock. 'She's a colleague of mine.'

The couple, looking rather bedraggled, stumbled out of their own car and shook their hands.

'Right, sir, perhaps you could take me to show what you've seen while Maxine has a chat with Ms Norris.'

Travers collected the boots and tackle. Then the two men set out along the canal towpath while the women claimed the only seat in the car park.

Fred was eager to stick to generalities as they walked along. Travers gathered that the couple lived in Boscastle and would often find out-of-the-way places to explore together. The men had walked half a mile along the path, the canal alongside them, before Fred fell into an uneasy silence.

For a second the policeman wondered what had made him lose his voice.

Then the man pointed ahead. 'I saw him – or her – under that bridge just ahead of us. I'd never have looked there at all, never seen anything, except that I was trying to recover our box of blackberries that Geri had dropped. She'd collected them, you see, before she fell in.'

The whole incident sounded too bizarre to have been con-trived. And it was supported by the wet, muddy state of the couple's clothing. Carefully the policeman made his way onto the bridge and then knelt down at the point which Fred had indi-cated.

It took a moment, peering through the murk of the canal, before he could see what Fred had spotted earlier. But once he had focussed, he was certainly looking at a body. It had wedged face down under a row of bricks which had been laid to form the edge of the bridge. There was no doubt that the person was dead, had been dead for some time.

Fifteen minutes later the two men had returned to the car park. Travers had hoped to phone his colleague at once from beside the body but, as Fred had pointed out, 'I tried that earlier. This is the back of beyond. There's no signal at all.'

At this point, mused Travers, it was unclear whether this was a natural death or the result of accident, suicide or murder. He had no idea if it was a crime so he didn't immediate have to call for the Regional Crime Squad. Under the new cross-charging arrangements brought in by the Coalition, any call to them would hit his budget.

He did, though, pull out his digital camera and take a number of shots of the sunken body and the canal from different angles. Then turned back to the car park.

The next thing to do, he decided, was to extract the body from the canal. The trouble was, even using his rescue tackle which he'd left by the bridge, that was at least a three person job.

Fortunately Maxine had done a good job in calming Geraldine. The woman had dried out to an extent and was now sitting quietly in her car. Seeing that his partner was alright, Fred declared he was keen to help the police in any way that he could.

'The first thing I'm going to do is ring for specialist reinforcements,' Travers explained. 'But they're stretched, may take some time to get here. While they're coming I'd like to get the body out of the canal. We can't tell how long it's been in there.' He shrugged, 'It might only be a few hours. But in any case we don't want it drifting any further along – or to decompose any more than we can help.'

'How are you going to do that?' asked Fred. He was a practical man and liked practical problems.

'Two of my colleagues are dealing with a case nearby, sir.' The policeman smiled. 'To be honest, that's how we got here so quickly. I'll get one of them to come over and join us.' He looked across to the women on the seat. 'Now she's calmed Geraldine, Maxine might help as well.'

'What will you do?'

'I'll do most of the heavy work using my rescue tackle. I carry that around in case I need to fish semi-conscious people out of a rough sea. I last used it in Boscastle, as a matter of fact.' He could see that Fred was angling to help. 'But it would aid us a great deal, sir, if you could give us a helping hand while standing on the bank.'

And that was more or less how it was done. First Travers, Maxine and Fred returned along the canal towpath to the bridge. Jamie Sampson was instructed to come after them as soon as he'd reached the car park.

There was only one pair of waders in the police car, which fitted the sergeant. Maxine could see that the bank was boggy; she'd already seen and smelt its effect on Geraldine. At least she could avoid that.

She quickly turned, removed her skirt and trainers and put them on the far side of the path, then pulled down her shirt as far as she could. It was slightly embarrassing but this was an emergency, no doubt any of the women police officers would have done the same. Her bigger worry was that she might have to go into the water as far as Geraldine.

Then Peter Travers stood in the canal in his waders, holding the rescue tackle in his hands. Slowly, with great care, making sure he kept his balance, he pushed the bars underneath the dead body until it was caught in the net hanging between them.

Next, as slowly as possible, he pulled the whole thing back towards himself. Then he swung it towards the bank where Maxine was waiting, up to her knees in the mud.

She reached out and helped him hold it but it was still too heavy to lift.

At that point they were all relieved to see Jamie Sampson walking down the path to join them. 'We'll have enough resources now,' said the policeman with a smile.

Travers and his two companions, with Fred holding the other end, raised the equipment up and, finally, lowered it onto the edge of the footpath. The sergeant had arranged a clean piece of groundsheet there, along the edge of the towpath, before the operation began.

The policeman could see now that it was – or had been – a man. The body was still face down. But there was a horrible stench emanating from it, plus the detritus of the canal. The whole thing gave a characteristic sense of decay.

Taking a hand from Maxine to steady himself and looking her

steadily in the eye, Peter Travers extracted himself from the water and stood beside his team on the bank. 'Well done, all of you, but it had to be done. Not a pleasant task.'

Instinctively Fred had turned his back on the man as soon as possible. Now he turned back and looked. But he was not used to such a sight. He turned away again and then, crouching, was violently sick over the far side of the footpath. After a minute he looked up. 'I think . . . I think I need to get back to the car.'

'Jamie,' said Travers quietly, 'we can't leave a body on its own, exposed on a public footpath. One of us has to stay and keep guard – move any passers-by on – until we have reinforcements. Hopefully the backup team will bring a covering tent. D'you want to do that or would you rather go back with Fred?'

A few moments later Jamie Sampson, Fred and a fully dressed Maxine had set off back to the car park while Peter Travers remained to guard the remains of the dead man. Fortunately, in terms of passers-by from either direction, the canal footpath was as empty as it had been all day.

The policeman took a few more pictures but took care not to disturb the body, which remained face down.

Last week his team's attention had been all on finding the lost: one escaped prisoner and a house-clearance man who had gone missing. Today they had been in a hideaway farm devoid of the person they had hoped to interview.

He glanced at the foul smelling remains on the footpath. Now he had the opposite problem: a dead body that was possibly – probably? – some sort of victim. At least there was nothing lost or hidden about this case.

CHAPTER 28

It was late Wednesday afternoon before Peter Travers and his team were in a position to return to Bude Police Station, either from the temporary morgue beside the canal or from the hide-away farm.

Acting police pathologist Dr Sarah Maxwell had conducted a preliminary investigation of the corpse as it lay in a white tent beside the canal.

'I'll conduct a post-mortem tomorrow morning at Stratton Hospital,' she told them. 'If you want an immediate report, please send a police representative.'

Unofficially Dr Maxwell had told Travers that it was clear from the facial decomposition that the death had not just happened: it must have occurred 'at least a week earlier, probably more'.

In view of this, Travers decided that there was little point in the police wasting limited time and energy on a detailed search of the banks of the upper Bude Canal. Not at this stage, anyway. Anything left weeks ago would have been soaked and blown away. Jamie Sampson had been pleased with this conclusion: he could see the bushes on the canal banks would be a horrendous challenge to search properly.

The pathologist had not yet given them any finding on the

cause of death, though the policeman himself had noted a gash on the side of the head. Travers hoped that a detailed examination at the post-mortem tomorrow might help narrow down the cause.

The policeman had taken a couple of pictures of the dead man's face as the body was turned over. It was scratched, mottled and swollen, not a pretty sight. In that state the pictures would be hard to look at and wouldn't identify anyone. The pathologist said that she would do her best to tidy the face so it could provide a recognisable picture for identification in due course. That might take her a day or two.

At this stage there were no clues on the body as to who the dead man was. His clothing was very rough. There was no wallet or notebook in the pockets, nothing with a name on it anyway. It would be difficult to do much investigation until the dead man had been identified.

If the man had died weeks ago, Travers reflected that at least it couldn't be Holdsworth. He'd been in prison until a week ago. It might, though, be Fairclough. Or someone from the hideaway farm?

Finally the body was brought back along the towpath on a stretcher and the mortuary van took it away. When it had gone Travers phoned the station to arrange for a team briefing. Jamie Sampson was sent back to the hideaway farm to pick up Joe Tremlitt and the two police cars headed back to Bude.

The events of the day were first outlined; on such an action-packed day it was important that everyone was brought up to date on everything.

First Travers gave a résumé of the Bude Canal mystery.

Fred and Geraldine had been allowed to go home, he explained, not least because they both urgently needed a shower and a complete change of clothes. 'With more thought,' he reflected, 'we should have offered each of them fresh clothing.'

The two had been asked to say nothing about what had occurred to anyone and to return to Bude next morning to make formal statements.

The police officers had no doubt, though, that the two were completely innocent. Without Geraldine's own mishap with the blackberries the body might have lain under the bridge for much longer. In that case the post-mortem, when it eventually did take place, would have been a great deal harder.

Since they would know more after next day's post-mortem, Travers held his team back from excess discussion. It wasn't hard to see, though, that the Bude Canal case might take much of their time from now on. Even if they were in partnership with the Regional Crime Squad.

Then Joe Tremlitt summarised events at the hideaway farm.

'The Bodmin SOCOs turned up half an hour after you left, guv,' he reported. 'I explained what had brought us there. They were excited: you don't often get a failed abduction, they said, where the prisoner has actually escaped. That encouraged them to search hard. They gave the place a real going over.'

'What did they find?' asked Maxine. It was a pity she hadn't been there. She had never witnessed a Scene of Crime search, apart from the snippets she'd watched on television.

'They got loads of fingerprints from the upstairs rooms and lounge but none at all from the kitchen. When they get back to base in Bodmin they'll see if any of 'em can be matched to anyone on the Crime Database. We should hear tomorrow.'

'What about the coal cellar?' asked Maxine.

Tremlitt remembered that she had spent a night there, uncomfortably perched on that rough pile of coal. 'They found one repeated set of prints, probably yours. We'll need yours for elimination, by the way.'

'But none on the hatch?' she persisted. 'They certainly touched that.'

Tremlitt shook his head.

'You know, the whole pattern is rather odd,' said Travers. 'It's almost as though the gang only used the kitchen and made sure they wiped it clean before they left. They had no problem with access, why didn't they spread over the whole house?'

He turned to Tremlitt again. 'Did they find any remnants of clothing that could give us some DNA?'

'Nothing. Not even a thread. No paper either, apart from a monthly calendar with a picture of a canal, left open on July. It'd slid down between the cooker and the cupboard. Someone had missed it – but not necessarily them. So that's probably irrelevant as well.'

It was all slightly dispiriting. The team had made so much progress in reconstructing Maxine's journey into Bude. The trail from now on was looking to be much harder.

'I've got to start tomorrow by attending the canal victim's post-mortem in Stratton,' said Peter Travers as he dropped Maxine at Ivy Cottage. 'Maybe you could get a lift in with George?'

She started to wonder if what he really meant was that their burgeoning friendship had hit the buffers. But the policeman sensed, belatedly, that she needed encouragement and gave her an affectionate squeeze on the arm as she got out of the car.

'You did well today, Maxine, very well indeed. Thank you. You'll be around Bude tomorrow, I guess? I'll give you a call when we encounter something where you could help us.'

He drove off before she could quiz him further. She was still puzzled as she went into Ivy Cottage.

'Hello, Maxine,' came the greeting from the kitchen. 'Had a good day?'

'I've seen a lot of Bude police work. And between us we've found where they held me. Trouble is, there's no one there anymore.'

'Tell me more.'

Maxine gave a succinct account of her exciting day, culminating in how she had helped drag a body from the canal.

Then she went back to the area where her friend had contributed. 'Your suggestion about dustbin lorries, George, was key. Given all the Tuesday routes from the Council we found the place without much difficulty. A small farmhouse near Tamar Lake, ten miles from Bude. We had to splash through a ford to reach it.'

Her face fell. 'But when we got there the place was empty. Been that way for weeks, probably.'

She went on to tell her friend the findings from the Scene of Crime team.

'That doesn't make sense,' George protested, after a moment's thought. 'So where did the gang sleep, the night they brought you from Bude and threw you in the cellar? Surely they wouldn't all spend the night in sleeping bags on a slate kitchen floor when there were beds ready to use upstairs?'

'They never went upstairs at all. The SOCO boys suggested they were very keen not to leave any traces in the hideaway.'

'In that case they must have slept somewhere else. Maybe in another farm nearby? It couldn't be too far away, could it? I mean, they left at midnight and were back before seven. Maybe, wherever that is, they're still living there?'

Maxine could see her line of argument. Then, glancing down to the tiles on George's kitchen floor, she remembered the highly polished kitchen floor at the farm.

'Hey, George, d'you think the hideaway was in a gap between two successive tenants? Perhaps the gang just moved in there for a day or two while it was empty, so they could deal with me without leaving any trace. If it was between tenants that might account for all the bleach I saw in the yard as well. It makes some sort of sense, you know: they were just squatters.'

George nodded. Her mind was already moving on to how that might have been done.

'Generally speaking, farming today is in a mess. Are there specialist estate agents, d'you think, that just deal with farms? Or might this all stem from some private deal that the gang latched on to?'

'If it's a private deal, George, the chances of us hearing about it are nil.'

'Right. So let's assume the farm appeared on the books of an agency. Say a small one around Bude. We might learn a lot via the internet.'

Maxine was already opening her tablet and asking Google the question. Five minutes later she turned the screen to George. 'This is a list of independent estate agents who deal in farmland around here. There's only half a dozen. Where do we go next?'

'What we need is any farm about the size of your hideaway, to get an idea of its market value and rental. Next, we use that to set a filter to find farms of similar value around Bude. Then we go through them looking for the hideaway. There's always a picture of the main farm. You've been there today, maybe you'll recognise it.'

For half an hour there was a purposeful silence.

'Eureka,' exclaimed Maxine. She looked exultant.

George stepped over to see what she had found.

'I've found my hideaway,' said Maxine, 'its proper name is Hallowdene. Offered by an estate agent with an office in Bude. Makes some sense, I suppose, it's only a small farm, the sale would be a small-scale operation.'

George leaned over and read her findings. 'The last lease ran out at the end of July, when presumably the leaseholder left. No replacement so far.'

'Look, George. You can see from the farm description that it's off the beaten track. Someone could squat there for a night or two – or even longer – without much risk of being caught.'

'And now we can ask the crucial question: are there any other farms like that which are currently between tenants?'

Maxine was hooked. For half an hour she stepped slowly through the properties on the firm's books. Then she stopped and looked up, a smile on her face.

'Only one, I'm afraid.'

'What's its address?'

'Warren Farm. And d'you know what? It's all of two miles from my hideaway.'

'Well, well. Maybe your days of being a key witness on a police raid are not yet over.'

CHAPTER 29

Peter Travers was long used to travelling to work on his own. But that Thursday morning his car seemed emptier than usual.

'Grow up,' he told himself crossly. 'Just 'cos you've met someone who's simultaneously pretty, bright and with a job in Cornwall is no reason to think the friendship will last. She only came with you 'cos she wanted to help find the villains. Who d'you think you are?'

Despite these worries he kept thinking of Maxine as he drove along. He hoped the friendship would endure beyond this case, special though those links had been.

He tried to convince himself that Maxine would have quailed at the thought of leaving home at seven thirty in the morning, the time needed for him to be with Dr Maxwell in Stratton Hospital by eight fifteen. But part of him thought – hoped – that she'd have been glad to be alongside, any time of the day or night.

Attending post-mortems was a new experience for the police sergeant. It had only happened once since he had moved to Bude and it wasn't the best part of the job. He tried to make himself look beyond the gruesome task to the findings that might emerge.

'Morning Peter,' Sarah Maxwell greeted him, as he entered the facility. 'I hope you'll find this a profitable experience.'

She held out the surgical gown he would need to wear. The dead man from the canal, now completely naked, had been pulled out of cold storage and allowed to thaw. Now he reclined on the green cloth that covered the examination table. Travers was glad to see that the pathologist was going to use a voice recorder to track her findings; at least he wouldn't have to remember anything. His role was simply to watch.

Afterwards he found that he'd wiped out the most gory details of the morning, probably as an act of mental self-preservation. Fortunately the doctor recognised his fragile state and made sure that she emphasised the key findings as they arose.

There were a lot of preliminary measurements which didn't seem to prove much, though they would help firm up his description. 'The man was just over six foot tall,' the doctor reported. 'And weighed just under thirteen stone. Not overweight, anyway.'

What else would help with description? 'Can you give me a medical estimate of his age?'

Dr Maxwell spent a few minutes looking into the man's mouth. 'His body hasn't changed much yet. You can get a fair idea from the ageing on his face. The teeth change in the mid twenties, he's past that. I'd say mid thirties?'

That seemed plausible to him, anyway.

Then Sarah started to feel the body more tenderly.

'There's plenty of bruising but as far as I can tell no bones are broken. No sign of stab wounds; just a couple of small tattoos on his wrists.'

She examined the body more intensely. 'I can't see any evidence of holes from needles. So he's probably not on drugs, legal or otherwise.'

Blood samples were taken but an initial test showed no alcohol in the blood. 'He didn't just fall in drunk,' she concluded. 'I'll send the samples off for more tests but we'll have to wait a day or two for the results.'

The first striking result for Travers, as she delved deeper and sliced further, was that she could detect no water in the lungs.

'That means the death was not caused by drowning,' she said. 'This man was already dead when he entered the water. Hm. That makes an accident a lot less likely.'

'So what was the cause of death?' asked the policeman.

'I'd say the probable cause was being hit very hard over the head. Look here.' She pointed to the gash on the left side of his head, which the policeman had noticed the day before.

'Have you any findings on the type of weapon that might have been used, Sarah?'

'Hm. You're pushing me hard.' The doctor bent down and examined the victim's head more closely.

'It's a very regular wound, Peter. Straight and symmetrical. I'd say it was probably done by a single blow with a long, heavy stick.'

'No chance that he just hit his head on the bank, say, as he fell in?'

'If he'd done that, Peter, the wound would have been much rougher; and he would have collected more injuries. No, I'm sorry to say that in my expert opinion it's been inflicted by

211

someone else.'

'In other words, Sarah, he's been murdered?' The doctor nodded slowly.

It was as he had feared. The policeman took a deep breath. 'Right. Can we say how long ago it happened?'

'It's hard to be precise. Look. See how the skin has swollen; it's got a soapy, almost greasy feel. The rate of change on the skin will depend partly on the average temperature of the water, which of course we don't know.'

'It's summertime, Sarah. No frost or anything.'

'No. But if he'd been kept dry in a freezer, say, he could have been preserved for longer. But assuming nothing peculiar, I should say he's been dead for between three and four weeks.'

It couldn't be Holdsworth, Travers decided as the doctor continued with her investigation, steadily dissecting the body. But that timeframe might fit with Fairclough: he hadn't been seen for several weeks.

He wished he had taken something from Fairclough's cottage that would give them a DNA sample, to compare with the corpse here. But he could go again. He would look for something on his way back to the police station.

'This is the stomach,' warned the doctor. Travers glanced but did not focus and turned away quickly. She smiled and continued to probe.

'I reckon his last meal was probably fish and chips,' she pronounced.

'It'd be more helpful if he'd had something less ordinary.'

'I'm sorry, Peter, I can only report what I find.'

The post-mortem was almost concluded now. 'What happened to his clothes?' asked the policeman.

'Ah yes. That's this pile over here.' She led him across the room. 'Nothing very distinctive, you see. Jeans, a check shirt and a heavy-duty sweater. Nothing at all, I'm afraid, in the pockets – no money or anything. But he was wearing good strong boots.'

'If someone had gone through his pockets after killing him, might they have left traces of DNA?'

'Oh, certainly.' But the doctor quickly dashed any hopes he might have of a way forward. 'Two weeks immersion in the canal would just as certainly wipe it all out.' She shrugged. 'There's no point in even trying. We can give you his DNA, of course. I imagine that will be helpful in the long run?'

'Thank you, Sarah. And how quickly might you be able to tidy up his face to make a presentable photograph? Publicising that as widely as possible is our best chance of being told his identity.'

'Not a problem. I'll send it through to you by tomorrow. Plus a written record of my findings.'

Not too far from Stratton to Fairclough's cottage, Travers decided, as he left the hospital. And the house clearance man's DNA was needed.

It would be better for the police to know the identity of canal-man, if possible, before any confrontation with the media.

Finding the place again was not difficult. He drove down the drive, opened the gate, drove into the yard and then headed for the door. A couple of unanswered knocks told him that the place was empty.

The policeman tackled the obstacle course round the side of the cottage to the back door, slipped on some plastic gloves and grabbed the key from under the doormat.

'Police here,' he shouted, though of course there was no answer. What would give the best chance of capturing DNA, he wondered.

He had an odd sense that someone else had been in there since his last visit but he couldn't be sure. There was a carton of milk on the worktop, was that there last time? A sniff revealed it was still drinkable. Fresh milk implied continued life: was the elusive Fairclough still alive?

Even so it would be good to have his DNA for elimination purposes.

After a moment's thought, Travers strode up the stairs and into the bathroom. He peered into the cabinet, spotted a razor and seized it. Then saw a dark-red face flannel draped over the sink. If anything would capture and retain DNA it was surely that.

The policeman transferred the items to an evidence bag and set off back down the stairs. Once more he reversed his route out of the cottage and back to his car. A moment later he was on his way.

Once more a solitary figure gazed out at him from the woods nearby.

The policeman finally reached the station at half past eleven. He immediately called his team together to tell them the news from the post-mortem.

'So we're dealing with a murder,' he concluded. 'Action to solve that has to take precedence over everything else – including the failed abduction we were working on yesterday.'

'Unless the two crimes happen to overlap,' said Jess Holland. She could see that Travers had taken a bit of a shine to Maxine – the effect might go both ways. He'd been very keen to tackle the abduction, anyway.

'Yes, I suppose so. But let's focus on the murder for now.'

'A murder must mean a call to the Regional Crime Squad?' asked Jess Holland.

'I've already talked to them, Jess. They say they won't start work until we've had the post-mortem report. So let's give ourselves an hour or two to mull it over. What ideas have we got?'

There was a moment's silence. His team were not used to being asked to ponder.

'The first challenge is identifying the victim,' said Travers, trying to push them along. 'We'll have his photo and DNA by tomorrow. There's no point in briefing the press until we've had a look at those for ourselves.'

'How d'you mean?' asked Tremlitt.

'Well, if his DNA is on the police database, we'll know his name; and that the man has form. A strong possible motive in that case is revenge. He might have been dumped here, say, after being murdered in Bristol.'

'In that case the sooner the Regional Crime Squad takes over the better.'

'It's not an obvious place to dump a body,' agreed the sergeant. 'Hard to find in the first place, especially if they came at night.

It's just bad luck for the dumper that the body wedged under the bridge, almost out of sight. Nine times out of ten it'd have been spotted next day.'

'But you said he had no scars. He'd not even been drinking. What if he has no record?' asked Holland.

'Then he's a local, purely innocent. Hey, maybe he was like Fred and Geraldine, walking the Upper Bude Canal? In that case the question is what on earth did he see on that quiet towpath to invite sudden death? Has anyone got any ideas?'

Silence. Some of Travers' questions were just too hard.

'You said the post-mortem showed that his last meal was fish and chips,' asked Tremlitt.

'Yes.'

'Well, doesn't that suggest he was more likely to be out in the evening rather than earlier in the day?'

Travers considered. 'Probably.'

'But no one goes walking late in the evening, guv. Especially beside a canal. Think of all those midges. You'd be bitten to death.'

'Well if he wasn't walking, what was he doing?'

'If it was evening, isn't it more likely he was out fishing? Not in the canal, maybe around Tamar Lake? It's only a mile upstream.'

There was another pause for reflection.

'My Dad used to fish in Tamar Lake,' remembered Jess Holland.

She mused for a moment. 'Dad took me with him in the school holidays. Mostly in the daytime, once or twice at night. He liked the company and I guess I liked the countryside – or perhaps the smell of his pipe.'

She sighed. 'That was a long time ago. But I bet they still fish there today.'

CHAPTER 30

On Thursday morning Maxine decided that as she had not been invited to the police station she would put in an appearance at Cleave Camp. George took her as far as Tee-Side and left her to make the rest of the way with Sam Hudson.

She wasn't sure which reason she would present for her recent absence. She had a sick note from Dr Brian Southgate following her escape from abduction but she rather preferred the ring of 'helping the police with their enquiries'. She hoped that might come into play again before too long.

She had worried about how much she could or should tell Sam. Could she assume they were on the same side? It turned out, though, that this was not a problem. Sam had plenty to tell her about this week's stresses in the Camp, which took almost the whole journey.

'Have you ever studied the water supply systems at Cleave?' he began as they set off through the early morning traffic.

'I seem to remember it's something to do with local boreholes. The Camp is on a big hill of sandstone and shale with several springs. Don't we pump our own supply from inside the Camp?'

'That's right. It's supposed to be a security device – stop the risk of the whole Camp being poisoned. Tapping into the public supply is deemed an unacceptable risk. But with all this fine weather it seems the water table's dropped, fallen to an almost untappable level. The pumps are struggling, producing more air than water; not much is coming out.'

Maxine had never taken much notice of the science of water tables or the impact of pumped wells. 'The Camp has reserves, surely? A couple of massive tanks, buried below the surface, which are left full unless there's an emergency. We've only got to survive till the next heavy rain raises the water table again. This is Cornwall, Sam – it's never dry for long.'

'That's what's supposed to happen. Reading between the lines, I'd say no one noticed the pumped water shortfall for a couple of weeks. Maybe the person who should have done so was on holiday. They just used the reserve tanks instead. So now those tanks are empty as well.'

Cleave Camp normally operated on a steady, regular pattern. Calmness was key to careful analysis. Maxine could imagine that an unexpected water shortage would ruffle a few feathers. Senior staff wouldn't want to muck about with buckets of water. But there was no equipment here that was too water intensive, was there? They had big computers but they were not water-cooled.

'In short, I shouldn't expect to have a long shower when we get there?'

Sam gave a hollow laugh. 'Huh. We're rationed on how often we can flush the toilets, Maxine. It's like living in a refugee camp.'

Maxine doubted it could be that bad. When they reached the Camp, anxieties about the water shortage and being told the restrictions they needed to accept choked off any questions on Maxine's absence earlier in the week. So neither reason was invoked.

Once she'd registered for the day she slipped past reception and down to her usual working area.

The thing about Camp, as with GCHQ in Cheltenham, was that there was always a need for decoding. Today her in-tray was piled high with the backlog from her absence. Soon she was working through a fresh pile of signals relating to the United States' view of the war in Syria.

She had been toiling away there, catching up for a couple of hours, before Colin Caldwell discovered she was back in the Camp.

A brusque call asked her to come at once to his office. This could be interesting, she thought. Her new relationship with Peter Travers had given her more confidence in dealing with Camp authority, and in recognising its limitations.

'I was expecting that you'd be here on Monday,' he began. 'I thought we had an arrangement that you'd come and vouch for me at Tee-Side.'

Maxine noticed that there were no preliminaries about her health or questions on how her recovery from her abduction was faring.

'Oh, you don't need to bother about that,' she smiled. 'I met the local policeman over the weekend. Peter Travers. He and I went to Tee-Side together on Monday. I've been helping him with enquiries ever since.'

Caldwell's face blackened. 'What on earth was it to do with him? This was a Camp matter. He's just the local plod. I have to sit through their meetings from time to time – boredom on boredom.'

'Well the local plod has made a great deal more progress so far in three days than you did. Anyway, what makes you think it was a Camp matter at all? After all, they took me from a local guest house.'

Caldwell humphed. 'So how's the great Travers getting on then?'

'Between us we found the farm I was taken to. It's a back-of-beyond place, out towards Tamar Lake. We went there and I recognised it. The trouble is, over the past week the gang have moved on.'

Caldwell was obviously in the mood to close down every problem he could. The least-hassle route was always preferred.

'Right. If they've moved on, you can at least safely go back to Tee-Side.'

'But, as Camp Security Officer, aren't you interested in chasing them down?'

He sighed. 'Not unless you can prove it's something to do with the Camp – an ongoing threat of some sort. Has Travers been able to show that?'

Maxine pondered for a second and then shook her head.

'We've enough troubles here, anyway,' Caldwell went on. 'I presume you've heard about the water shortage?'

'Yes. I was surprised that a place as vital to UK security as this didn't have a contingency plan. I mean, the water table under here must have dropped before?'

Caldwell sighed again. Maxine could see he wasn't the most endearing of characters. He probably didn't have many supporters among the senior staff. 'There was a contingency plan.'

'What was that, regular water tankers from Barnstaple?'

He looked at her aghast. 'Water for Camp brought on the public road? For days on end? That's much too risky. No, our plan was much more subtle. The trouble was, when the time came it didn't work. I've commissioned an investigation but so far we don't know why.'

Maxine would have been interested in knowing the details of the plan, maybe she could add ideas of her own, but she could see she wasn't going to be told. Caldwell was enacting the 'need to know' maxim. That was his default behaviour.

It was time for her to gently rock his boat.

'One angle Peter Travers and I worked on was how the abductors got access to the keys to Tee-Side. There was no break-in, you see.'

Caldwell was still brooding over the water shortage and showed only a smidgeon of interest.

'There's only one locksmith, you know, in Bude. He's very security conscious. We got the list of people who came to him to have keys copied and checked it against the Tee-Side guest list. There were two overlaps this year. Would you like the names?'

'Go on then.' Grudging acceptance was better than none.

'One was giving both places the name "Jan Smith". The other was "Geri Hartley Brown". I wondered if you could check: did either have anything to do with the Camp?'

This was an acid test. Maxine could remember the name Hartley Brown from the latest senior management list circulated to staff at Cheltenham a few months ago. But would Caldwell admit that or would he brush the whole thing aside? She could see from the way he tensed up that something about the name was familiar to him.

'I've never heard of Jan Smith. Sounds like a name you'd make up. But Geri Hartley Brown is one of our Personnel managers; she visited here quite recently.' He checked his laptop. 'Yes, that's right. She was here for a week in June.'

Then something struck him, his face became more animated. 'That's interesting. The record shows that she stayed in Tee-Side as well. Well, well. Maybe your abduction has something to do with Camp after all. But I have no idea what.'

It seemed the interview was over. 'OK,' he said, 'you can leave that side of things to me. And do let me know, please, if Travers makes any more progress.'

Despite the size of her in-tray Maxine decided to take the early bus back to Bude and call in on Tee-Side. She had no intention of staying there until she was sure nothing more would happen, but she did want to ask a few questions of the Murdochs.

She was given a warm welcome. Irrationally they seemed to feel the need to make up for her kidnapping. Soon she was sitting in an easy chair in the kitchen enjoying a mug of tea.

'We did find one or two names of people that stayed and got new keys with Sandy Jenkins while they were here. What I wondered was if you had any memory of what they looked like – or any other distinguishing details?'

'Might have, I suppose,' said Mrs Murdoch. 'Trouble is, we get so many visitors. Most of 'em don't stand out in the mind –

unless there's something odd about them, of course.'

'Go on. What names did you find, then?' asked her husband.

Maxine took a sip of her tea. 'The first was someone called "Jan Smith". He was here in May.'

'Let's have a look.' He grabbed the guest book and sifted through it. 'Hm. We've had several Smiths staying with us this year. Ah, yes. Here we are: Jan Smith. May 10th to 12th.'

He shut his eyes for a moment. It didn't help his recall.

'The trouble with a common name like Smith is that they tend to blur together in the mind. I can only picture a composite Smith, made up of all of 'em. Our guestbook indicates that this one came on his own. We note down any links with other guests, you see. But what he looked like I really have no idea.'

It was as Maxine had feared. 'What about Gina Hartley Brown; she came in June?'

'Oh, I remember her,' said Mrs Murdoch. 'It's only a few weeks back, of course. D'you remember, John? A smart looking lady, dressed for the office more than the beach, all padded shoulders and high heels. She was on her own too, I recall. She was never a tourist.'

Mr Murdoch had found the name by now. 'She came for a whole week, I see. June 10th to the 16th. Yes, generously built: a very pleasant visitor.'

His comment gave Maxine an idea. 'Hey, do you keep a visitors' book? Could we have a look for what these folk said?'

A minute later the book had been brought back from the hall and Maxine was browsing it.

'Jan Smith left no trace or comment,' she said. 'What a surprise. But Hartley Brown, she left you a warm accolade. You could use that for your future marketing.'

Ten minutes later Maxine was on her way down to the Bude Exhibition. She had called George and agreed a place to meet.

'Trouble is, not having seen Peter today I feel out of the loop,' she said, as the pair joined the modest evening traffic home (it couldn't possibly be termed a rush hour).

'Huh. I haven't seen him since Sunday,' replied George. 'But we can do something about that. Once we're home I'll give him a ring, invite him to supper. It'd give us chance to bounce some ideas off him.'

CHAPTER 31

Despite Maxine's fears that he would be far too busy, Peter Travers could not resist the invitation to supper. 'Though I won't be able to stay too long afterwards,' he warned, 'I've brought plenty of work home with me.'

He turned up just after seven, armed with a fine bottle of Merlot which George reckoned was a Delabole Spar special.

'I'm afraid it's only Shepherd's pie,' said George as she lifted the dish out of the oven and onto the kitchen table.

'That's great,' said Peter. 'Better than beans on toast, anyway.'

Maxine felt a little sad. This was a man who needed some looking after. The food was served and the meal began.

George had known Peter Travers for several years and evolved various ways of getting behind the official line of police secrecy when she needed to. By far the easiest way was to draw him in with some minor indiscretions of her own.

'We had a rare event at the Exhibition today,' she remarked, as she poured the Merlot into their glasses. 'They brought a steam car down through the town on a slow-moving trailer, towed by a tractor. Very exciting, especially for the kids. It was a good advert for the Exhibition.'

'What was wrong with the car already in the Exhibition Tent?' asked Maxine.

'They'd sold it. It was collected by an investment banker on Wednesday evening.'

'How much did this millionaire pay?'

'That's a closely guarded secret. But I had a word afterwards with the Operations Manager. He reckoned it was at least fifty grand. His friend, a venture capitalist, had bought one the week before, you see. Basically this part of the Exhibition trades on high-class envy. Each car is handmade, they're facsimiles of Gurney's originals – though with more robust boilers.'

'So where do they keep them?' asked the policeman. George sensed he wasn't as interested in the cars as in the scope for skulduggery around them.

'I gather there's a unit they've hired for the summer on the Kings Hill Estate. You'd pass it on the side road into Bude.'

'Yes, I know where the estate is. There are all sorts of businesses there. We take our police cars in there for servicing and tuning.'

Maxine already knew most of this. She was impatient to get on to Peter's news.

'So what's happened on your cases today, Peter?'

The policeman gave a sigh. 'Police work doesn't often give much excitement, I'm afraid.' But he could see his hostess and her house guest were not that easily fobbed off. They would undoubtedly offer a more radical sounding board than his official work colleagues.

'How was the post-mortem, for a start?' asked Maxine. 'Have you identified the victim yet?'

'When will you be holding a press conference?' added George.

Peter Travers smiled. 'I'm only sharing this as you're both involved anyway. It's not for wider dissemination.' The two women nodded.

'I'm holding back from talking to the media until we've got the dead man's DNA. That's been promised for tomorrow. The way the case will go, you see, will depend heavily on whether the victim's already known to the police.'

'D'you have any local, recently missing person that it might be?' asked George. 'I mean, in case the DNA doesn't help.'

'That's one thing we've been working on today. Lots of people go missing, of course. Most of 'em turn up again a few weeks later. The most promising one from my point of view, that might be the corpse in the canal, is someone we're not even certain is missing. A chap called Barry Fairclough. He has a small business clearing houses. The sort of chap that gets called in when an owner's died and the relatives want to sell an empty house. He's about the right size and age, and hasn't been seen for several weeks.'

The women were gripped. This was new information. Peter went on to sketch out the details.

George remembered their earlier conversation, her mind still on logistics. 'Presumably this man – Fairclough – must have a vehicle that's big enough to move furniture? If it is him in the canal, whatever's happened to that?'

'After a bit of a struggle we got his home address from the DVLA in Swansea. I was over there this morning. No sign of a large white van, or even a small estate car.'

There was a pause, a chance to eat, as options were considered.

'If it was abandoned by a roadside somewhere two or three weeks ago,' said George, 'it would surely have been reported by now?'

'That's what we reckon. Even if it was left on a side road.'

'Could it be dumped underwater?' asked Maxine.

'The estate car might be. But it'd be hard to hide a big van that way. There are not many places round here that would be deep enough for it to be fully submerged.'

'So if Fairclough is dead,' concluded George, 'both his vehicles must be hidden away in some building or other – maybe a barn on a farm?'

There was silence as they finished their second helpings of Shepherd's pie. 'If you've got any room left there's some black-currant cheesecake,' said Maxine. 'It's not homemade, I'm afraid; I bought it at Morrison's on our way home.'

The offer was hard to refuse. Plates were quickly cleared and the dessert brought in. Maxine made sure Peter had an extra large portion and the conversation continued.

'If you do end up visiting farms around the canal, it'd be easy enough to glance in their barns as well,' said George. 'Maxine and I had an idea about that, by the way.'

'Oh yes?' The policeman had just taken a mouthful of cheese-cake and couldn't say more.

'The only reason we could think of, why the pair that ab-ducted Maxine might not sleep in the place where they'd just brought her, would be if they already had somewhere else to sleep nearby.'

'I'd already got that far,' said the policeman.

229

Maxine took over. 'Then we started to wonder how the gang might have found the hideaway farm in the first place. So we looked up estate agents in this area on the internet. We found the farm was advertised as "to let" since the start of August by just one local estate agent in Bude.'

'Burrows on Fore Street,' George added. The policeman might need reminding, she thought, that this was a joint effort.

'Then we started looking at other farms that Burrows were handling. And we found another back-of-beyond farm also available to let, even more remote and less than two miles from the hideaway. Warren Farm, it's called. George and I reckon it'd also be worth a visit.'

Peter struggled with information overload that threatened to swamp his cheesecake. It was a minute or two before he could speak.

'Look. If, tomorrow, we have no match for the DNA from the corpse, we'll be starting to visit nearby farms, showing owners the poor chap's picture. It'll be a slog but if he's local it might be how he's identified.'

He gave them a puzzled look. 'Now you're saying that's what we should do for the abduction case as well. I don't understand. Are you telling me these two cases are linked?'

'Peter, I don't know. We don't have hard facts on why either of them happened. But if they're not linked, it means two different gangs enacted two different crimes of aggression at almost the same time and much the same place. Isn't that even more unlikely?'

It was an unanswerable question on the data so far. Coincidences did sometimes happen. There was a pause as they each finished their cheesecake.

'Can we think about Warren Farm again?' asked the policeman, once their desserts had been consumed. When you invited outside-the-box thinking, he mused, you had to try and respond. 'Can you remember anything about when it could be let?'

'It had been empty for much longer than the farm where they took Maxine,' said George. 'I think since June. Why d'you ask?'

'I was thinking, might that be one reason why the gang found it attractive? They found it first, maybe, as their headquarters; used the second farm as a short-term expedient. OK, I'll make sure my team visit it tomorrow. And I'll also have a chat with Burrows. See what they can remember.'

Later, as they enjoyed mugs of coffee and chocolate mints (another luxury Maxine had bought for their guest on the way home), the conversation turned to Cleave Camp.

'I went back there today. I was surprised to learn they've got a water shortage at the moment,' said Maxine. 'There's no water for showers or anything and any water you drink is taken from a plastic bottle. It's happened 'cos the water table beneath the camp has dropped so much. But that is just a mishap, they think, due to the dry weather. It's not a deliberate disruption.'

Peter looked disturbed. 'There are a lot of "mishaps" going on around here at the moment. Are there any links between them? If you had any time, Maxine, it'd be worth talking to a geologist about water tables: check that the lowering is natural.'

'I've got nothing else to do. Is there anyone you'd recommend?'

'Well, there's a local geologist called Roger Higgs. He consults internationally for oil companies. When he's at home, he does two-hour geological walks for holidaymakers from out of the Visitor Centre. I went on one when I was transferred to Bude. He talks a lot of sense, got a doctorate from Oxford. He'd be a good place to start. And if he doesn't know, he might know who would.'

After that the conversational turned to more everyday and personal matters. Without any conscious planning, Maxine and Peter were sitting snugly together side by side on the settee and looked set for a long haul. George doubted that Peter would make much of a dent in his homework that evening.

CHAPTER 32

On Friday morning Peter Travers drove into Bude early to start work on reducing a massive in-tray. Maxine arrived later, being brought in by George just before ten. She was rather disillusioned with Cleave Camp and had resolved to take advantage of the last day of her sick note.

'After last night's conversation, we may all have different tasks but at least we're starting from the same page,' commented George, as she parked at the rear of the Exhibition car park.

She had an interview lined up that morning with the Finance Director. He was based in Exeter so she had to make the most of a rare appearance in Bude. In the afternoon she would repeat her talk to the Exhibition on "Invention and Implementation". She had given it several tweaks since its first outing a week ago.

Maxine's task was to do her best to contact Dr Roger Higgs and obtain his take on the water shortages at Cleave Camp.

Frank Clark, the Finance Director, was already hot-desking in the Operation Manager's office, laptop open, when George arrived and introduced herself. An older man, smartly dressed in a suit and a tie that would have done credit to Jon Snow of Channel Four, the Director still looked to have plenty of energy – and to have acquired considerable wisdom in his time.

'Your Chairman had a hunch that there was something going on with these exhibitions,' explained George. 'So in the gaps between my talks and when I'm not investigating alternative charging regimes, I'm trying to give the whole organisation an independent take. Also to meet all the senior staff and see if there's anything odd you think I should be looking into.'

'I'm afraid, George, the Chairman's known to be slightly paranoid. He's always having these hunches. He's renowned for them in the City. There are bound to be things slightly awry in an enterprise of this size, but I for one haven't any sense of something seriously criminal. We are audited, of course . . .'

'The Chairman didn't say it was this particular spot, Frank. It could be any of the exhibitions – or all of them. If there *is* anything, I would say it's more likely to be one of your bought-in services – or special events. By the time those are audited any scam will have long since ended.'

'Right. Well, we do have a Renewable Energy Display at Exeter this coming Sunday – "RED Alert", as we call it. Companies from all over Europe are setting up stalls as we speak. Been doing so for days; it's a big event. There are lots of ideas on better ways to manage energy. The government's Business Secretary and Energy Secretary are both due to make an appearance.'

'Ah, that explains it. I noticed a mention of renewable energy in the leaflet for Limelight, but I couldn't find a stall that matched.'

'Yes, in the initial planning it was meant to be here – Cornwall is the top spot in the UK for renewable energy, after all – but the politicians over-ruled us, said it was "off the beaten track".'

234

'You mean Bude is too far to drive from Westminster.' The Finance Director thought for a moment and then nodded.

There was a pause while George consulted her notebook.

'Well, how about steam cars,' said George, glancing up to a large poster of a nineteenth century vehicle, a smoke cloud billowing behind, hanging on the office wall. 'They are for sale to big bidders, I gather. That's a sort of bought-in service. There must be scope for skulduggery there.'

'That's mostly down to Nicholas Jupp,' said Frank. 'Though I think it was the Head of Research that first alerted us to their possibilities. A full-sized metal vehicle, with all the mechanisms visible on the outside, that we might be able to replicate. Nick had contacts in the Midlands, a specialist engineering firm that could make the idea a reality.'

'Yes, I saw one being driven slowly through the town yesterday. A fine sight. And a good advert for Limelight.'

Frank nodded. 'Yes. Poor old Goldsworthy Gurney: it was a rotten time to invent the thing: just two years before railways took off. I hope that care on when you first announce your invention – its timing – is something you emphasise in your talk?'

'It is. But I also tell them that the initiative belongs with the inventor; and he or she has to own it. It's entirely their choice how and where they push it.'

'How d'you mean?'

'Well, for example, the steam car might have been a non-starter by 1831 but Gurney could easily have applied the idea to boats. Imagine steam-powered craft powering up and down the Bude

Canal. It might have made the idea last a lot longer.'

The Finance man smiled at the thought. He was into unusual investment schemes. How much money might have been made: for a second he wondered if it was too late to start.

'Anyway, what part of steam car economics are you interested in today?'

'My remit is to be super-critical. So let's just for a moment fear the worst. I've not a shred of evidence that there's anything wrong, mind . . .'

'But you'd like to see what a car-based scam might look like. Alright, fair enough. I suppose the only person who knows much about the firm in the Midlands is Judd. So he's the one person around here who knows how much replica cars really cost to build.'

'And he handles the bidding process as well, doesn't he? So could he be making a lot more money on each car than he claims?'

Frank frowned. 'That'd be easy enough to check on, anyway. I'll give 'em a ring.' He picked up the phone, reached Judd's secretary and asked her for the appropriate number. A half-hour conversation ensued.

'Well,' he said, putting down the phone, 'the firm seemed clear enough on the production costs: around thirty five thousand pounds per car.'

'That's roughly what Judd told me. So there isn't any villainy on price, anyway.'

'No. They did, though, claim to be making more cars than I would have expected. More than I've seen being reported as sold, anyway.'

'D'you know where they're kept down here, before they're sold?'

'It's "Unit Four" on the Kings Hill Estate, I believe.'

'It wouldn't do any harm for me to go and see how many cars are there now, would it? I could go over to the Exhibition and get the key from Judd, then have a look tomorrow.'

Frank Clark mused for a moment. 'Let's not bother Judd, shall we. No need to upset him. I insist that we keep a spare copy of every key used by the Exhibition in the safe behind the reception desk, just down the corridor. I'll get the Kings Hill Estate one for you when we've finished this conversation. Now, what else are you apprehensive about?'

CHAPTER 33

Getting hold of Dr Roger Higgs, the geologist, was harder work than Maxine had anticipated. She tried the Bude Visitor Centre but they said they weren't empowered to hand over his personal details. They advised her instead to send the man an email. The trouble with that was she knew he might not reply for a while.

And she knew Peter Travers wanted an urgent consultation.

Eventually she decided that the best way to get hold of Higgs in a hurry was to enrol on one of his geology tours. There was one today, the Visitor Centre told her, starting just after lunch. That was alright, she used the spare time for some personal shopping. Then she settled down to plan the interview, obtain maps and learn about the conical impact of boreholes.

The tour started on the outside front steps of the Bude Museum. Roger Higgs was easy to pick out, he was the authoritative one with a rucksack, boots and sturdy shorts. There were only half a dozen in his group so Maxine decided it would be easy enough to catch him for a private chat afterwards.

The tour itself lasted two hours and was fascinating. Roger certainly knew his subject. The wonderfully specialised nature of UK education meant that Maxine knew a huge amount about mathematics but almost nothing about geology. But that was alright, Roger always started his tours assuming a low knowledge of geology among his audience.

He gave his listeners a summary on geology and how society utterly depends on it, then produced various sorts of rock from his rucksack for them to examine with a hand lens.

Later the geologist led them down to the sea-lock gates at the end of the Canal and across the beach to the cliffs. The group was fascinated by the sharply folded beds of Carboniferous-age sandstone and shale.

There he gave them the edited highlights of his doctoral thesis on the origins of the Bude Formation: how it had been deposited in a large tropical lake. 'That was 300 million years ago,' he explained, 'when there was just one single supercontinent called Pangaea.'

On the way back from the beach Maxine contrived to walk next to the geologist. She asked him if he had time for a private chat on a geological matter, once the tour was over.

'As long as you're prepared to bribe me with a cream tea,' he replied with a grin. 'The Lock Gates Tea Room does one; it's just around the corner.'

Soon they were settled in a quiet corner with servings of scones, clotted cream and strawberry jam, plus a large pot of tea.

'So exactly how can I help you?' the geologist began.

Maxine had decided that the "need to know" in this context had to include the need to tell Roger something of her background. She had grown increasingly impatient with the Cleave Camp security protocols.

'My name is Maxine, I'm a mathematician and I work at

Cleave Camp, just up the coast.'

'Yes, yes, I know about the whole coastline along here. What's the problem?'

'What I want to tell you is not public knowledge . . .'

'Maxine, I've been around long enough. I know how the security services work. This conversation has to be confidential. Of course I accept that. Please carry on.'

'Great. Well, what's bothering me is the height of the water table under Cleave Camp.'

Dr Higgs looked at her thoughtfully, slowly constructing a reason for this bizarre opening question.

'Is this something to do with the boreholes in the Camp?'

'It is. You see . . .'

'I think it'll work better if I make intelligent guesses, then all you have to do is nod yes or no.'

Maxine smiled. This seemed to be the local way to share Official Secrets.

'Are the boreholes producing less water than the Camp needs because the water table has dropped?'

Maxine gave him another smile and a nod.

'And you're wondering if the water table should vary as much as that?'

Another nod.

'Well, the rock below the Camp is the same sandstone and shale of the Bude Formation. The water table rises and falls with the season. As there's more rain in winter it possibly drops twenty or thirty feet in a typical summer. But the boreholes should have been drilled deep enough to cope with that. Unless the Camp has substantially increased its water demand recently? With more people on site, say, or some new water-guzzling machinery?'

This time a firm shake of the head.

There was a pause. Roger took the chance to slice another scone and coat each half with jam overlaid with clotted cream, the Cornish way; then took a big bite. For a few seconds speech was impossible. Eventually he continued.

'So the next question one might ask is . . . is there any way the water table might be lowered over a few weeks, say by malevolent external forces?'

Maxine wondered if Roger had taken a course on mind-reading along with his geology. She smiled at him again and helped herself to a second scone as she pondered what the geologist was trying to suggest.

'Is that possible, Roger?'

'Hypothetically, yes. In any landscape made of permeable rock, like our highly fractured Bude Formation, the water table dips down towards the sea and meets the coastline exactly at sea level. You'd need to find, along the cliff face, a series of fractures, each wide enough and long enough that you could shove a long, flexible plastic hose far enough into the cliff to pass below the sloping water table. You'd then attach a pump. The main difficulty would be that you'd have to keep refuelling the thing – topping up the petrol – maybe for weeks on end.'

'But surely, if you did that, the noise of the motor would be a giveaway?'

Roger gave a grunt and stopped to think (and to eat another

piece of scone).

'Well, the pump would have to be above beach level, beyond the reach of high tide and storm waves. I suppose it wouldn't have to be driven by petrol. What if you leased a cottage nearby? Then you could use an electric pump, kept inside the cottage. That'd be a lot quieter. You'd simply need a much longer hose which connected to the ones going into the cliff. Or else a very long power cable.'

There was silence. Both were thinking around the idea and eating more scones. It wasn't certain the exact scheme would work or how long it might take to have much effect but it seemed promising.

'OK Roger, that's brilliant. I've got one other question that's related to this.'

He smiled. 'Go on.'

'Well, I was told that there was a contingency plan for water at the Camp but that this year it had failed. For security reasons they wouldn't tell me what the plan was. But I know it wasn't as simple as regular water tankers from Barnstaple, that'd be too easy. So have you any ideas?'

The geologist produced a map from his backpack and studied it carefully.

'You'd need a separate fresh-water supply. The most obvious one would be the Tamar Lake. So how about if you laid a pipe from the lake, up this valley here, under the A39 and then down this valley on the other side till it runs close to Cleave. You'd need to pump water up to the Camp from there – but that's OK for an emergency supply. The pipe could have been installed years ago.'

'It's an idea, anyway. Thank you.'

'I thought you were going to ask me something else altogether.'

'What was that?'

'Maybe as a Cleave Camper you know it already. I was thinking about the undersea internet cable that they brought ashore here in 2001. It came in on Crooklets Beach.'

This was a surprise to Maxine. 'From where?'

'Southern Ireland, so rumour has it. I found out as much as I could in case my geology tourists had questions about it. As they do from time to time.'

'What happened to the cable once it came ashore?'

'It caused a massive disruption here in Bude. They first had to dig a trench through the beach sand for the cable, about two metres down. Then they took it all the way up to the British Telecom Unit on the Kings Hill Estate. That's where it gets joined into the rest of the internet. I think the Unit decomposes the various signals, duplicates them and reassembles them. Then, I presume, loads them onto the land-based internet system for distribution to the rest of the country.'

Maxine had expected that she would be the one with the Official Secrets. It seemed, though, that Roger Higgs knew a lot more than she did.

CHAPTER 34

Peter Travers had been at work since seven o'clock. He had cleared much of the routine paperwork that had built up over the last, intensive week before the first of his staff appeared.

At half past nine the analysis of two sets of DNA arrived on the station email. One was from the corpse in the canal; the other was DNA taken from the razor and flannel at Barry Fairclough's cottage.

Travers was disappointed but not altogether surprised that the two sets did not match. The corpse was not the long-missing house clearance man after all.

Further analysis using the police database showed that neither was he a known criminal.

He called his team together. 'I've been talking to the Serious Crime Squad. They'll be here after the weekend,' he said. 'It'd be much better, though, if we had already found out who he was. So I'd first like us to give a bit of effort with "routine policing" to trying to find the man's identity. I mean, there's no reason to think he's not a local, maybe an angler who lives on his own.'

The policeman went on, 'Dr Maxwell has also sent us an image of what the victim looked like, tidied up a bit. It's not very detailed but still a lot better than nothing. We've also got the man's height and weight. What we need to do, I think, is to show the pictures to as many house-owners as we can within, say, a five- mile radius of where the body was found.'

There was no dissent and the search was quickly organised. Four police officers would go out, each in a separate car, and each targeting a different quadrant of the area around the canal car park.

Jess Holland would remain in charge of the station and act as the link person coordinating the search. Officers would each call in every half hour to give their latest search findings and plans. They would also note any houses where, apparently, no one was at home: one of these might belong to the corpse they were trying to identify.

Peter Travers had the north-east quadrant. He had taken this one as it included Warren Farm. He would approach it with care but had no real reason, apart from Maxine's suggestion, for suspecting it had anything to do with her abduction.

Warren Farm was in fact one of the first places he had to visit. But there was no one at home and no sign of habitation. It looked like a farm awaiting a new tenant. If it had been used by Maxine's abductors they were now long gone.

Other farm owners were supportive but none recognised the picture of the corpse which he showed them. He duly clocked in with Jess Holland but was told no one else had made progress either.

After a while he came to a car park for Upper Tamar Lake. This one had a couple of small huts beside it. Then he recalled Jess Holland's schoolgirl memories – how she had been out at night fishing with her Dad. Quickly he gave her a ring.

'Jess, you know you told us you went fishing with your Dad at Tamar Lake once or twice at night?'

'Yes.'

'Well, did you stay out all night; or did you spend part of the night sleeping in a hut?'

There was a pause. 'You're asking me about thirty years ago, Peter. But I have some vague memory that once we did spend the night in a hut of some sort. Beside the car park, I think. Give me five minutes and I'll do my best to check.'

It was a good excuse for a short break and some coffee from his thermos flask. In a few minutes his colleague rang back. 'I've looked on the Tamar Lake Fishing Club website. Use of a hut is one advantage of joining their club. I've got the number of the secretary if you like.'

Ten minutes later Peter Travers had contacted the secretary and discovered that the hut keys were to be found hanging over the rear doorways. 'It's not very secure, I know, but there's nothing worth stealing anyway,' the man said.

Soon the policeman was inside. Both huts were very simply furnished, each with a couple of single beds and a pair of arm-chairs. There was, though, a visitor's book in each.

The kind of guys who would use this type of shelter during their overnight fishing were fairly methodical, Travers decided. There were plenty of entries for each hut. He took one of the armchairs and started to work through the record. What he wanted was the name of someone that came regularly until three or four weeks ago but had not appeared since.

Half an hour later he stepped outside and rang Jess Holland

again.

'Are you alright, sir?' she asked anxiously.

He was about to laugh it off when he realised that in his search he'd missed the agreed call time by a good fifteen minutes.

'Jess, I'm very sorry. The thing is, I got into both of the huts and found each one had a visitor's book. Since then I've been looking for names which appeared regularly but not for the last three of four weeks.'

'Some of us care a little about you, sir. And we need to watch out for one another. Have you found anything?'

'I've got just a couple of names that would fit. Both come as loners – or at least they don't mention a companion. One's called "Ben Farthing" and the other is "Walter Madson".'

He paused to check his notes. 'Walter's from Bude so we'll try him later but I see Ben lives in Alfardisworthy. I've just found it on the map, that's not far from here. I might try that one first. But I will ring you in twenty minutes, Jess, I promise. Thank you for your concern.'

Alfardisworthy was a ten-cottage hamlet with no shop or pub, about a mile across the fields or three miles by road from the hut. Ben's cottage was in the centre of the group of houses but no one came to the door when Travers gave the knocker a hefty thump. After two more tries he went to the cottage next door.

After a while an elderly man came out. 'Ah, you're after Mr Farthing. He's gone away. Leastways, I've not seen him for about four weeks. It's very odd. He always tells me when he's off on holiday.'

Gingerly the policeman felt in his pocket for the photograph sent by Dr Maxwell. 'Is this Mr Farthing by any chance?'

The man squinted at it. 'It might be. Let me get me glasses.' He returned with them a couple of minutes later. 'Let's have another look.'

This time he gave the picture a thorough examination. 'You know, I reckon it is. My, oh my, he looks the worse for wear. Did you find him in the lake? Or has something else happened to him?'

An hour later lots of procedural activity had taken place. The police search of the area had been halted. The neighbour had provided a spare key to Ben Farthing's cottage and two of the Bude policemen were giving it a preliminary search.

The neighbour himself had accompanied Peter Travers to the morgue at Stratton. There he had been shown the corpse from the canal and had identified it, with great sadness, as being Ben Farthing.

So at least the corpse now had a name. For some reason that made his death more tangible, more personal.

Travers had brought the old man home again and used the journey to ask him a few gentle questions.

It seemed, though, that there was nothing suspicious about Ben. He was a single man who earned a modest living from casual jobs on nearby farms. Hence no one would miss him when he did not turn up for work. Fishing was his passion and he would regularly walk the mile across the fields to Tamar Lake.

Back at Alfardisworthy, Joe, Jamie and Holly had found nothing suspicious in Ben's cottage. There was no suggestion of violence. Nor could they find a fishing rod. There seemed little doubt that the man had met his end while night fishing around Tamar Lake.

'We'll have his DNA confirmed. But I've no doubt that we've answered the question "who",' commented Travers, once he had heard their reports. 'Where we have no answer, so far, is to the question, "why".'

But further discussion was forestalled by a call from Bude Police Station that was very peculiar indeed.

CHAPTER 35

'I was keeping track of you all,' said Jess Holland over the speakerphone, 'when the thought came to me. We'd checked that the DNA from Fairclough's cottage was not the same as that from the corpse in the canal. That's what started the search you guys have been conducting. But I wondered, as I kept waiting for you all to ring in, did it match anyone else?'

'Not very likely. We'd already checked that Fairclough had no form,' commented Holly.

'Not under the name "Barry Fairclough", Holly. But suppose he had been done for something and then changed his name? Anyway, it wasn't difficult for me to search the national database. And that was when I found the match.'

Peter Travers was puzzled. Jess seemed to be making a huge meal of this. 'So you found a match? Fairclough does have a record?'

'Possibly.'

'But if you found a match . . .?'

'The trouble was, guv, the name it matched to. That was . . . Christian Holdsworth.'

Travers drew breath ready to demolish the statement and challenge the officer. It was only a week ago that Regional police had told him that Holdsworth was dead, drowned in Lake Wim-

There was no need to be confrontational. He took a deep breath. 'Jess, let's think about this calmly. We've been told that Holdsworth has drowned. But no one's had sight of the body yet. So I guess that might be some sort of hoax.'

He paused to order his thoughts. 'And if we're being really precise, the DNA from Fairclough's cottage is not straight from the man himself: it came from a razor and a flannel in his bathroom.'

'So what if Holdsworth used the cottage as a hideaway, guv, after Fairclough disappeared? He might have left his own DNA traces on the flannel. I mean, he's a convict on the run. He'd hardly be likely to go into Boots and buy a new one.'

'No. It wouldn't be a priority. But isn't it more likely, Jess, that Holdsworth might be the reason that Fairclough's disappeared? I mean, the conman might have done the poor bloke in – Sooty topples Sweep, as it were. Then buried him in his own garden.'

'But Fairclough disappeared weeks back, guv, when Holdsworth was still behind bars. Unless Fairclough started hiding before Holdsworth even escaped, the two events happened in the wrong order.'

There was silence at both ends of the line as the various known events were considered and tried in different orders. Finally Travers gave his opinion.

'You know, Jess, we've been having this conversation despite being told that Holdsworth drowned in Lake Wimbleball. But we've no hard evidence he's gone. The DNA shows he was in the cottage and he might be still hiding there. That could account for the fresh milk Holly found in the fridge. There are four of us here and Fairclough's place isn't far. It must be worth another visit.'

Two of the cars were left for the time being outside the late Farthing's cottage in Alfardisworthy. Holly travelled with Peter and Joe with Jamie.

As they drove, Peter Travers thought hard about how this visit must be handled.

'The thing is, Holly, Holdsworth is a wily criminal. We've no idea how he landed on the place, what his links with Fairclough are or how long he's been there. But if he's settled on it as a long-term hideaway, the chances are he's got some sort of early warning system so he can get out of the cottage and into the woods if he sees someone coming.'

'It'd be a very primitive system, guv. I mean, he's not had the chance to go to Maplin's to buy some technical wizardry.'

'OK, what would you do?'

Holly mused for a moment, imagining herself back at the cottage.

'Anyone going to Fairclough's cottage would have to come by car. It's too far off a bus route for anything else.'

'Yes?'

'That means they'd drive in via that long track through the woods. What if ... what if he put some sort of tripwire there?'

'Right. It must be something like that. Which means?'

'We'd better park the cars a short way down the road and walk in. With two of us first making their way round the back.'

Travers was encouraged at this demonstration of planning

nous. Holly had more potential than his other colleagues; he would need to encourage her further. But that was for the future.

'Great. So can you call Joe and Jamie, tell them the plan. They can be the ones hiding round the back of the cottage. Ask 'em to give us a call once they're in position.'

As they waited, two hundred yards down from the entrance track, Peter Travers wished that he had Maxine with him. She had raised his spirits, made him feel young. Then he scolded himself. This could turn out to be a dangerous operation; he didn't want Maxine at more risk than was necessary. Besides, if there was a fight, Holly had more training; she'd be far more useful.

There was a call. It was Joe. He reported that he and Jamie were in the woods at the back of the cottage, with a good view of the back door. But there was no sign of life within.

Time to put ideas into practice. Peter Travers and his junior colleague advanced carefully down the track.

They were within sight of the gate to the yard of the cottage when Holly spotted the green string, running low across the track. Travers gave her a thumbs up. It was just possible there was some sound equipment nearby as part of the early warning, so they had agreed to speak only in whispers.

Carefully they stepped over the string and continued to the gate. Silence was important now and surprise was essential. Quickly the two officers climbed over the gate and up to the front door. There was no noise from within.

Travers grabbed his phone and called his colleagues, speaking as quietly as possible. 'Joe, can you two approach the back door.

There should be a key under the mat. Enter the kitchen as quietly as you can. Holly and I are by the front door, we'll stay here until you open it for us or else Holdsworth comes out. If he does we're ready for him.'

The two police officers got out their batons, stood either side of the front door and waited.

Their vigil lasted only a few minutes but seemed much longer.

Then they heard shouting from inside the cottage. Suddenly the front door burst open and a large man appeared. Peter Travers thrust out his foot and the man tripped over it as he ran past. Before he could stand up again the policeman was on to him and had his wrists handcuffed.

A few seconds later Holly applied a second pair of cuffs to his ankles.

By the time Joe and Jamie appeared there was nothing left to do except to fetch one of the police cars so he could be taken away.

It was not yet clear what further crimes the man had committed; or his relationship (if any) to the disappearance of Fairclough or the sudden death of Ben Farthing.

Some of that might emerge from the interviews which were yet to come. What seemed certain was that Christian Holdsworth's days of freedom were over.

CHAPTER 36

By now it was almost lunch time but Peter Travers was too busy for serious food and asked Holly to bring him a tuna baguette. Christian Holdsworth would be back in Dartmoor before too long. But while he was in the cells of Bude Police Station there was chance for the apprehending officer to interview him and make some sense of his surprise appearance at Fairclough's cottage.

And while he was doing so, to look for any connection to other recent events in Bude.

They were being victims of their own success. Travers had to remind himself that this morning had also seen real progress on the case of the corpse in the canal. At least they now knew who the man was. That would require further attention before long. They didn't even have a single option on the question of "why" he had been killed. He knew his team's limitations but didn't want to arouse scorn when the Regional Crime Squad eventually arrived.

The first priority was Holdsworth. After some thought, Travers decided that it would be best to conduct the interview in the usual room with its recording device, but to first handcuff the man's wrists and ankles to the chair. Whatever went on at Dartmoor, he didn't want to be part of any inquiry into how the man

255

had escaped from Bude Police Station.

Holdsworth was smouldering at being recaptured but realised that he was not in the same position as someone who had not yet stood trial.

When the interview began the once and future convict made no attempt to deny his name or that he had recently escaped from Dartmoor.

A brief survey of Fairclough's cottage kitchen before they had left had suggested to Travers that the man had run out of food. There would be no point in him faking his own death if he then started appearing in local shops – even assuming he had the cash to do so. So apart from the vegetables he could dig up from Fairclough's garden he was stuck. He was probably very hungry – he was certainly more docile than the policeman had expected from the prison profile.

The policeman decided that a small amount of psychological pressure would do no harm and enjoyed munching his own baguette as noisily as possible as the interview continued.

'I'm sure others will want to question you about your escape from Dartmoor,' he said. 'That's for later. What I'm interested in is your recent activity around Bude. You grew up here, I believe?'

The man nodded.

'Out loud please, for the recorder,' requested Travers. Scowling, the man complied.

'So you still have friends around here?'

'Not many. Most of 'em gave up on me when I was nicked.'

'"Most of 'em". Huh. I bet there's no one here that gives a damn about you. They didn't miss you in the snooker place, anyway. I checked.'

Holdsworth looked like he was torn between the criminal tradition of keeping mum and demonstrating that he still had one or two real friends even after so many years in Dartmoor.

'Well, there's Harold. Harold Lockwood.'

'OK. That's one. Any more?'

'And Barry Johnstone.'

Travers was elated to have been given a name they didn't already know but chose not to give this away.

'And have you caught up with them in your time around here?'

'I tried ringing Harry. But he said not to call him again. He's married, got a kid.'

'What about Barry?'

'I tried ringing him a few times. But he never answered. I was hoping he'd come home and we could have a good catch-up.'

Travers decided to take a punt. Barry wasn't that common a name. 'You mean, to the cottage where we caught you?'

'That's right. Hey, hope I got the right place.'

'You probably did. But he's changed his name, I'm afraid. He calls himself Barry Fairclough these days. Maybe he's changed his number?'

'Don't think so. I recognised his voice on the answering machine. Now I think about, he did use some name like Fairclough. I only listened to it the once.'

'So why did you want to see Barry? Other than to ask him about staying in his place, I mean.'

'We're old mates, go back a long, long way. We were in the

same class at school. In the early days he'd help me dispose of any jewellery I picked up. Landed us both in porridge, that did. After that he went straight, got a job as a chimney sweep, while I got dragged deeper and deeper into crime. It'd be good to see him before you send me back into stir.'

'The reason I'm so interested, Mr Holdsworth, is that Barry has disappeared. Our officers have been looking for him for over a week.'

It took a second for the statement to sink in. Then the convict responded angrily. 'So you're saying, someone's done him in? Bloody hell, is nowhere safe these days? I'll help you find the one that did him in. He's my only mate.'

Holdsworth was either an outstanding actor or was extremely upset. Given that he had been locked inside Dartmoor Prison for some time after Fairclough was reported missing, Travers judged it was the latter.

'I don't suppose you have any memories of secret places he might have hidden away in? You see, we've looked hard but with no success. We're starting to wonder if something dreadful has happened to him.'

'Barry didn't hide away at all. He was always cheerful, that's why we got on so well. My, oh my. ' The convict looked to be close to tears.

'Right, Mr Holdworth, we'll leave it there for now. I'll have you taken back to your cell and then I'll send you down a meal. Maybe you'll think of something that will help us while you eat. I've told Dartmoor that you're here but they said they wouldn't be able to send anyone for you until after the weekend. So you'll have a bit more time in Bude, anyway.'

By now it was late afternoon. Travers decided that he wasn't going to get any more out of Holdsworth and he'd devote the rest of the day to the case of Ben Farthing.

He went into the office open-plan, announced he was going back to explore the path around Tamar Lake and asked if anyone fancied coming with him. But they were all busy dealing with routine tasks that had been shelved in the week's excitement, trying to complete them before they went off for the weekend.

He didn't mind too much. For years he had worked entirely alone, patrolling a huge area of Cornwall, north and south of Delabole. Going round the lake was a task that could be done single-handed. It was simply a question of looking for anything that might hint at why Ben had been killed. It was now a month after his death and broad daylight, there was no way it would be dangerous.

But as he walked to his car he wondered what Maxine was doing. She might enjoy a walk round the lake. And he would certainly enjoy the company. Quickly he called her number. Ten minutes later he was driving down to the long-stay car park beside the canal to pick her up.

It took the whole journey to Tamar Lake for them to bring one another up to date on their progress over the day.

'You certainly keep busy,' observed Maxine, once Peter had told her about the identification of the canal corpse and then the recapture and interview of the escaped convict.

259

'It's not often like this,' replied the policeman. 'The thing is, I want to get as far as possible before the Regional Crime Squad arrive on Monday and start bossing us about.'

'Are you calling them in over the canal murder?'

'I am. We've found the name of the victim, which is good. But that leaves a major question of what brought about his murder. It seems almost certain that he was killed while out fishing one night beside Tamar Lake. That's why it seemed worthwhile to walk right around the lake: we might spot something that could give us a clue.'

'Oh, Peter. And here was me thinking you wanted my company for a summer stroll.'

The policeman turned to look at her and saw to his relief that she was smiling. He needed to get used to being teased. 'Maxine, of course I want your company. But if we can tackle this together that's even better. I'm not normally this busy.'

They parked in the car park beside the two fishing huts. 'That's where I got the name of Ben Farthing,' commented Peter. 'There was no car though, it's walking distance from where he lives.'

'Presumably his fishing rod ended up in the bottom of the lake?'

'I guess so. It's no longer in his cottage, anyway.'

'So there's no clue where he was fishing?'

'None at all, Maxine. We'll just have to walk round. It's about three miles. And perfectly flat.'

It was a perfect summer evening with no breeze and an almost azure blue sky. The view was less dramatic than that seen from the cliffs around Tintagel but still green and pleasant. Best of all, there was no one else in sight.

Maxine slipped her hand into Peter's as they started to walk along. As she did so the policeman felt the burdens of the heavy caseload slide away. But he still kept examining the side of the footpath as it meandered along the lakeside. It would be a shame to have completed the whole walk and noticed nothing at all.

For Maxine, her experiences less than two weeks ago had galvanised her approach to life. Whereas before she had been content to accept the straightforward demands of her job – and to regard it in some way as a vocation – now she was minded to regard every day as special, even when the days had nothing to do with Camp.

She had no idea how many days she had left – hopefully it was many thousand – but she wanted them all to count.

The encounter with Peter Travers – was it really less than a week ago? – had shown her how much richer life could be when lived to the full. Maxine had fallen head over heels in love, in a way that only made sense if you knew that this had never happened to her before.

In truth, though he would hesitate to admit it, Peter Travers was almost as smitten. A small part of him, though, was still on duty. He listened to his companion more than he spoke to her, his eyes continuously combing the shoreline for some reason why an innocent fisherman might possibly have been attacked.

They walked along steadily. Maxine was in no hurry to bring the promenade to an end and Peter was equally content to walk slowly and watchfully. It is often said that a man cannot tackle two things at once but on this occasion a valiant attempt was being made.

They had almost reached the northern end of the lake when Peter spotted it. There was a piece of machinery between the path and the lake, a metal frame of scaffolding, about three feet wide and six feet deep.

'What on earth is that?' he asked as they came to a halt and peered more closely. Standing right over the frame and looking down, they could see a sizeable pump at the lower level, connected to a four-inch pipe that ran away under the path.

Maxine crossed over to the other side and looked down for the pipe's continuation. 'I can see where it comes out,' she announced. 'But it drops down beneath the meadow. I can't see where it goes after that.'

'I wonder what that's all about,' said Peter. 'It seems to be a lake outflow. Do you reckon someone is taking water directly, without bothering to pay their water rates?' He looked across the grass but there was nothing there except sheep.

'D'you have a map of this part?' asked Maxine.

The policeman had many items in his rucksack that years of experience had taught him might occasionally be needed. Among them was an Explorer Map that covered the lake and the area over to the coast.

'There's my Camp,' said Maxine. It was rather cryptically marked but anyone who knew about the Camp would have no difficulty spotting it.

Suddenly she remembered part of her conversation earlier in the afternoon with Dr Higgs. 'You know, this pipe might just be something to do with the Camp. It could be the contingency water supply they're supposed to use when the boreholes fail.'

'There's a bench just over there,' said the practical policeman. 'It'd be easier to look at the map sitting down.'

A minute later they were seated at either end of the bench with the now-unfolded map spread out between them.

'So if you were a water engineer, Maxine, asked to link the Camp to the lake, what's the route you'd take?'

The mathematician considered the options for a moment. 'You'd want to climb as little as possible. But you can't help doing some. And you'd have to run under the A39. The best way would be up this slope here, cross the A39 there and then run down this obscure valley and finally up the hill to Cleave Camp.'

'Hm. In all that's about five miles.'

'That's OK, Peter. The Camp has plenty of funding. I mean, it's a key part of national security. All the expense came when the pipe was laid. After that it costs nothing until you have to use it – which is perhaps a few days a decade. Good value for money – provided it works.'

'And of course it's not advertised or talked about: secrecy is deemed the best form of security.'

'No. Provided it stays secret. But you and I've worked it out by seeing this pump and using a map. So others could do the same.'

'In fact, Maxine, could this not, somehow or other, be the key to poor Ben's death?'

CHAPTER 37

Maxine took it for granted that Peter would be invited for supper when they finally completed their circuit of Tamar Lake, drove south past Bude and got back to Treknow.

Seeing the two drive up outside Ivy Cottage in the police car, George could have felt like the proverbial gooseberry. But she knew the pair well, had known them both individually at different times over the years. She could sense there was something going on between them and it needed to be encouraged.

The trouble was, she couldn't face cooking another proper meal. 'Right guys, we're all in regular work. It's the end of the working week, time to celebrate. Or if necessary commiserate. How about us having some fish and chips in the Port William?'

There was no dissent. Half an hour later the three had walked down the narrow path into Trebarwith Strand and had claimed a quiet table at the back of the dining room. 'We can talk here without any risk of being overheard,' announced the ever-cautious policeman.

Soon Peter had set up a tab, ordered them all sea bass and chips and brought them each a pint of Rattler cider. 'It's strong stuff mind, ladies. At least six percent alcohol. I'm on ginger beer after this. You've only got to stagger up the hill to Treknow. I've got to drive on to Delabole.'

264

They had all had busy days and it took some time to bring one another up to date. They had all finished their fish and chips by the time they were back onto the same page – though it was a later page than they had reached the evening before.

'I'll get the dessert menu,' said George. It was no trouble to wait her turn at the bar and give Peter and Maxine a little private time on their own. Eventually she returned and handed round copies of the menu.

'I'm for Eton Mess,' announced Peter. Maxine remembered that he had chosen the same option in Boscastle. Maybe, if all went well, she would need to learn to make the dessert herself. It looked horribly difficult.

The two women each chose the fruit salad; there was no point in adding to their waist lines. George returned to the bar to place their order and came back this time rather more quickly.

'Right,' said Peter. 'So we've all got all the facts – plus plenty of extra ones that don't fit into this case at all. Where do we go next?'

'A lot of the facts seem to relate in one way or another to Cleave Camp,' observed George. 'Isn't it likely that it's about to be placed under some form of attack? If so, isn't our responsibility simply to tell all we know to the Camp Security?'

'The thing is, George, you've not met Colin Caldwell, the Camp Security Officer. Whereas Peter and I have. Neither of us has been overwhelmingly impressed.'

'His initial instinct is always to minimise trouble,' added Peter. 'That's trouble for him, I mean. He's got so many items on the back burner that they won't all fit. Anything we told him would simply be added to the pile. My instinct, though, is that the threat we're dealing with is more urgent.'

'OK, Maxine. You know the place best. Peter and I don't want to know any details, but what sort of threats can you imagine? What are the biggest worries facing management at the moment? Is there anything that's got a time deadline associated with it?'

There was a pause. Desserts arrived and took their attention for a moment. Maxine notice how Peter's eyes lit up at the sight of the Eton Mess. She hoped he would stay tuned in to their discussion.

'It's blindingly obvious,' Maxine said, 'but the world's a dangerous place. I'd say the biggest problem at the moment is the civil war in Syria. There's pressure from the United States for the UK to get involved directly. That might lead to a vote in the House of Commons before too long. Obviously the government would want to be as up to date as they could with the intelligence before that happened.'

'Huh. The last time all that came round was the so-called intelligence reporting on Iraq,' observed George. 'Trouble was, in the end it didn't do us much good. We solved one problem but created a lot more. You might even say that it prompted the Middle East war that's still lingering on.'

Peter Travers looked up from his Eton Mess. 'If you were driven by geo-political forces I doubt you'd start in Bude.'

There was something in that. Bude was hardly the centre of the political universe. He took another mouthful of Mess and then continued. 'What about the issues raised by that American leak-smith? You know, unrestricted spying, reading everyone's email? Doesn't that worry anyone in high places?'

'Oh, you mean Edward Snowden?' said Maxine. 'What he's reported – or at least what's been published – might make our security system less popular, I suppose. Harder for government to support, easier to have its budget cut. We'd be more vulnerable to someone else making the Camp look like fools.'

George remembered what her friends had said about the pipe they had found leading out of Tamar Lake, which they suspected went on to the Camp.

'I guess that a Camp that can't even manage its own water supply won't look good. If it ever gets out, that is; the media would have a field day. But wrecking the pump or the pipe that provides the emergency supply, if that's all they've done, seems a lot of work for what can only be a short-term disruption.'

'It's not just a lot of work. Remember, George, some innocent angler died as a result of stumbling across their efforts in the dead of night. They must have been after more than bad publicity.'

'Abducting Colette and later me was serious stuff as well,' protested Maxine. 'What on earth was all that about?' George remembered that this question had started the whole case. They'd not yet found the answer.

'Going back to the water supply,' said Peter, 'your conversation with Dr Higgs implied there might indeed be ways to lower the water table, if you could extract more water for long enough.'

'But he was talking about putting pipes into fractures along the shoreline and linking them to an electric pump. That'd be hard to keep secret for long. There are lots of walkers along the Coast Path,' George went on. 'It'd only take one of them climbing down to explore the shoreline for the hum of the pump to be heard.'

'If you can pump out from the water table via a fissure,' said Peter, 'then maybe you can do the same via an artesian spring. After all, they're a sort of pressure valve for the water table.'

'I believe there are springs all around the Camp,' said Maxine. 'One of them might be much easier to get at – and easier to keep secret once it was installed.'

'It'd be worth a walk round to have a look,' said Peter. 'If you lowered the water table for the summer and the contingency supply is sabotaged, then that could lead to a serious shortfall.'

'I'd be happy to walk round the Camp with you tomorrow,' offered Maxine.

Peter smiled. 'Let's see. I'm supposed to be on duty in Bude. Sunday might be better.'

George was still exercised on deadlines. 'Maxine, can you remember any significant dates for the security team in the near future?' They had so many facts, she thought, yet they seemed to know so little.

'The only date I've come across,' answered Peter, 'that could be significant was on that calendar we found behind the oven in the hideaway cottage.'

'What was it?'

The policeman got out his notebook and looked it up. 'Well, well. It's this coming Sunday, actually. There were no words, just a big cross.'

'So it's possible that something is planned for this weekend.' George looked pensive. But she couldn't think of anything specific.

'Why don't we have coffee back at Ivy Cottage?' she suggested. 'These chairs are getting a bit uncomfortable. A change of venue might give us new ideas. I'll go and settle the tab, it's my treat this evening. Then we'll battle back up that hill. The exercise will help us sleep, anyway.'

Half an hour later they were back at Ivy Cottage, preparing to enjoy some of George's special blend, together with a box of After Eights.

'I did have one idea,' she reported as she emerged from the kitchen with the coffee. 'Oddly, it was prompted by the notion of the date.'

'Go on,' said Peter. He enjoyed outside-the-box thinking, though he didn't see much of it inside the police station.

'Well, it occurred to me that tight deadlines and target dates are much more likely to be linked to the internet than to general security. So is it possible that all this is to do with the internet links in Bude, and not directly with the Camp?'

There was a pause as the idea was considered.

'It's possible, I suppose,' replied Maxine. 'I've been told the Camp has a direct connection from the internet as it passes through Bude. I don't know how it's done, though. Fibre optic cable is much more efficient, you see, than satellite links.'

'So you ladies think this might all be something to do with intercepting a communication that's being sent over the internet?' Peter Travers was struggling to keep up now. He was no techno-freak.

'Not directly,' said George. 'If you're hoping to track a message, and that's all you're doing, you wouldn't need to be anywhere near Bude. I mean, the internet is accessible everywhere. All you'd need would be a connection of your own, plus knowledge of the sender and the password of the intended recipient.'

'The trouble wouldn't come in getting hold of the raw message but in making sense of it,' added Maxine. 'If it was important then it would certainly be encrypted. But decrypting it without the key would not be easy. That's the sort of thing I do at Camp, you see. Decryption isn't easy, in fact it's very advanced mathematics.'

'What sort of message might an intruder be interested in?' asked Peter. 'Let's not worry about decryption for the moment. If it's for a foreign power, say, they must have decryption facilities of their own. I'm interested in the big picture here, not the fine detail.'

'There's a staggering amount of data on the internet,' said George, Maxine nodding in agreement. 'There's ordinary communication – emails and the like. Then there's technical detail or updates. And security details, of course. It's hard to think, at this time of night, of something that's time critical but I'm sure there must be stuff like that as well.'

It sounded like they weren't going to get much further that evening. It was late by now and everyone was very tired. George made a tactical retreat up to bed and left Maxine and Peter to say goodnight to one another in their own way.

CHAPTER 38

Saturday morning looked to be the start of a brilliant weekend. There was no wind and scarcely a cloud in the sky. Both George and Maxine had slept soundly, helped no doubt by the slog back up the hill from Trebarwith Strand the evening before.

But it was not the day for a lie in. As they tucked into their muesli and toast the questions raised by the case refused to be ignored.

'Are you game for more investigation?' asked George as she spread a spoonful of lemon marmalade across her toast.

'I'd prefer that to going for another swim,' replied her guest. 'At least until I've bought a wetsuit. What did you have in mind?'

'Well. I've been lent the keys for one of the Units in the Kings Hill Estate, that's round the back of Bude. The one that stores the steam cars before they're delivered to the Limelight Exhibition. I had a long conversation with the Finance Director, managed to persuade him that it was worth seeing what was in there. And while we're there . . .'

'We could have a look for the Unit that's supposed to be handling the internet cables. Assuming we can find it. See if anything strikes us about ways it might be accessed. That'd be great,' Maxine enthused. 'Even though it's fabulous weather I don't feel like being a tourist while we've got a live case to work

271

on. There'll be plenty of time to walk on the cliffs later.'

They set out soon after nine. It was the weekend, both women were off-duty and each wore short-sleeved shirts, shorts and trainers. George took the precaution of adding a torch, a penknife and a set of maps to their rucksack of useful items for the day.

'We can buy lunch out,' she remarked. Maxine had rather hoped they could have lunch with Peter but decided, diplomatically, to stay silent.

George had done some research on Google and found out how to reach the Kings Hill Estate. It was accessed by taking the first road off the A39 into Bude and then turning off to the right a few minutes later.

This was new territory for them both. They drove slowly round the industrial estate at first, seeing the kinds of business which operated there. It wasn't very large, perhaps fifty businesses in total on various spurs, and there was only the one road in.

George was surprised at how few people there were about. Most of the units had locked doors; hardly anyone was open for business. Maxine had been looking at the names on the units as they went past but had seen nothing obviously linked to internet processing.

'Maybe it's hidden away behind somewhere else,' she remarked.

'I'm nervous about all these cameras. Let's walk around for a few minutes,' said George.

She parked the car at the far end of the estate, seized the rucksack and the pair strolled down the road.

'You know, George, the BT Unit might have been made deliberately hard to spot. If no one knows which one it is, that's one way of keeping it low profile. More sensible than that big sign at Cleave Camp, anyway.'

'Well, how about that unit over the road? Don't look for too long, I can see a camera fixed to the roof.'

'Mm. It's got a ten-foot high wire fence round it, with razor wire on the top. And one or two more cameras round the side.'

'Yes. Maxine, it's got no posters of any sort and no windows. Let's keep walking, shall we. We'll come back in a few minutes on the far side of the road.'

The women kept walking, talking inconsequentially about other units they were passing. Most were marked though one or two offered no clue as to their owner. Five minutes later they turned and came back.

'Look, George, they've got generators sticking out round the side. That's the sort of thing you'd expect for an internet station. It'd take a huge amount of electricity boosting all those signals. You wouldn't want to rely on the local power supply – much better to generate your own.'

'We've seen nothing else with half those features, anyway. I bet that's the place.' As she spoke a large British Telecom van drove up. The gates of the unit opened automatically and the van drove in, the gates then shutting behind it.

'I'd say that confirms it, Maxine. Security is pretty good. It wouldn't be the easiest place to force your way in, would it? Right, let's go and find Unit Four.'

It didn't take long. Unit Four was next door to the BT Unit, probably just a coincidence. There was a pair of Yale locks but the keys fitted and the women were quickly inside. It wasn't easy to spot a light switch.

'Good job we brought the torch, Maxine.' She swung the beam round.

'OK. I can see several steam cars lined up – half a dozen in all. The unit is all one large space, there's no door in the back, anyway. What are we looking for?'

'Anything out of the ordinary. Signs of some sort of scam. In other words, things with no connection to the Exhibition.'

They inspected the unit carefully. One set of equipment was probably something to do with Gurney's lighting inventions. There were a few more mirrors and several cobalt lights. Other bits of kit looked like items that might have been planned to help partition the Exhibition but then discarded.

Then they came to a heavy tarpaulin. Carefully George seized the edge and lifted it up. Below was a square of heavy-duty metal, hinged at one side and bolted at the other, with a padlock holding it down. There was a massive, battery-powered bolt cutter lying on top of it. Alongside was a huge piece of machinery with a set of sharp blades at the front. There was also something that looked like a small piece of radar equipment.

'What on earth is that?' asked George. None of it had any connection with the Exhibition that she could think of.

Then they heard the noise of a vehicle drawing up right outside and an engine being turned off.

Quick as a flash, George lowered the tarpaulin. Then she nodded towards the nearest steam car and whispered, 'Best if we're not found here. Don't know who it is. Get inside.'

A quick scramble and both were hidden inside the steam car's cab. George remembered, just in time, to turn off the torch. There were no doors but the car faced away from the peculiar items of machinery. It wasn't an ideal hiding place but it might do, depending on what the newcomers were doing.

They were only just in time. The door opened once more. Contrasted against the light beyond they could just see a couple of men, dressed in dark clothing. Evidently they didn't know where the light switch was either. Instead, though, they had a small torch.

George and Maxine lay side by side, as still as a pair of dormice.

The men weren't here to inspect the stock, anyway. Confidently they strode forwards to the tarpaulin, lifted it up and threw it off. One of the men picked up the giant bolt cutters and moved them aside. Briefly the torch caught his figure as he too moved forward.

Beside her George sensed Maxine quivering but she had no idea why.

Then the second man undid the padlock, drew back the bolt, seized the square of metal and lifted it up. It was hinged at the rear and he rested it back against the wall.

Then he grabbed the piece of machinery with the blades and precariously lowered himself down the hole that the square of metal had previously covered. He was followed a few seconds later by the other man, still carrying his bolt cutters. The whole sequence had taken place in less than two minutes and in almost complete silence.

George and Maxine were now alone with half a dozen steam cars.

It seemed likely that the men would be down the hatch for some time. They could hear them shuffling around underground, some distance away. It was their chance, George thought, to get away.

Slowly, silently, she raised herself from the floor of the car and eased herself out of the doorway. She daren't use her torch in case the beam, or even its diffused glow, shone into the shaft where the men had disappeared.

She waited for Maxine to follow her out of the car and gave a reassuring squeeze when her friend stood beside her.

George was sure these men were up to no good; there was one more thing she needed to do. Carefully she tiptoed towards the shaft, lowered the door of the hatch and then slid the bolt across. She didn't have a key to padlock it but she was sure it could not be opened from below.

There was a glimmer of light round the edge of the unit door that told them which way to go. George went first, taking small steps in case anything lay on the floor. Once further from the shaft she turned on the torch, making sure it was pointing towards the doorway. Two minutes later they were both at the door, opening it and slipping out into the daylight. Then George put both keys into the locks so she could close it once more without making a sound.

Outside, on the unit forecourt, stood a dirty blue Skoda. The car meant nothing to George but a great deal to Maxine.

'George, I'm almost certain those were the two guys that

abducted me. I saw one of them in the torchlight. And I'm sure this is the car they took me away in.'

George was a woman of action. 'Quick, Maxine, we've got to let the tyres down. They shouldn't be able to get out but if they do we can at least make sure they won't get far.'

Matching actions to words, George knelt down, unscrewed the valve cap and then used the bottle-opener on the pen-knife to push in the valve. A hiss showed she was having the effect wanted.

Maxine saw what was needed and knelt at the next tyre. She used her hairclip to push in the valve, with the same result.

Five minutes later the car was essentially immobilised.

The women weren't waiting around any longer. Two minutes later they were back at George's car, at the far end of the estate.

Maxine grabbed her phone and called the police station. 'Hi, is Peter Travers there?' A minute later he was on the phone.

'Peter, George and I have just captured the two guys who abducted me. We're in the Kings Hill Estate. The guys were digging a tunnel from the unit where they keep the steam cars – that's Unit Four – through under the BT Unit where they process the internet signals. We've shut the hatch they went down and bolted them in. But an immediate arrest would probably be a good idea.'

CHAPTER 39

'We might as well drive down so we're nearer to Unit Four,' said George, once Maxine had finished her call. 'Then we'll be able to see what happens when Peter arrives. I hope he brings some reinforcements. There's no reason to think those guys inside are armed but there's no guarantee that they aren't.'

As soon as the words were out of her mouth she wished she hadn't said them – not in Maxine's hearing, anyway.

But Maxine didn't seem to notice. 'We need to give Peter the Unit Four keys, anyway.' She sounded just as excited. The thought of her abductors trapped down the shaft and the prospect of them being arrested was one that she could relish. Especially if she could witness it in person.

Five minutes elapsed. Then two police cars were seen entering the estate and heading for Unit Four. Maxine got out of the car, ran across to greet Peter Travers and handed over the keys he would need.

'Get back into George's car now, please,' he responded. This was no time for emotion. 'Then keep it locked until we've made the arrests. Two of 'em, you say? And there's only one way in to the unit?'

'The hatch to the tunnel they went down is at the far end, the right corner as you view it from here. We shut it and put the bolt across, so unless there's another tunnel exit they're trapped inside. But take care, Peter. I don't want anything to happen to you.'

Maxine was swallowing hard as she returned to George's car. Security came with heavy responsibility but police work was about direct danger.

The women watched and waited. Ten minutes went by. It was hot inside the car, instinctively George opened her window. Then they heard the noise of shouting, coming from inside the unit.

After that the unit door swung open and two men emerged. But they weren't the policemen. 'That's the two abductors.'

They headed for the blue Skoda. Then one of them gestured as he saw the state of the tyres. This was no sort of getaway car.

Where would they go? George started her car, ready to give chase.

Looking back later, she realised that was a mistake; it drew the men's attention towards them. Maxine picked up her phone to redial the police station – if there was anyone still there. The men started walking towards them. One of them still held the pair of industrial-strength bolt cutters.

It came to George that it had been a misjudgement to deflate the tyres. It made them the alternative getaway vehicle.

But there was no time for her to take evasive action. The men were beside the car now, one on each side. The bolt cutter appeared through George's open window and its jaws were wrapped round her wrist. He wasn't exerting pressure yet but there was no doubt he could.

'Open the doors,' the man commanded.

If the window hadn't been open George would have put her foot down and driven away but she had no doubt he would use the cutter if necessary. She didn't want to lose a hand and moved her other one to the internal unlocking button.

Two seconds later the men had occupied the rear seats. 'Now drive.'

George kept looking straight ahead as she started down the road of the estate and out to the road beyond.

'Into Bude or out to the A39?'

'Out!' came the instruction from the rear seat.

That was a pity. A traffic jam in Bude might give them chance to escape. She drove steadily towards the A39. Maxine was silent in the seat beside her.

Soon they had reached the A39. 'Which way now?'

'Left. Towards Barnstaple.'

George decided there was no choice but to obey. For now the bolt cutters were critical. Maybe, once they were away from the town and in the middle of nowhere, she and Maxine would be dumped and the car taken over by the men.

No doubt they would remove their phones in the process. These were professionals.

For a few miles there was silence in the car. Then George heard the men arguing in the back seat. It was some European language or other but not English. Unfortunately it was one she didn't speak.

'Go right at the next turning.' Now he was talking in English.

George slowed. There was only a minor side road. The signpost said it led to Thursdon, a village she'd never heard of.

'You mean, to Thursdon?'

'Yes. Just do as you're told.'

Up to now Maxine had been silent as she sat beside her. George wondered what the long-term effect would be, seized for a second time by the same men. Poor girl, it might crush her completely.

George turned her head ever so slightly and glanced at her companion. To her surprise Maxine looked almost animated.

'Keep the Focus, George.'

So she was hanging on.

'It's hardly a Fiesta of Fun, is it?'

It was an odd comment. Bizarre. Suddenly George realised that her friend was speaking to her in code.

'We could do with a Lone Ranger,' she replied.

'Or some sort of Explorer, to help us escape,' came the reply.

'Shut it, girls,' came an angry command from the back. But it was too late, the warning had been given and the plan made.

It was a very minor road. George speeded up now, eyes alert to the hazard she expected ahead. There was no warning but she saw the steep dip and a fast-flowing stream crossing the road beyond.

George waited until they had dipped into the middle of the ford. Then she hit the brakes and the car stalled. At the same instant she pushed open her door and leapt out into the knee-deep stream. She sensed rather than saw Maxine doing the same thing on the other side.

Then, a moment of genius, she pushed the button that would

lock the car doors. The men were locked into the rear seats, while the stream was gushing in through the front doors that the women had left open.

They didn't wait to see what would happen next. Both splashed to the rear of the car and started running back down the road. It was unlikely they would be chased down a public road but neither wanted to take the chance.

'Have you still got your phone?' panted George as they got round the next corner.

'It's been on all the time, George. On my lap. I'd just got through to the station when the thugs turned up. If they've been listening to our various directional discussions they should be here soon.'

And, indeed, George could hear a police siren approaching in the distance. A second later the car appeared.

On seeing the women the car slowed but Maxine waved it on. 'They're stuck in the ford, just along here. They're too wet to get far. But I'd turn off the siren. No point in giving them warning.'

CHAPTER 40

In the end it took nearly four hours for order to be restored. And it wasn't restored in every case.

Jamie and Holly had driven on and apprehended the two abductors while they were still trying to reach the front seats of the car. They had been charged with abducting George and Maxine (that crime at least was well-attested; other charges would no doubt follow). They were now being safely held in separate cells at Bude Police Station.

George and Maxine had waded back through the stream and into their car and managed to restart it. Then George had driven out, turned round and driven carefully back through the ford and on to Bude.

They had gone to the station to recover the keys from the abductors, then on to Unit Four on Kings Hill Estate; what on earth had happened to Peter Travers and Joe Tremlitt, were they safe? George bitterly regretted her comments earlier about the risks involved in making an arrest.

They parked next to the abandoned police cars, unlocked the unit door and went inside. George shone her torch round carefully. There was no sign of the two policemen in the main unit, either standing to greet them or lying injured on the ground.

She saw, though, that the hatch had been re-bolted and padlocked. It was a good job they had the key. Soon the metal door had been pulled back and George could shine her torch into the tunnel. What would they find?

The women's first emotion was relief. There was an unnerving pause and then Peter Travers' face looked back up at them. He seemed not to be injured and extremely relieved to see them.

But something had happened to Joe. 'Can you ring for an ambulance, please. Then help me to make him more comfortable.'

Maxine lowered herself into the tunnel while George went outside to phone the emergency number. 'I'm ringing on behalf of Police Sergeant Peter Travers,' she said. 'One of his colleagues has been injured while making an arrest.'

She paused to hear the immediate response. 'No, I don't know the nature of the injury,' she answered, 'we've only just found them. We're currently inside Unit Four on the Kings Hill Estate. But Sergeant Travers says please send someone as quickly as possible.'

Then, leaving the unit door open ready for the ambulance men, she went back inside to see what she could do to help.

For a small woman the first stage of getting into the tunnel was easy. Once she was down she shone her torch along: it was longer than she'd expected. It went far beyond the area covered by the unit above. Peter and Maxine were out of sight.

For a second she wondered whether to wait to show the ambulance men where to come. But even with lights flashing they would be a few minutes. She surely had time for a quick look.

The tunnel was only a couple of feet across and had been cut roughly through the soil. If it had been a rock base they would have been stymied, but if you were strong enough earth was moveable. Suddenly it dawned on her what the machine with blades was for: it was a tunnelling device. Probably electric powered, she thought, a petrol engine would make too much of a racket – might be heard in the unit above.

Getting a patient out via the tunnel would be no easy task. Especially as Joe was quite tall. She wondered how he was injured.

George crawled along, regretting now that she was wearing shorts. They had been useful earlier when she plunged into the stream at the ford; now she wished she was wearing jeans. This wasn't doing her knees any good at all.

The tunnel had several bends but she could hear Peter and Maxine talking at the far end. She struggled on. At one point a water pipe crossed the passage just below the ceiling and she cracked her head against it. A brief pause to check she wasn't bleeding, then she carried on.

Finally she emerged into a small, brick-lined chamber that, she reckoned, must be below the British Telecom unit.

Joe was sitting on Peter Travers' jacket, just about conscious but in a great deal of pain. Then she looked down, saw his arm and felt sick. The arm had been smashed: the wrist was hanging at a strange angle and there was blood everywhere. The thugs must have gone for him with the tunnelling device.

Maxine saw her distress. 'Sorry George, there's nothing we can do except make him a little more comfortable.'

'I'll get back and wait for the ambulance,' responded George, straining to hold herself together. She wished she had not come in. But at least she could tell the ambulance men what to expect: a tiny passage and a traumatised patient.

George had been an enthusiastic caver in her younger days. It always seemed further back than it had been going forward. Eventually she reached all the way back into Unit Four. She went outside, then lost control and was violently sick into the gutter.

Up to now she had not really believed the thugs would use their bolt cutter on her wrist. Now she knew that they had not been bluffing.

The ambulance arrived a moment later. 'So where's the patient?' asked the driver as he stepped out. His mate, an equally cheerful woman, came round from the other side.

'It's a challenge,' George replied. 'He was attacked by a criminal with a tunnelling device, his arm is shattered. He's conscious but in agony.'

'But where is he?' asked the driver's mate, repeating the question.

'In a chamber, the far end of a narrow tunnel. It's about two feet wide. The gang dug it between here and the place next door. The chamber's about six feet square, four feet high. Sergeant Travers and my friend Maxine are with him.'

The two paramedics looked at one another for a moment.

'I reckon the first thing is to give him morphine. Sounds like it'll take a while to get him out. I'll go, Danny. I'm slimmer than you.'

'OK, Sal. Meanwhile I'll grab the narrow stretcher that's got castors. And a rope to pull it out with.'

In the end it took another two hours before Joe was retrieved from the tunnel and whisked off to the main Cornish hospital in Truro. But was his arm damaged beyond repair? Only time would tell.

Once the recovery process was under way, Peter Travers did a swap with Jess Holland, who he learned had been called in to the station as an extra pair of hands.

Peter Travers wanted to be with Joe but had a station full of criminals to interview. There were only five police cells and three of them were occupied. If they kept arresting at this rate, he mused, they'd need to rent out cells in Barnstaple.

He took Maxine back to the station with him. 'I need you for an identity parade.' Maxine looked puzzled and he realised he had not been clear. 'I mean to *judge* it, not to be part of it as a pretend villain. I want those thugs clobbered for everything.'

'What about me?' asked George.

'Ah. I know it's a bit unofficial but maybe Jess could help you. I need a full account of what's gone on in the chamber. I can see they've done damage but it'd be good to have a professional description and some accompanying photos. Can you find out which cables have been hacked, for example?'

'Couldn't British Telecom tell you that?'

'No doubt they will when they do the repair, but I'd like something to charge these guys with today. Though seriously injuring a police officer is plenty to be going on with. Mindless thugs, I saw the attack myself.'

Once Travers had returned to the station and Tremlitt had been whisked off to hospital, George Gilbert and Jess Holland had Unit Four to themselves.

George first made sure the unit door was locked. She didn't want any more interruptions. Then she took a few minutes to explain to the policewoman what had been going on and why they needed to struggle through the narrow tunnel.

'You'd better go first, Jess. I'll come right behind you. Fortunately Peter Travers left his torch, so we can have one each.'

George pretended it was a caving exercise in an attempt to stop herself worrying too much about Joe. She was much slimmer than Jess so the journey took longer than her previous entrance. She managed, this time, not to crack her head.

Finally they reached the chamber and could each change from a crawling posture into a low crouch.

'Right. Let's get this done fast,' urged Jess. Her new position made her knees ache.

George shone her torch round carefully. There were just three encased internet cables coming into this chamber, all at floor level. Two were four inches in diameter, the third was smaller.

As far as she could see, nothing had happened to the larger cables but the small one had been sheered completely in two.

'I reckon that's been caused by that bolt cutter,' said George. 'Can you take a few photographs, please, Jess?'

'There are no clues as to where it comes from,' observed Jess.

There were no labels on the cables. George hoped she might be able to work out which the sheered one was – specifically, where it had come from – using cable maps from the internet.

'I can't see any other damage,' she concluded, after scanning the chamber carefully. 'Right, let's get out of here. You first, Jess.'

Visiting the internet connection chamber had been an interesting experience. But it was one that she hoped never to repeat.

CHAPTER 41

In the end Peter Travers decided that an identity parade would take too long to organise at this moment. It was irrelevant, anyway, for the crimes that had been committed that morning.

Instead Maxine viewed the two thugs through the one-way glass of the interview room and confirmed that they were indeed the two who had abducted her a fortnight earlier. It would be better, he decided, to conduct an interview on this crime when he was ready.

In any case there should soon be more evidence available. The blue Skoda in which the two had arrived at Unit Four was now in the hands of Scene of Crime Officers. Peter Travers hoped they would find some trace of Maxine's DNA inside it. The boot, at least, didn't look to have been used much in the past fortnight. There was a good chance the ski slot in the rear seat hadn't been used at all.

There was also Maxine's bathrobe. This she had secured from George's linen basket and handed over in a large plastic bag. Unless the kidnappers had both worn plastic gloves throughout the abduction there was a good chance of finding the criminals' DNA on that too.

Peter's interviews with each of the thugs had been unproductive. Neither had said anything significant.

'Your sentence might be reduced if you helped with our enquiries,' he urged them. But there had been no response at all.

After the interviews he had rung Truro Hospital. Joe was already prepped for the emergency operation. The patient might be ready for a short visit, the doctor advised, by Monday afternoon.

Peter had agreed to have a light lunch with the women in the Falcon, partly because he was hungry after the morning's excursions, and partly because he wanted to know more of their side of the events. So Maxine got her lunch-date after all.

He wouldn't admit it but he was also keen to tap into their outside-the-box thinking.

Maxine and George first brought him up to date on how they had captured the two criminals who for a time had used their vehicle as an escape car.

'I had no idea where we were heading when we hit that ford,' said George.

'I do,' responded Maxine. 'They were taking us back to the hideaway farm. To put us down the coal hatch, leave us to fester without food or water and make off in our car. No one would think to look for it, would they? I mean, it's got no connection with them at all.'

'Huh, I can't even claim it's my car. And no one would think to look in the hideaway farm for us. It could have been a slow lingering death for us both.' She turned quizzically to Maxine. 'But how did you know?'

'Do you remember them starting to talk in some foreign language? That was Dutch. I don't speak it fluently but I had a

291

two-year course in the Netherlands soon after I joined GCHQ, so I understand much more than I can speak. That was the plan they cobbled together.'

'So that was how you knew we were coming to a ford?'

'Yes. It was the one I first heard splashing outside the car a fortnight ago. Peter and I drove through it again on Wednesday.'

'OK,' said the policeman. 'I haven't got everything but that'll do for now.' He turned to his other lunch companion. 'George, what can you tell me about what our criminals were doing in Unit Four? And what on earth took you both there in the first place?'

'Well, d'you remember, last night we were wondering what crime you could commit by accessing the internet. And in particular, what crime might bring you to Bude?'

'Yes. We hadn't a clue.'

'Well, I woke up this morning with the glimmerings of an idea. Just suppose that the motive for this elaborate crime was not hacking the internet but rather bring it to a halt. Or to be more precise, bringing one limb to a halt for a few days. That might be a rational reason for coming to Bude.'

'But I thought you said access to the internet could be done anywhere?'

'Yes, but blocking is a different problem. The internet has massive redundancy, you see.'

She could see that Peter was looking puzzled and realised she needed to avoid technical terms. 'I mean, there are lots of internet routes from one place to another, so a break in one route doesn't stop traffic altogether.'

Peter nodded slowly. 'Just as there are lots of ways to travel from Bude to, say, Exeter?'

'That's right. So if you're going to block the internet, you don't want to work on the arcs that link places together, you want to be at one of the nodes – I mean a point where they come together. Like Bude.'

Maxine could see where her friend was heading. 'And Bude is a good place to choose, Peter. It's where the various cables that come ashore have to be processed and their signals boosted. A sort of internet junction box.'

'And to answer your original question, Peter, our criminals were using Unit Four to access the British Telecom Unit next door in order to get at one particular cable from Crooklets Beach. Which, I'm sorry to say, they've cut through completely using their bolt cutter.'

'D'you know which cable that is?'

'Not yet. I need to spend some time browsing with Google. There are maps of all the underground cables somewhere if you look hard enough.'

'Right, Peter,' said Maxine. 'George and I have each given you something new. So what have you got for us?'

Peter looked downcast and Maxine realised she hadn't done much for his self-confidence. 'For example, what did you learn in this morning's interviews?'

'Damn all,' the policeman said, looking frustrated. 'They've been carefully trained by someone very clever to say nothing at all. Which means, ladies, that we have no clue at all as to their leader. These guys are brutal technocrats, they'll do as they're told but they couldn't have invented the whole scheme.'

George, too, wanted to give him some encouragement. 'OK, leave that for a moment. Can you tell us anything interesting about your interview yesterday with that convict?'

'Christian Holdsworth? Yes, I did learn something. It turns out that he was an old school friend of Fairclough – that's the chap we started looking for a couple of weeks ago. He had a different surname in those days. They went into business to-gether – at least, Fairclough would use his contacts in the trade to dispose of anything that Holdsworth could pinch.'

'It was some sort of partnership,' said Maxine doubtfully.

'Yes. They both ended up in jail, after which they went their separate ways. It was that friendship, years later, which led Holdsworth to head for Fairclough's cottage. Couldn't under-stand where he'd gone. He was very cross when I told him that Fairclough had gone missing.'

There was silence for a few moments.

'Don't you think it would be very odd, Peter,' asked George, 'if there were two lots of serious crime going on here at exactly the same time?'

'How d'you mean?'

'Isn't it at least possible that Fairclough has been finished off by the same gang that's committed all these other crimes?'

'You mean, happening to be in the wrong place, like Ben Farthing?'

'But we know what happened to Ben. He was just very unlucky.'

'And couldn't Fairclough have been equally unlucky?'

Maxine added, 'For example, how could a house clearance man find himself at the wrong house?'

'Easy,' the policeman answered. 'There are loads of cottages round here with the same name. You could easily get into a muddle and go to the wrong one.'

'And if he did that, there'd be another cottage around here of the same name, which he never turned up at, which is still waiting to be cleared. Peter, what's the matter?' For the policeman seemed buoyed with hope, remembering something.

'You know, we had a call via the Visitor Centre sometime last week. They reported a call from some chap in Crackington who said he'd been let down by Fairclough – his mother's house was completely uncleared.'

'What was the name of his cottage – the let-down man's mother, I mean?'

'I don't think they said. It didn't seem very important at the time. But we could go round to the Centre on the way back to the station.'

'There's one other thing from what you've just told us,' said George. 'It's probably not important but did you say something early on about Fairclough having changed his name?'

'Well remembered. He used to be called Barry Johnstone.'

'Am I right in thinking that your team will have carried out lots of searches under the name Fairclough, finding out, say, where he stores the furniture from all the houses he clears?'

'Yes. And all of 'em a dead loss.'

'But have you done those searches under the name Johnstone? I mean, he could have hired the warehouse before he changed his name and never found a plausible way to change it.'

'Damn, damn, damn.' The policeman looked cross with himself.

'Easy, Peter. You only had the name yesterday afternoon. It's Saturday afternoon, will there be anyone else in the station? George and I could come back with you if you liked and try it out.'

CHAPTER 42

On Saturday afternoon in high season the Bude Visitor Centre was crowded. The staff on the counter didn't look too pleased to be asked to undertake an urgent administrative task by the town's senior policeman.

'Going through our old contact records will take us half an hour,' protested the manager. 'Couldn't you wait till Monday?'

'Why don't I wait to collect the answer?' asked George, smiling sweetly. 'You two can go on up to the station, start on the other business.'

The offer wasn't completely unselfish. There were desk-top computers for hire in the Centre. George wanted to find out which internet cables landed at Bude. That could be done as well here as anywhere.

Maxine and Peter headed off and George hired a Centre computer for half an hour. Then she started to search for maps of the world's undersea internet connections. There were dozens, in differing levels of detail. Most showed the spread of cables across the Atlantic and the Pacific but there were a few charts that focussed on Europe.

Most of the maps gave a broad sweep. When she tried zooming in to look at connections into Cornwall, and specifically Bude, the lines showing individual cables were hard to distinguish. She read that Cornwall carried a quarter of all the UK's internet cable traffic. Bude and Widemouth, three miles down the coast, were often lumped together.

Then she found one. The map showed a thick line coming in from New York – maybe that meant a pair of cables. And there was a thinner line linking Bude to Curracloe, a small town on the coast of southern Ireland.

There was more work needed to take this clue forward but her time was up. The Centre manager hastened over with a slip of paper. 'Can you get that to Sergeant Travers as soon as possible, please?'

George didn't even look at it, put it into the top of her ruck-sack. 'Thank you very much indeed. That might be very important. I'll take it straight away.'

When she got back to the police station, there was an officer on the front desk that she hadn't seen before. It was the officer with the mysterious lurgy, back to find out what was going on. Peter Travers and Maxine were the only two present alongside Jamie that she could see through the frosted glass, working in the office behind.

'I've got an urgent message for Sergeant Travers,' she explained and hastened past him before he could stop her. He started to chase, then was reassured when he saw that Peter Travers knew who she was. Dutifully he plodded back to his desk. Things seemed to have livened up here since he was last on duty.

'We've found one or two possible locations for Barry Johnstone,' said Maxine excitedly.

'Yes, the most interesting one – would you believe it – is another unit in the Kings Hill Estate . . .,' said the police sergeant.

'. . . only three units along from where we were this morning.'

Maxine seemed more enthused by the low-level security side of policing than she'd been by the long term national security at Cleave Camp. There she would never be more than a small cog in a large machine. If this case had opened her eyes to alternative careers, thought George, then it might have done some good after all. It might not be too late to change.

'The Visitor Centre gave me the name of the man from Crackington who had a bad deal from Fairclough – or whatever we should call him.'

'I don't care who it was, did they give you an address?' growled the policeman. It sounded like the pressure was getting to him.

'Yes. But that's not the address you want, is it, Peter? It was the man's deceased mother who was supposed to be having her cottage cleared. According to this note, anyway.'

She paused and then offered, 'Would you like me to ring him to find out what that address is? Then we can start to look for anywhere else with the same name, the place that Fairclough might have gone to by mistake.'

'Right. Sorry, George, it's been a hard day. I've been worried about Joe. Could you ring Crackington for me? Take care, though, he might still be grieving. You could use the phone in my office if you liked.'

Jamie was seated at his own desk. He looked up from his latest search, shook his head in a bemused fashion but made no comment. Today was obviously not a day for tight protocol.

George went into the sergeant's lair, sat at his desk and composed herself to make the call. For the police this could be a vital step forward. But it was more important to think herself into the attitude of the man she was calling.

Then she dialled the number, it was a landline. Was he in or was he out walking the cliffs? She could hardly blame him if he was, as it was a fabulous day.

'Hello. Samuel Wollacombe here.' He had a strong West Country accent.

'Good afternoon, Mr Wollacombe. My name is George Gilbert. I'm ringing from Bude Police Station.'

'Oh yes? What do you want?' He was polite enough, anyway.

'I'm chasing up a phone call you made to the Bude Visitor Centre a month ago. It was about Barry Fairclough and a house clearance.'

'Oh, don't get me going on that again. I told the woman at the Centre I wuz real pi . . . upset. I'd paid the deposit, like, and the man just didn't turn up. But I found someone else in the end. Mother's old cottage is cleared all right now.'

'Right. Would you mind telling me the address of the cottage he was meant to clear, please?'

'Longridge Cottage, it was. Out in the wilds, a mile down a country track, near Nether Crackington. It's been there for centuries. I haven't sold the place yet, mind. Why are you asking?'

'We're just trying out a few ideas, sir. Mr Fairclough's disappeared, you see. No one's seen him or even heard from him for about a month. You're the last person we know of where he was expected.'

'Oh dear. And here's me giving the bloke a bad name. I hope I've not judged him wrong. Well, if you wants to check the place out, let me know. Trouble is, I've had someone else clear it in the meantime. Won't that take out the evidence?'

'The name of the cottage might be the vital clue. We'll let you know if we need any more information, Mr Wollacombe. Thank you very much indeed.'

'So the question is,' said George, as she rejoined the others, 'can we find another Longridge Cottage around here? One that's also out in the country. With the only access via an unmade track.'

'If it's an old place on its own, out in the country,' said Peter Travers, 'there's some chance it'll be on one of these large-scale maps.'

'Or even Google Earth,' added George.

'I don't suppose you'll want us with you in Kings Hill Estate,' said Maxine. 'I can't think of any excuse for you to take us there, anyway. Neither of us has even met Fairclough.'

She mused for a moment. 'Why don't you leave George and me here to scour all the sources and the maps, looking for another Longridge Cottage? That duty bloke out there will look after us. In the meantime you and Jamie can go and check out the estate unit we've just identified.'

'That's fine by me,' said Peter. 'Jamie, would you like another trip? See where all the trouble was this morning, where poor old Joe nearly copped it. I found a spare key in Fairclough's cottage, remember. If it fits and we can get in, we might even find his van.'

CHAPTER 43

'They've been an awfully long time,' observed Maxine. 'I hope there's not been more trouble on the estate.'

'I shouldn't think so,' replied George. 'Not with live criminals, anyway. They're all locked up down below us. It's more likely they've found something in the unit that needs extensive analysis. Maybe even another call to the Scene of Crime people.'

'They might be assembling all the evidence there before they go to check out Longridge Cottage 2,' said Maxine thoughtfully. 'Trouble is, they won't want us to go there with them.'

'We've done the task we set ourselves, Maxine. Found one more Longridge Cottage, anyway. I reckon we've done our bit for the day. It's a fabulous day, not one to spend indoors. We could leave a note and go for a walk. We can catch up with Peter this evening.'

Maxine thought for a moment.

'If you don't mind a drive before we start, there's one more place we talked about in the pub on Friday – crumbs, that's only yesterday – where there might be something to find. It means going up towards Cleave Camp?'

'Fine by me. My car's survived one dousing today. It should be able to get us as far as the Camp.'

The car that George had borrowed from the garage did not

have a Sat Nav fitted, so Maxine did the navigating. The route toward Cleave Camp, through the back of Stratton and then along a series of winding narrow roads, was not that easy to follow.

'They don't bother much with signposts in this part of Cornwall,' observed George as they came to a T-junction where it was guesswork as to whether she should turn right or left.

'It's left here. It's probably part of a security system designed by Colin Caldwell. Designed before Sat Nav was invented, I should think. I mean, most terrorist can't read a map.'

'That's 'cos they're too young,' suggested George. 'But I presume there are sensors linked to the Camp somewhere under all these roads?'

Maxine did not reply, either out of respect for an Official Secret or because she knew the answer and that voicing it would bring ridicule. George decided it would be best not to take this discussion any further.

They drove down a steep, wooded valley. 'Can you park over there?' asked Maxine, pointing to an off-road area near the bottom.

George reversed in and the pair got out and then fetched their walking shoes from the boot.

'Cleave Camp is on top of the next hill,' said Maxine, pointing through the wood. 'The valley that runs up the far side of this stream is the only place where you might extract water from one of the springs. There are springs on the coastal side too, but that's all open slope. There would always be a risk of Coast Path walkers spotting it.'

She pointed. 'There's a path winding up the valley. I suggest we walk up through the woods for a couple of miles, see what we can find.'

It was a pleasant enough stroll through the woods, anyway. They were sheltered by the trees from the burning heat of the afternoon sun.

'The thing we need to watch,' said Maxine, 'is that slope on the far side. That's got Cleave Camp perched on the top. If our composite theory is correct, there should be a pipe running down it somewhere from a spring near the top.'

'We'll do well to spot it,' retorted George. 'It's a hundred yards away, there's loads of bracken everywhere. And plenty of trees. It'd be easy enough to hide a pipe in there, wouldn't it?'

Maxine had to admit she was correct and looked a bit disconsolate.

'How about climbing up the hill to look for the spring itself?' asked George.

'Trouble is, although only one spring is marked on this map, there may be half a dozen running now. It could take us hours to find them. And it'd be hard work struggling up that steep hillside without a path.'

'OK. So that's a non-starter. But could we listen for the sound of pumping?' George continued. 'I mean, for the idea to work it's got to be pumped more or less continuously.'

It meant walking without talking, which was next to impossible for the two women, but they managed it for an hour without hearing anything except the distant calls of birds and the quiet tinkle of the stream below, cascading over the stones.

Then, in the distance, a little further up the valley, they spotted a small thatched cottage.

'That's off the beaten track,' said George, breaking her silence. 'It's not obvious how you'd reach it by car,' she went on. 'There's no proper road for some way.'

'I reckon we'll stop when we get as far as that. We're starting to get well away from the Camp now. If you were going to do anything to the water you wouldn't want to come as far as this.'

That was true. At least, it made sense from their logic.

But as they drew closer to the cottage the pair could hear, just about, the steady sound of a whirring electric motor. It was going on for a long time. If someone was running a hoover round the place, they were giving it a very long clean indeed.

George stopped and looked at her friend quizzically, received a shrug in reply. If they hadn't been looking for such a sound there was nothing strident or outrageous that would catch their attention.

But if you were looking for the sound of a continually operated pump, sucking water out of some spring high above, then it was a very suspicious sound indeed.

CHAPTER 44

Maxine's imaginings about problems for Peter Travers on the Kings Hill Estate proved, later, to have been slightly exaggerated. But the visit to Barry Johnstone's unit took far more energy than he had expected.

He and Jamie had driven past Unit Four, where they saw a Scene of Crime van parked outside, alongside a blue Skoda with four flat tyres. They continued and parked outside Unit Eight.

The unit was next door but one to the place he had been earlier. Was that merely a coincidence? No doubt George would tell him it wasn't, though he could see no possible connection between the two units.

The two policemen got out. Travers tried the spare key he had found the week before in Fairclough's cottage. Would it work?

If it didn't, then this unit must belong to some other Johnstone altogether and the pair could go back to the station. It was true that Travers had broken into Fairclough's cottage – or at least used the key from under the doormat. But as an official keeper of the law he could not justify breaking into a well-locked unit simply because the tenant's name matched one that had come up in his inquiries.

The key fitted without even a struggle, like a hand inside a glove. This must be Fairclough's furniture store, the place where he kept items between collection and disposal. The two police-men exchanged glances and pulled open the unit door. Then they stepped inside.

Travers had his torch with him and quickly shone it round. Irritatingly, the light switch in this unit was also hidden. But there was nothing grotesque in view, as far as he could see.

There was, though, an unpleasant smell. Both policemen had smelled such an odour once or twice before. It was not good news.

Travers shone his torch round a second time, now more slowly. At the back of the unit, behind some settees and a pair of kitchen cabinets, he now saw a large white van and beside it a green Astra estate. Some instinct told him that these were the places to start their search: one of these might well be the source of the smell.

He didn't have a key to either of the vehicles. They were both locked. But holding up his torch to the window of the Astra, he could see a set of keys had been inserted in the ignition. Carefully he shone his torch over the car's interior. No, there was nothing untoward at all. Fairclough wasn't in here.

What about the van? Even standing outside, the smell seemed stronger here. He shone his torch into the cab: nothing except for more keys in the ignition.

'Must be inside,' said Jamie.

Travers agreed. He had no qualms, now, about forcing his way in. The owner had been missing for several weeks. He had a horrible feeling about what he would find inside.

Both policemen looked around for something to help them

force open the door.

'This'll do,' said Travers, seizing an iron bar from beside an old coal-fired oven – it had probably served as a poker. He turned and jammed it through the door handle. Then both men took a deep breath and gave it a massive heave.

There was a crack and one of the doors swung open. The smell went from being a minor nuisance to being an intolerable stench. A large swarm of flies flew out.

Looking in, the policemen could just see the remains of a man. An inspired guess would be that he had been dead for several weeks. And it would be amazing if the body was not the remains of the missing van owner, Barry Fairclough.

Coughing, waving away the flies, the two policemen retreated to the front door of the unit.

'That's handy,' said Sampson, 'we can collect SOCO from two doors down. They'll be glad to get to a crime so quickly.'

Peter Travers and Jamie Sampson were down in Unit Eight for a couple more hours. They had to make sure the SOCO were focussed on the objects most likely to affect this case. Dr Sarah Maxwell, acting police pathologist, joined them soon after they had arrived.

'I don't think this can be anything but manslaughter or murder,' said Travers. 'The poor chap was locked in the van. He could have hardly driven it into the unit and then committed suicide.'

'Unless there was someone helping him to do it,' replied the pathologist. She knew it was always a mistake to draw conclusions too quickly.

She went on, 'He might have wanted to end his life in this unit because his business here had gone horribly wrong. One important question, I think, is whether he died inside the van or was already dead when he was put in there.'

'Have you any idea what caused his death in the first place?'

'I won't know that until I've conducted the post-mortem. What are you doing first thing tomorrow morning, Peter?'

The sergeant was not keen to attend but knew that this was part of his duties.

The policeman turned from the pathologist to the Scene of Crime chief. 'There's not much point in you spending ages dusting every item of furniture for fingerprints,' said Travers. 'Collecting this sort of stuff was what the man did. Some of it's been here for ages.'

'The key item has to be the van,' added Sampson. 'Not just because that's where we found his body, but because, on our current theory, it was going to the wrong property by mistake that got him killed.'

'Right,' said the chief. 'Let's assume for a moment it was murder. It's certainly not an accident. I guess what we find will depend on whether the villains wore plastic gloves for the whole sequence. But first I'll need the vehicle keys.'

The question fired another one in Travers' mind. 'That's another thing, I suppose. How did the car get here? Who drove that? I can't believe the dead man kept it here. He'd got plenty of space to park at his cottage. And he'd need a car there for everyday life. It's not near any village, I've been there. So DNA from it might be helpful.'

'We've been looking for this chap for nearly a fortnight, you see.' Jamie Sampson added this nugget, it was part of the overall picture.

'One more thing,' added Travers. 'We've not come across his working diary. He must have had one. He couldn't possibly remember every address he was supposed to clear and the date he had agreed to clear it. It isn't in his cottage. Can you check if it's in either of his vehicles?'

'Right,' said the SOCO chief. 'That's plenty for us to be getting on with. We'll let you know how we get on. I fear it could all take some time.'

The man's body was not the only remains they had to work on. As the team delved further into the depths of the van they found a second body.

This one was a young, red-haired female.

CHAPTER 45

Peter Travers and Jamie Sampson returned to the police station at four thirty, leaving the Scene of Crime team to collect what evidence they could. The policemen discovered that George and Maxine were no longer present, they had gone off for a walk.

Their note, though, identified another Longridge Cottage, in addition to the one Fairclough had failed to visit.

'D'you reckon it's too late to make a call, Jamie?' asked Travers. 'It'll be after five by the time we get there – on Saturday evening. Whoever lives there might be getting ready to start a barbecue.'

'A lot's happened today, guv. We can't be sure what Fairclough's murderer has picked up. For instance, he might have seen the SOCO van outside Unit Eight. If Fairclough went to this place by mistake it might be the crucial location. I'd say we'd best strike while the iron is hot.'

Travers was pleased to see that the man was not bothered too much by his official hours. There'd be plenty of other days, quieter days, when he might be sent home early. Today the adrenalin was pumping through both of their veins.

Travers opted to drive, relying on his younger companion to coax Sat Nav into picking their route. Longridge 2 was certainly off the beaten track, the last half mile looked to be across country.

As they drove the two men discussed how the interview should be handled.

'The key question is whether or not this chap encountered Fairclough: was this the place he came to and visited in error?' said Sampson.

'True. But that might not be the best question to ask. After all, the mix-up happened a month ago. If nothing took place he might have forgotten all about it. And it'd be easy enough for the owner to deny there'd been any clearance visit at all. Then we'd be stuck.'

'So what do you think would be better?'

Peter Travers told him what he had in mind. A broad grin spread across Jamie Sampson's face. His boss had some wisdom after all.

They traversed various minor roads, with fewer and fewer signposts. Finally they came to a dead end. The gate ahead of them proclaimed " Longridge". Beyond was a gravel track with grass in the middle.

'No reason for Fairclough to suspect he was in the wrong place if he came this way,' observed Travers. Sampson got out and opened the gate, closing it once they were through.

Half a mile further, heading steadily down a wooded valley, they reached another gate, this one marking the entrance to a small, attractive, thatched cottage. Once again Sampson dealt with the gate while Travers parked nearby.

'Remember, Jamie, someone or other killed poor old Fairclough. We owe it to him to find out who that was. It might have happened here.'

The two walked over to the cottage and Travers gave a hefty knock. For all he knew the owner might be out in the rear garden.

A minute later a slim man, aged around forty, came to the door. He was obviously surprised to see a pair of policemen. Travers had deliberately given him no advance warning of their visit.

'Good afternoon, sir. I'm Sergeant Travers and this is Constable Sampson. We're both from Bude. Could we come in for a few minutes, please?'

The man hesitated for a second and then bowed to the inevitable. 'By all means. My name is Jagger – Nick Jagger. Not the singer, I'm afraid. My wife is out for the moment. Would you like a cup of tea?'

He led them inside and they took seats on the settee in the lounge. Travers declined the offer of tea.

'What we've come about, sir, is house clearance.'

He was watching the man carefully and sensed that he flinched. It was only for a millisecond, he might have been mistaken. But it gave him confidence to continue.

'I'm sorry. I don't need house clearance. I'm not going anywhere.'

'To be more precise, sir, we're investigating a man who does house clearances in the Bude area. You see, he's disappeared.'

Again Travers caught a sense of unease. Only this time it seemed to last longer.

'I don't understand. What's this got to do with me?'

'Well, you can imagine, we've been checking the places where the missing man would go to sell items he'd removed. Making a list of dates he'd been seen at each. He'd visit them all regularly, so it's easy to tell when he was last seen. Our conclusion is that he disappeared around July 12^(th).

Jagger was perceptibly uncomfortable now, his back arched and his body tense. 'I still don't see what this has to do with me.'

'The thing is, the antique shop where he called on July 11^(th) remembered the conversation. I think there was a gentle romance going on between him and the owner. "I've got a good clearance job tomorrow," he told her. "Place called Longridge Cottage. So I might have one or two fine antiques for you next week." That was the last time she ever saw him, he never came again. And that's why we're here, sir.'

Jagger was so tense now that he stood up. 'Really, sergeant. This is just hearsay. I've never called for a clearance man, never wanted one, never paid for one.' He looked upset.

'But the thing is, sir, have you met one?'

Jagger must have realised he looked ridiculous standing up and sat down again. He took a few deep breaths. Then he faced Travers again.

'The thing is, I may have met him. I can't remember the date but it must have been around then that someone came here in a large white van. Announced they'd been asked to clear the place. I told them they must have got the wrong name or the wrong address. Like I told you, I told him I wasn't going anywhere. After a while he saw he was getting nowhere either and drove off. I've not seen him since.'

'Right, sir, that's the essence of your story. I'd like you to come with us back to the police station. There we can conduct this interview at greater length, record all the details.'

'What if I don't want to come?'

'We'll arrest you. You've just admitted being the last person to see someone that we know has disappeared. If necessary we'll come back here with a search warrant. The van must be around somewhere. So, will you come with us, sir?'

Jagger was trapped between a rock and a hard place. He swallowed hard, then said, 'OK then, I'll come.'

The two policemen stood on either side of him to make sure he did not deviate in his path out of the door.

CHAPTER 46

'What on earth do you make of that?' George and Maxine had sat on the path through the valley, looking over to the thatched cottage beyond, for over forty minutes.

The reason for stopping so long was simple. Just after they'd got to the log by the path and sat down for a rest, Maxine had spotted a car coming down the track on the other side. As it got closer she realised that it was a police car.

Then, when it parked inside the gate and two policemen got out, she saw that they were Peter Travers and Jamie Sampson. She was about to give them a call and a wave when George managed to stop her.

'Maxine, they're on some sort of raid. We can't interrupt them, it might muck up everything. Let's just sit here quietly and watch what happens.'

They waited and waited. And then, after forty minutes, the policemen emerged again, this time accompanied by another man, presumably the owner, in weekend attire. They all got into the police car and it drove off.

'George, I reckon the man was the only one living there. There was no sign of a wife or anyone coming to the door to say good-bye. Why don't you and I go over there and have a look?'

'I can still hear the humming noise we caught earlier. The

chap's gone off and left it. Maybe the police didn't know anything about it.'

'It'd be good to have a look at that electric motor and see what it's powering anyway. If it is a water pump, and if it's drawing water out of a pipe and into that stream, that would be a crucial finding. It would explain why Cleave Camp is so short of water. That would be something for me to tell Caldwell on Monday morning.'

'Whereas if it was simply a fountain aerating the goldfish pond then we'd save ourselves a great deal of hassle by saying nothing at all.' Avoiding needless embarrassment was very important in George's line of work.

Both reflected for a moment.

'How long have we got?' asked Maxine.

'We can assume, I think, they were taking the man to the police station. That's a half hour journey each way. Then they'll have to question him when they get there. That's not a five minute job, even if he's completely innocent and handles it well. I'd say he'll be gone for a couple of hours at least.'

'So the next question is, how do we cross that stream?'

'And the answer, Maxine, is using those stepping stones over there, just above the cottage. I reckon that's how the owner gets onto this path. So let's go.'

It was harder work than they expected. If the cottage owner did indeed use the stepping stones to reach the path he must use a different route from the one they had taken. Their path involved what seemed like acres of nettles and brambles.

'Maybe wearing shorts was not such a good idea,' mused Maxine.

In the end they reached the stepping stones and crossed them without either of them falling in. Finding the path on the other side was easier. They knew it had to start at the stepping stones and they could follow it fairly easily up to the front of the cottage.

The women approached the cottage carefully but it was clear there was no one inside. Their attention was now on the noise of the electric motor.

'It's coming from round the back,' said Maxine.

They fought their way round the cottage: the garden had not been well maintained. Once they reached the rear it was obvious from where the noise was coming. A steady hum emerged from a wooden shed which stood away from the cottage.

'We might still be stymied,' warned Maxine. 'The question is, is it locked?'

Carefully they approached the shed and then tried the door. Evidently the cottage owner was not as security conscious as the Camp he was trying to disrupt. Or maybe living in the back of beyond had made him careless. Whatever the reason, the shed door was easy to open.

Inside a medium-sized pump was humming away steadily. It was attached on one side to a three inch pipe that they could see winding away across the hillside below Cleave Camp. On the other side was another pipe, this one led down into the stream below.

'Bingo,' said George. She took her camera out of her shorts

pocket and proceeded to take pictures in all directions. Some showed the cottage, others the pipe winding away from the pump towards Cleave Camp, and the remainder the pipe that ran down into the stream.

'Let's not push our luck here, George. We need to take these pictures back to show Peter. It might help him with his interview. We'll see which way the pipe water's going when we get down to the stepping stones.'

It was a sound plan and easy to follow. It was relatively easy to find their way back to the stepping stones. Then George spotted the place where the pipe came down to the stream and was able to confirm that the pump was indeed adding to the stream flow. Looking carefully they could see that the stream was flowing faster below the cottage than it was above.

Now came the scramble back to their original footpath. This time there was the hint of a path to follow, though it was still hard work.

'I bet the owner doesn't do this in shorts,' muttered Maxine.

Now they had to reverse their earlier route up the valley. The fact that they were now going downhill made it seem easier, though George suspected that the main factor was the knowledge that they had important information to impart.

An hour later they were back at the car and half an hour after that they were back at Bude Police Station.

CHAPTER 47

Back in Bude, Peter Travers was still looking utterly determined to solve his case, though no longer quite as certain that he could do so.

Fortuitously, George and Maxine had arrived back during a short break in the interview with the man from Longridge. He was still in the interview room downstairs, apparently, being guarded by Sampson.

He had, though, been given a cup of police station tea. The stuff was absurdly strong. That would give him something to think about.

Travers was pacing the open-plan office upstairs, seeking inspiration. He noticed the women come in but his mind was clearly elsewhere.

'Trouble?' asked George. She had known Peter Travers a long time and sensed when he could do with some help.

'He's not giving me anything, George. Refused to talk at first, even to repeat what he'd already told Jamie and me in the cottage.'

'So he's denying Fairclough even went there?'

'No, he'd admitted that in the cottage, realised he could hardly deny it later on. But he insisted Fairclough just went away again, once he realised he'd got the wrong place.'

'So can you prove that he didn't – go away, I mean?'

Travers sighed. 'Not yet. Somehow or other the man's picked up on Fairclough's work diary. Started asking me what was the next entry in it. Fairclough was a professional, he said: where else was he due that day? And why weren't we questioning them, the way we were questioning him?'

'But what made him think of that?'

'I had alluded to the diary in an attempt to trick him. Implied that was how we'd found him. But it didn't work. He's very clever.'

George reflected for a moment. 'Don't you think he's concentrating on the diary precisely because he knows you haven't got it?'

Maxine saw where she was heading. 'And the reason he knows that, Peter, is that he destroyed it himself, after he dealt with Fairclough. He probably found it in the man's clearance van and realised it had to go.'

'You mean, the non-diary is his "Get out of Jail free" card?'

'That's right. The thing is, Peter, he's desperate to get back to Longridge without having the place undergo a thorough search.'

'You think he's got something in there? The diary, for example? But surely, like you said, he would have destroyed that. I mean, it'd be dynamite.'

'The thing is, Peter, Maxine and I have been to Longridge. This afternoon, on our walk. It was pure chance. We were sitting in the wood opposite when we saw you arrive in the police car with Jamie, and later drive off with the owner.'

'So we knew there was no one there,' added Maxine. 'That

gave us chance to inspect it.'

Peter Travers boggled at them, looking puzzled and then very angry. 'What the hell were you two doing barging into my investigation? If his lawyer ever gets hold of this he'll make mincemeat of me. I'm shocked . . . really disappointed in both of you. We do have rules, you know.'

George knew that managers sometime got angry, especially when they were under pressure. When that happened she needed a rapid, objective response. 'I think you should see our pictures before you go back in.'

'We know what he was trying to hide, you see.'

The policeman eyed them for a second, realised they were serious. 'Let's have a quick look then. I've got to be back there in a minute. He'll have finished his tea by now.'

George pulled her phone camera out of her shorts pocket. 'Here.'

'We talked about it yesterday evening,' added Maxine. 'We were talking about the water table at Cleave after I'd talked to Roger Higgs. He said it might be lowered by extra pumping, say along the shoreline. We wondered if another way would be to put a pipe well inside the spring and then add a pump.'

'So we decided to use our walk to look for it – or rather, to listen for the sound on the hillside.'

'And that was what we heard coming out of Longridge. It was a low hum, the sort of thing you wouldn't notice unless that was what you were there looking for.'

'That's why he wants to get back there, Peter. He's threatening the water supply in the UK's top security post outside GCHQ

Cheltenham. Surely you can hold him on that while you go and look for yourself?'

A minute later the policeman had disappeared to continue the interview. He was more certain now where he was going. Nick Jagger – if indeed that was his real name – was not going home at the end of the session.

George and Maxine found themselves alone in the open plan.

'The trouble is, George, threatening Cleave Camp security can sound like a technical offence. It's not likely to be dealt with in open court, you see. They'd be worried that doing so would expose their weak security. The man might even get away with a suspended sentence.'

'That's ridiculous. Is there no way he can be linked to Fairclough?'

'Well. Suppose that Fairclough made some comment about the pumping when he was there? Asked if he could see it working, for example? Or asked why all that water needed to be put in the stream and where did it come from?'

'Yes, that would be a much stronger motive for doing away with an unexpected visitor like Fairclough. Can we get Peter to try asking him about that?'

The idea would be tried one day. But something else happened that evening which proved even stronger.

Travers spent another hour with Jagger. He didn't talk about the pumping at Longridge, he would need more preparation on that. But he did tell the man that he could consider himself arrested, would be spending the night in a police cell. The news seemed to dishearten him.

Travers took him down to the cells himself. Christian Holdsworth was in Cell 1 and looked at them carefully as they went past.

A few minutes later, as Travers returned alone from Cell 4, he heard a 'Pst' from Cell 1.

'I got something to tell ya,' the man said.

'We can't talk in the corridor,' the policeman replied. 'Let me put you in handcuffs, just so there's no problems, then we'll go to the interview room. But it had better be worth hearing, I'm very tired.'

A few minutes later Holdsworth sat in the chair recently occupied by Jagger.

'You're still looking for the bloke what did in my mate?'

'Fairclough? Or Johnstone, if you prefer. Barry, anyway. It's still an ongoing case.'

'You know that guy you've just taken to the cells?'

'Yes?'

'Well, he was the one what done it, I reckon.'

'And what makes you think that?'

' Well, you know I was staying in Barry's cottage?'

'Yes?'

'Well, he came there – that bloke I mean, the one you've just arrested. It was the first evening I was there.'

'Go on.' Peter wished now that he'd started the voice recorder when they began, but Holdsworth seemed calm enough. If it was worth hearing he would no doubt be happy to repeat himself.

'I'd got that string, see, across the way in, to warn me. So I knew when it pinged that someone was coming. It might have been Barry; but then again it might have been someone else – the police, for example.'

'So what did you do?'

'I hadn't got the hang of slipping out the back yet. So I hid in one of the wardrobes upstairs. Dunno why Barry hangs onto them, the door was starting to swing open.'

Travers was starting to realise that Holdsworth loved to talk. Probably because no one ever bothered to listen to him. He would need some encouragement to get to the crux.

'And what did you see?'

'It was that man – the one you just took to the cells. I was about six foot away, it was definitely him.'

'And what did he do?'

'There was some sort of large diary beside Barry's bed. I'd seen it when I first got there. I reckon it had his appointments and such like. This bloke picked it up, glanced inside and then looked very pleased with himself – very smug. He slipped it into his jacket pocket and walked back down the stairs.'

Holdsworth paused for a moment and looked at the policeman. 'D'you reckon that'll help prove he did it?'

CHAPTER 48

Sunday morning was another fine day and one for an early start. George had persuaded Maxine to join her at the Innovation Exhibition in Exeter.

'After all, your friend Peter is busy all morning at Fairclough's post-mortem. Lucky old him. And I need to be in Exeter anyway.'

Maxine looked unconvinced so George continued, 'It's an hour's drive, we don't need to stay all day. Can't you catch up with Peter this evening?'

Maxine had finally agreed to come. Peter was busy and she wanted the chance to synthesise the events of the last fortnight. Somehow George seemed to have a better grasp than her of the big picture.

As they set off up the hill past Delabole, George seemed keen that her friend took in the view. 'Look at those wind turbines, Maxine. They're really massive.' A few minutes later she was pointing out some more, closer to Launceston. 'Those ones are a lot older. But there's more of 'em.'

'Why are we bothering with wind turbines, George?'

'If they're properly coordinated they could be the fuel of the future. That's one of the things today's exhibition is all about.'

Something in her friend's voice suggested this was not just

small talk. But now she had more urgent questions of her own. 'George, I've not got the whole story. Can you help me?'

'You know as much as me, Maxine. Which parts don't make sense?'

'Well, for a start, what was achieved by cutting through that internet cable in Kings Hill Estate? I mean, the world's not come to a halt, has it? So what linked sabotaging the internet to disrupting Cleave Camp? And . . .'

'Maxine, I'll try and answer all your questions, but I can only do it one at a time. Why don't you sit back, enjoy the view and let me sketch out how the gang's plans evolved? You might see more wind farms.'

'That would be great.'

George drew a deep breath and then she began.

'The gang started with a major miscalculation. They knew internet cables came ashore at Bude. For reasons which I'll explain they were interested in a cable from Ireland. British Security had a site in Bude, said to process internet data. So they mistakenly assumed Cleave Camp was the internet hub and the place they needed to access.'

'So that was why I was abducted?'

'Maxine, I'm trying to tell the story as it unfolded. Be patient. Phase one was to disrupt the Camp by attacking its water. That meant pumping water out of the spring beneath the Camp so as to lower the water table. Eventually that would dry up the boreholes.'

'That's what we found yesterday.'

George nodded. 'Phase two was damaging the pipe from

Tamar Lake, so it could no longer offer a backup supply.'

'Peter and I saw that too. Both these phases were vital to their opening plan. I guess they hoped the Camp would call for water tankers from Barnstaple – which, one way or another, would give them access. So they dealt with Fairclough and then with Farthing, because they got in the way. They were collateral damage to the big scheme.'

'Sadly, Maxine. But, for whatever reason, the water shortage didn't trigger tankers. The gang had to know what was really going on in the Camp. They found that Tee-Side took its visitors as guests. Twice they kidnapped one of them. We can only guess exactly what happened to Colette but we know that you got away. Your escape was the end of phase three.'

'Any idea on why they picked on Colette and me?'

'I'd like to say it was because you were especially intelligent. I fear the truth, Maxine, is that they went for females because they thought it would be easier to make you admit what they wanted to know. After all, their main question by this stage was how the internet connected to the Camp. They didn't care two hoots about security.'

'Puts me in my place, anyway. I was seen as an easy touch.'

'Then somehow or other they learned that Bude had its own connecting hub in Kings Hill Estate. They'd been working on the wrong place.'

'I've an idea on that, George. The only reason we got onto it was an aside from Roger Higgs. But he implied that was a question he was asked quite often. Maybe he told them as well?'

'It'd be worth asking. So now, in phase four, they focussed all their efforts on the cables in the British Telecom Unit. After all, there was a deadline on their efforts – today – which I'll explain shortly.'

'They daren't go inside the unit, I suppose; there'd be cameras. They knew the cables came in underground. So how did they find them?'

'When you went back to the station with Peter, I had a look at the equipment beside the hatch. There was a bolt cutter for cutting the cable and a boring machine for digging the tunnel. There was also a device that looked like ground-penetrating radar.'

'Wow. How did that work?'

'Undersea cables have an outer layer of steel to protect the inner cable. Radar might have been able to pick that up. Or else detect the hollow chamber under the BT unit and guide them towards it. However they did it, they were successful: the cable was ruptured.'

There was a pause as George overtook a heavy lorry on a hill near to Exeter. Then Maxine spoke.

'Thank you George, that makes a lot of sense. But what did they hope to achieve by rupturing one internet cable?'

'Ah, it was a cable from Ireland.'

'Come on, what difference does that make?'

George went back to answer her earlier question. 'That bothered me for ages. I mean, the messages weren't lost for good. Once the Irish realised they'd not got through, they'd send them again. You might introduce a delay of a few days but nothing would be stopped forever.'

'You mean, all this effort – including two men being killed, two women abducted and a policeman with a smashed arm – was all just to delay some message from Ireland? That's barmy, George.'

'They didn't intend to hurt anyone. Events got out of control.'

Maxine was silent for a moment. There had been some points where she feared the worst but overall she'd had a lucky escape.

'You still haven't answered my question: what was it all for?'

'That's why I wanted you to come to the Exhibition. Wait ten minutes and I'll show you. "Show not Tell" is a sound slogan, don't you think?'

The Innovation Exhibition in Exeter was far larger than the one in Bude and looked more permanent as it was housed in a large Meeting Hall.

'This one is focussed on Renewable Energy and all its possibilities,' explained George as the pair wandered through the various sections. Sunday's exhibition had only just opened, there were not many visitors at this stage.

'We should find the answer to your question in here.' She led her friend into a section marked "Integrated Control Systems". There were a number of stalls from all over Europe, each with many pictures and leaflets. The stalls also had huge computer monitors hanging on the rear walls.

'The critical one that led to all the trouble is over here.'

Maxine found herself being led to a stall in the centre with a large team of men and women, all with strong Irish accents. They seemed cheerful and full of energy.

At the rear, on the monitor, was a diagram of the Irish Republic. Across the whole map, right across the country, were shown tiny diagrams that mimicked wind farms. The farms were pictured in a variety of colours and had small numbers beside them, which twinkled and occasionally altered. There were also arrows showing the direction and strength of wind.

'We only got hold of this whole thing yesterday evening,' the expert who had adopted the girls explained. He'd introduced himself as Paddy.

'It's taken us all night to pull it all together,' Paddy added. '"Something wrong with the internet," they told us. Huh. Old technology, it gives you the creeps. I told 'em our guys shouldn't be fine tuning the whole thing right up to the wire.'

Paddy went on to demonstrate the system in detail. 'It's a live system, you see. Takes account of wind speed and wind direction in deciding which farms to run. Also predicted electricity demand. That varies hugely over the day, of course. It also takes account of other energy sources and their marginal costs.' He was obviously very proud of his system and could talk about it for hours.

Maxine could see her question starting to be answered. 'There was a problem with the internet yesterday,' she admitted. 'Something happened to the cable from Ireland to Bude. But this thing is still working. How did you manage that?'

'We realised there was a problem just after lunch,' admitted Paddy. 'It didn't affect the phone, though. Once we told the systems guys, they went for their contingency plan. One of their team was coming over for today anyway. He flew over to Exeter in the afternoon, brought a copy of the whole thing with him on a portable hard drive. Face to face communication, you see. Still the best.'

George and Maxine eventually extracted themselves from Paddy's enthusiastic attention. The system was dazzling in its complexity. A subsequent tour of the other stalls showed nothing remotely comparable.

'Alright, I can see that's part of the answer,' said Maxine. 'It's a great system. But what's so special about today?'

'Ah. I guess that's one fact I knew from talking to the senior managers at Bude. Today is an Energy Decision Day for the European Union. Their big man will be here this afternoon, along with the UK Business Secretary and Energy Secretary. They're going to pick out the best system on display and adopt it for general use to manage renewable energy across Europe. To the winning system that's worth millions and millions.'

'Sounds like a sort of glorified beauty competition.'

'It is. That's why all these journalists are here. A non-show from the Irish would have been disastrous – both for them and the rest of Europe.'

'So were our gang sponsored by one of their rivals?'

'I guess so. But we'll never know which. There are a dozen stalls here, it could have been any one of them- all done through intermediaries. That's why some say the "European Dream" is just warfare conducted in a higher plane.'

'And why some call it the "European Nightmare".'

CHAPTER 49

'So you see, Peter, the whole thing was driven by doing down the Irish in some wretched European competition.' It was Maxine speaking; she and Peter were sitting in the Ivy Cottage living room in Treknow. They had all just enjoyed a splendid celebratory roast dinner cooked by George. Now was the time to share their day's findings.

'There's one thing I still don't understand . . .' she continued, after explaining her previous comment more completely (the policeman was looking slightly bemused).

'In the end the Irish had a backup plan that worked fine. So hacking the Irish internet cable didn't do the gang any good anyway.'

'Mm. But who instigated the backup?'

'It was . . . I assume it was their people in Exeter, when they didn't receive the system that morning.'

'How do you know when you've not received something? I mean, it takes a while before the internet reports itself as broken, doesn't it? I mean, it might just be suffering a short delay.'

George had stayed silent during this previous exchange. Now she spoke. 'Alright, I confess. It was me.'

'You?'

'Yes. After lunch, when you left me in the Visitor Centre.

333

Various maps showed me where the cable linked to, you see. When I saw it was Ireland, that reminded me about the system coming from there to our Exeter exhibition.'

'Whatever gave you that connection?' asked Maxine, sounding sceptical.

'I'd been talking to the Finance Director about that exhibition just the day before. Then the date on that calendar that you found, Peter, made a lot more sense. The whole business of blocking a bit of the internet only worked when there was a deadline that could not be missed.'

There was a leisurely pause and some sipping of coffee. This was one conversation that did not need to be hurried.

'George, how come you spot all these things and I don't?'

The hostess thought for a moment. 'Perhaps it's the difference in our roles at work? Your job, I understand, is to flog to death any information you're given. Decode it, translate it, interpret it, report it.'

Maxine considered. 'I suppose so. Whereas . . .'

'In my work, hard data is generally hard to come by. Industry regards it as a waste of resources to measure things properly. So most of my time is spent doing intelligent expansions of limited data, to work out what it really means. In other words, Maxine, you interpolate and I extrapolate.'

'While I simply ask loads of questions of the people I've managed to arrest.' Peter sounded doleful. For sure it wasn't that glamorous.

'Peter, you're the only one that applies whatever we find. That's the most important task of all.' Maxine didn't want her special friend pulled down, she sounded protective.

'I know you can't tell us much,' added George, 'but did anything special come out of your interviews today?'

'Or the post-mortem on Fairclough?' added Maxine.

'There was no problem with that. Dr Maxwell wasn't holding back anything.' He looked as if that had not been a happy experience.

'Great. So what do we know about how Fairclough died?'

'He was hit over the head, she said, with the proverbial blunt instrument. And it was murder, he'd been moved from the place where he died. Unfortunately she couldn't tell us what weapon to look for.'

'But Jagger's under arrest, isn't he?' asked Maxine. 'Might there be something that would match the wound, to be found in his cottage?'

'To be honest, I've not had time to look. Today was pretty busy. Holdsworth was the only one who really wanted to talk. But it's an idea.'

'How's Joe?' asked George.

Peter looked more cheerful. 'Some good news there. They're brilliant surgeons in Truro, they've managed to pull his arm together. It'll take a while, they say, but he should make a full recovery. I'm going to see him tomorrow.'

'Can I come with you?' asked Maxine.

'I had one more idea,' said George, speaking quickly before the two started to ogle one another like a pair of springtime blue-tits.

'It was about your man Nick Jagger. That's a very odd name, you know. Like a name he'd made up on the spur of the moment.'

'I agree. When we get to Longridge Cottage we'll look for confirmation but it may not be easy. There may be no documentation at all. If he ends up being tried in a special court then the media won't see him either.'

'No. The thing is, there was an Operations Manager associated with the Limelight Exhibition that I interviewed, called Nick Jupp. He was meant to be in Exeter today to help with the special exhibition day but he didn't turn up. Nor did he send any apology. And then I started wondering . . .'

'What?'

'Well, was it coincidence that the unit next to British Telecom contained the steam cars? They were Jupp's baby, after all. Or did it all run the other way round? In other words, did he choose the unit for the cars so it was next to the internet unit? Did that give him the crucial idea?'

'Hold on. I thought you saw me arrest him?'

'Yes, but I was a long way away across the valley. There were policemen alongside him. And he was dressed for the weekend, not the office.'

George mused for a moment then continued. 'It'd be easy to check out. I'll drop into the station tomorrow if you like, peer through the cell doorway. He might talk more if he knows he's been identified.'

There was plenty more they could talk about but the case seemed to be well in hand. Peter Travers would have a lot more to do but as far as they knew all the guilty parties had been identified, arrested and charged.

George wondered if his success would help make a case for him to be promoted to inspector.

And what would happen to Maxine? George sensed that she was uninspired with her work at Cleave Camp. She had told George that her future there depended on the way she was treated by Colin Caldwell – and the way he responded to all the new information provided.

Peter would accompany Maxine to the Camp tomorrow morning with questions on the redhead victim whom the police had found alongside Fairclough. His guess was that it was almost certainly Colette. What would Caldwell make of that?

George was sure Peter Travers would be unhappy to see Maxine return to Cheltenham. Was there any change that would keep her down in this part of the world? Maybe, in her new state of emotional bliss, decoding was no longer so important.

She observed that the two were cuddled up now, entangled in one another on the sofa. That was good. She did not want to be a gooseberry, slipped out of her chair and headed off to bed.

AUTHOR'S NOTES

As with my earlier "Cornish Conundrums", this story is a work of fiction, set in the present time with made-up characters in a real location. It is NOT an authority on the police, the internet or national security.

I have delved into various sources on the web to learn about cables, connections and the like; also about security. I have stood outside Cleave Camp and walked past it on the Coast Path. I have viewed its white satellite dishes from Pentire Head. But I know no one in the security services (as far as I know). My conjecture about how the place operates stems only from my imagination.

Dr Roger Higgs does provide excellent geological tours around Bude. I'm glad to have him in my story.

Tee-Side is a great bed and breakfast guesthouse. My wife and I stayed there while researching this book.

I met John and Diana Murdoch while selling books at a Gala. I'm sure they'd make great bed and breakfast hosts if they ever moved to Cornwall.

I hope this book may inspire you to visit the small town of Bude and its neighbouring coastline. Sir Goldsworthy Gurney did live here, with his various lighting inventions – including lime-light. These lit the Houses of Parliament for fifty years.

Please send your comments via the website below. But most useful of all I'd like ideas for future stories.

David Burnell *www.davidburnell.info*

May 2017

DOOM WATCH describes George Gilbert's first encounter with crime as she helps Padstow plan an upgrade.

A body is discovered behind the Engine House of the old quarry at Trewarmett; but identification proves tricky.

It takes the combined efforts of George and Police Sergeant Peter Travers to make sense of a crime which seems, simultaneously, to be spontaneous and pre-planned.

"A well-written novel, cleverly structured, with a nicely-handled sub-plot..." Rebecca Tope, crime novelist

SLATE EXPECTATIONS begins as George Gilbert buys a cottage overlooking Trebarwith Strand.

The analyst finds herself part of an outdoor drama based on 19th century events in the Delabole Slate Quarry – a drama heightened when one of the cast is found dead in the opening performance.

The combined resources of George and Police Sergeant Peter Travers are needed to disentangle the past and find out precisely how it relates to the present.

"Slate Expectations combines an interesting view of an often overlooked side of Cornish history with an engaging pair of sleuths who follow the trail from past misdeeds to present murder." *Carola Dunn, crime author*

LOOE'S CONNECTIONS finds George Gilbert conducting a study of floods in Looe when, without warning, her colleague disappears.

Without really trying George is drawn into a web of suspense and foul play. But when her personal and professional lives begin to overlap, is she the unwitting suspect or the next victim?

The trail covers ways of reducing the flooding in the town and events over many centuries. Even the Romans have a part to play.

"History, legend and myth mixed with a modern technical co-nundrum makes this an intriguing mystery." Carola Dunn, crime author

TUNNEL VISION begins with a project to turn the old North Cornwall Railway into a cycle trail. Then journalist Robbie Glendenning, exploring the only tunnel on the line at Trelill, finds first a peculiar side chamber and then a skeleton.

Making sense of a death half a century ago is a huge challenge. Who were they? When and why did they die? Who had reason to intend them mischief? And who intends more now?

It takes George Gilbert's late arrival to rescue Robbie and move the case to a dramatic conclusion.

"Enjoyable reading for all who love Cornwall and its dramatic history." Ann Granger, crime author

Printed in Poland
by Amazon Fulfillment
Poland Sp. z o.o., Wrocław

50423882R00195